I0617801

DRAWING FIRE

Art of Murder Series
Book 1

Pam Fox

Bright Fox Books

Bright Fox Books
Copyright © 2018 by Pam Fox
ISBN-13: 978-1-7328799-0-4

All rights reserved. No part of this book may be reproduced or transmitted in any form or by any means, electronic or mechanical, including photocopying, recording, or by any information storage and retrieval system, without permission in writing from the author.

This is a work of fiction. Names, characters, places, and incidents are the products of the author's imagination or are used fictitiously. Any resemblance to actual events or persons, living or dead, is entirely coincidental

ONE

In the gravel parking lot, Kate Corliss sat behind the wheel for a minute, letting the hours of road noise ebb away. The truck engine ticked, cooling, and then the quiet was vast and delicious, scented by pines and cedars. A sign with crossed pen and paintbrush above ARTS CENTER in gold letters hung over the porch steps of the big house in front of her.

A few weeks ago her old friend from college, Danni LaMaze, had called to invite her to spend a month at the Eastern Maine Arts Center. Kate had protested she hadn't done much artwork in the last few years, but Danni was insistent. "I remember how you drew when we were roommates, so I know you've got the chops," she said. "But honestly? It's a little lonely out here. And I work with guys all the time. I'd love to see you. If you do some drawing here, hey, that's a bonus."

"Wait, all the artists are men?"

Danni laughed. "Oh, God, no. I meant the electricians, plumbers, landscapers—those guys are guys. So can I count on you for some sisterly solidarity?"

Pretty lucky timing, although Kate hadn't said so to Danni the first time they'd talked. Kate had gotten laid off by the daily newspaper in Danvers where she'd been a reporter for three years. Not to mention her boyfriend Mike had dumped her just before Christmas. She'd been in a funk since then, looking for a job and finding only temp office work, which paid the bills but wasn't much fun.

And then Danni had called, and a door in Kate's life opened. Things were going to be much, much better.

* * *

Kate took the place in. Good job, Danni. What must have been an ordinary farmhouse looked like an upscale bed and breakfast. Its paint was fresh—a sage color with maroon trim—and baskets of bright yellow flowers hung along the front beam of the porch. She could see part of a barn to one side of the house: it needed paint, but managed to look picturesque.

One part of Kate wanted to get out of the truck; another part didn't. Despite three years at the *Danvers Daily News,* where she interviewed people every day, she wasn't crazy about meeting strangers. And she was anxious about how well she'd work now that she had no excuse not to.

Wait, she could just stay in her camper tonight. What a good idea. The slide-in, with its double bed over the cab, had everything she needed, the house batteries all charged up from the long drive, half a Subway sandwich in the fridge—no, Kate. The last thing she wanted was to get a reputation for being weird, some kind of hermit type who couldn't face people.

She grabbed her daypack and dropped out of the cab, then gave the rig a quick walk-around. The turnbuckles holding camper to truck were tight. The kayak on the roof rack hadn't slipped an inch—the straps looked good and taut—and none of the compartment doors had shaken open. Good. She went up the porch steps, feeling her knees complain about the long drive. She didn't blame them. Not in bad shape for thirty-two, was she? But sitting for so long made her stiff. Usually she took stairs two at a time, but—

The door banged open and a big man barged out, yelling over his shoulder, "You're a selfish bastard, Farley! You'll be sorry, you stupid son of a—"

2

Kate dodged to her right, and when the giant caught sight of her he stopped yelling and scowled. Even more foul than his temper was the odor of cigar that hit Kate as he thumped past. She watched him go, hoping the rest of the artists would be easier to deal with. Spending a month with bad-tempered smoke-breathing he-dragons wouldn't help an artist struggling to get back to work.

The door opened again, more slowly this time, and a slender man in a tweed jacket looked at her. His dark hair, swept back from an alert face, was streaked with silver.

"See any charging elephants?"

She smiled. "A whole herd just went by."

"Their smoke is worse than their bite." He held the door wide. "C'mon in and pick up the key to your cabin. You can meet the rest of the inmates of the zoo later. I'm Farland McQuay—call me Farley—and you must be Katherine."

His name sounded familiar, but how did he know hers? "Er—right."

"Not a wild guess, my dear. You're the only incoming artist today. And your cabin's next door to mine."

"Ah. Call me Kate." She hoped she sounded casual, hoped he hadn't seen her stiffen at "my dear." She was going to have to work on herself. She was a wreck around men—rude ones and gentle ones.

Heck, she was a wreck around everybody, even herself.

"Kate, then. Welcome to the Eastern Maine Arts Center, EMAC for short." Farley's face said he was in his fifties, but his body language said older. His wrists were thin, and the arm against the door shook. He had the hunched posture some tall people adopt, as if denying their height made it less apparent rather than more. He didn't offer to take her pack, although he had the sort of old-fashioned manner that suggested he might.

3

"The director isn't here today, she's off fund-raising, so I'll fill you in a bit. Oh, but you know her, don't you? I forgot. She said to expect her friend. So—Danni isn't here, and I'm all you've got."

She'd placed his name now: he was a very well-known artist. Definitely major league. She returned his smile, feeling out of her element. She hadn't talked to an artist since her college days, and some of the conversations with studio art professors hadn't gone well.

"This is the Big House, the main building where most of us eat breakfast and dinner," he said. "Lunch is put outside your door in a basket, so you can work straight through." He laughed at the astonished look Kate gave him. "First-class operation, our EMAC. Classier than anything else in Short Creek, Maine.

"We're in the lounge, where we all come to wait for dinner, served about seven. People show up at six, bringing their favorite fermented beverage with them, and wait for the honest-to-God dinner bell to ring. Very Pavlovian."

What an enormous room. With dark wainscoting and small windows, it could have been depressing, but Kate recognized Danni's touch in the comfortable furniture, bright cushions and rugs that made it look snug instead of somber. A couple of accent lamps, mixed into the conversational grouping of couches and chairs near a huge fireplace, were turned on even though it was still daytime. The place looked like an ad from *House and Garden*. Its size even accommodated a Ping-Pong table off to the right without any sense of crowding.

A burly man in a Greek sailor cap got up from one of the couches. "Welcome to EMAC. I'm Hallsy," he boomed. "Just heading out."

"Hallsy, like Admiral Halsey," Farley said. "But not William. And never been near a naval vessel, if I understand correctly."

"Oh, I'm a landlubber, all right. Nebraska-born. Roland Hall, officially, but you'd better call me Hallsy if you want me to know

4

you're talking to me." He stuck out a big paw. "Nobody's called me Roland since I was too young to fight."

"Hi, Hallsy. I'm Kate."

"I just came in to check my mail, take a break. See you tonight, Kate. Watch out for this old geezer." He winked at her, moved toward the door. Quietly, for such a big guy.

"You'll meet everyone else tonight. No sense in my running over names you won't remember for the first few days. At least I didn't."

He was probably saying that to help Kate relax. Farley seemed comfortable with people, good at being around them. And Hallsy was friendly. She was glad to have met these two after her encounter on the porch.

Farley took her to the back of the lounge, to the left of the fireplace. "The dining room's back here, through these glass doors"—he opened them, went down a short hallway—"and the kitchen's around here. We bus our own tables to this pass-through. Erik, the cook, is a gem—you'll love the food. And here's your key, nice and secure. Not that we bother to lock our studios."

A board with rows of labelled hooks was mounted on the wall beside the pass-through. Farley took one of the two keys from the "Bobcat" hook and handed it to her with a small bow. "Your new life," he said.

Startled, Kate wondered how much Danni had said about her.

He showed her the cubbyholes where they got mail, and then led her through the dining room and out the back of the building, onto a patio scattered with Adirondack chairs and surrounded by a railing. "Sometimes we sit out here with our coffee, if the weather's nice." A small herd of no doubt communal bicycles crowded around a rack, old three-speeds with the dispirited look that came from being stored outdoors and lubed once a year. Only the one at the end, a red Specialized road bike, looked cared for, its chain gleaming.

"Your cabin's the first on the left, down this road. It's called the Loop, makes a circle past all the studios. We're not supposed to use our cars beyond the parking lot after we settle in, but new arrivals can drive right to their cabins. So you can do that, if you have a lot of luggage to unload."

"Oh, I don't have much," Kate said. "I'll walk."

"I thought so. See you around six, then."

* * *

The cabin was tucked into the woods at the left edge of the dirt road, a bench on the porch facing the field behind the Big House. Nothing fancy, but Kate was happy to call it home for a month. She let her hand rest on the doorknob for a few seconds and felt a shiver of—what? Anxiety? Or freedom?

The door opened on a bright room with a high ceiling and white walls. Table at the big front window, bed with a forest-green comforter. Kitchenette at the back with a smaller window over the sink. Shiny green kettle on the stove, floor lamp by a loveseat, area rug with a border of paddles and moose. Whatever she'd expected, it hadn't been this nice. She dropped her duffle, walked through the place and opened the back door. A trail on the left went up the hill to another cabin, sky blue with white trim.

That must be Farley's. The thought pleased her. She took a deep breath of the warm afternoon air.

She turned and dropped her daypack on the bed and stood at the screen door. Slant of sunlight on the road, a snug cabin across from a trio of birch trees, sweet scent of hay: things could be a lot worse. Things had been a lot worse. Danni had given her a fresh start. A new life, as Farley had said.

Watching the late light change the color of the field, the screen crosshatching it like graph paper, she tried not to feel the depths of her self-doubt.

6

* * *

"Here's our latest arrival," Farley said when she joined the group in the lounge. He introduced her around. Only eight faces were new to her, since she'd already met him and Hallsy, but eight was plenty. Kate tried to make some visual connection to each name, since her mind worked best with pictures. David Sterling, a writer, wore eyeglasses with silver frames that would call up his last name; Joy Grimm, painter and installation artist, had such high eyebrows that she looked permanently surprised, the opposite of grim; Kim Park, photographer, merely nodded. Was Kim a man or a woman? In dark clothes, glossy hair pulled back. The slim body merged with the chair's dark leather. Distracted by gender uncertainty, she couldn't do a thing with his or her name.

Two guys who looked like cowboys, in nearly-matching leather vests, jeans and boots leaned against the mantelpiece. "These gentlemen have the good fortune to be Canadians," Farley said. They nodded and said "Hey." Case Crenley and Gabriel Rousseau. "We're pencil artists," the one on the left said.

Kate came up with the image of a case of angels. Maybe it would help her remember the names, but good luck telling the two men apart.

Nava was an elderly painter with huge earrings and droopy eyelids; even seated, she looked tall. A cane was propped against her chair. Kate's mnemonic was concern for her ability to "nava"-gate with those eyelids at half-mast.

Farley surprised Kate by stumbling over the old woman's last name.

Nava smiled and raised a bejewelled hand. "Don't trouble yourself, Farley, dear. It's seven syllables. It's Polish. And I'm the only one who needs to know it."

He laughed. "That's the lot," he said to Kate, "except for Reggie Blair. You already met him when he almost ran you over this afternoon."

7

Hallsy guffawed.

Reginald Blair? The name rang a bell. Maybe she'd seen his work in a gallery or magazine. Not recently, though; she'd been losing touch with the art scene the last few years.

David said, "Don't worry about Reggie, Kate. I've known Farley a week, and he's the kind of person who takes it upon himself to keep the peace." He looked at Farley. "You should be in the diplomatic corps, not dealing with overfed artists throwing tantrums."

"Overfed is right," Hallsy said. "Stomach and ego both. The only thing more obnoxious than him is that cigar. Fortunately, he was outvoted. Thanks for handling him, Farley."

Farley shrugged.

"I wasn't there," David said, "but I bet Farley wasn't the deciding factor. I think it was you, Hallsy. The look on your face, or perhaps the flex of your biceps."

Hallsy smiled. "I don't work out for nothing."

"That man has problems," David said.

"Farley, you've forgotten to mention Reggie's side-car Sherri. Is she not memorable?" Hallsy said. To Kate he said, "She does watercolors. Sort of."

"Cut it out." Joy tossed brown bangs out of her eyes. "Why are women always accused of being gossips? You guys sound like a bunch of cats."

Kate was relieved. Even though she already disliked Reggie, it wasn't fun to see people talking behind anybody's back.

"By 'guys' I think she means you and me," Hallsy said to David.

A bell rang from the next room. Whatever David had opened his mouth to say was revised to "Ah. Dinner."

The mantelpiece loungers, already on their feet, were first out of the room; the others rose with varying degrees of speed. Joy unfolded her legs like a fawn, while Kim flowed from the chair without seeming to move a muscle. A dinner bell makes a good flexibility test, Kate thought. She stayed behind Nava, who was of course the slowest; Farley held the glass door open for them both.

Kim turned out to be male, with a feminine grace in his gestures and fascinating, unorthodox English; he was an immigrant from Korea. Nava laughed often. Joy, next to Kate, asked if she had a website and said she had a wise aura and wasn't the food great? They were lucky to have Erik to cook—wait until Kate had his Northern Lights Chili—and he did it all without gas, you couldn't get gas out here, he had an electric stove, yuck! Hallsy and David each assured the other of imminent and savage defeat at Ping-Pong, and Farley asked her if she played. "The table's pretty rickety, but that just adds an exciting touch of unpredictability," he said. "I don't play—but if you do, beware. These two are killers."

Erik turned out to be waiter as well as cook. He was about Kate's age, tall and lean. On his first trip to the table, his eyes found hers. "Hi," he said. "You're new."

"Kate, this is our renowned chef Erik DeLuca," Farley said. "Erik, Kate Corliss."

Erik set down two wooden bowls of salad. "Cor-liss? Rhymes with 'kiss,'" he said.

Kate blushed.

"Don't mind him," Hallsy said. "He's harmless. All talk. Right, Erik?"

Broiled snapper, an arugula salad, and potatoes au gratin disappeared from the serving plates. Brownies with ice cream followed, but she passed on dessert and fetched herself a cup of coffee from the big electric pot next to the pass-through. She had a flash of Mike's face, laughing at her concern about her weight. He'd always eaten whatever he wanted. Damn him.

Forget him.

Reggie had stalked in late, looking angry, with Sherri, a busty blonde. They barely looked at Kate or anyone else, touched hands often, and left early, Sherri with a couple of brownies wrapped in a napkin. Reggie paused conspicuously at the door to extract a cigar and lighter from his pocket.

After pitching in to clear the tables, the group split up, some of them heading out the back door and some staying to watch the Ping-Pong game or make phone calls from the landline, which was an old-fashioned pay phone tucked into a closet for privacy.

Farley called Kate "my dear neighbor," and they went out together. Gabriel and Case were on the back patio, smiling. One of them held up a hand and said "Listen." Case. At dinner she'd noticed his nose had a bit of a hook to it, and now she could tell them apart. Cases have corners.

The four of them stood there. A minute passed.

A series of short hoots floated from the woods, the last of them ending with a falling quaver. Kate and the men smiled at each other.

"The answer is Erik," Case said, and he and Gabriel laughed. A moment later Kate got it, and laughed, too.

Farley looked at her, puzzled, but it was Case who explained.

"That's the call of a barred owl," he said. "Bird-watchers identify it by its rhythm, which matches the rhythm of 'Who cooks for you, who cooks for you all?'" He laughed again. "In this case, Erik cooks for us all."

"I thought owls just asked Who?" Farley said.

"That would be your great horned owl."

"Not my owl. I don't have owls. I'm a city cat."

"The barred owl is smaller, but asks more pointed questions," Case said. "I don't know what he'd think about broiled snapper or salad."

10

"That wasn't a he," Kate said. The three men looked at her. "The last note, or hoot, of the call? Did you hear that shaky quality, that—"

"Vibrato?" Farley said.

"Yes. That's a female. The male's call stops short on 'you all.' It sounds clipped compared to this guy—er, gal.'"

"Women do ramble on, don't they?" Case said to Gabriel.

Kate felt stung. Then she realized Case was joking about the female owl's longer call, not criticizing her own comments. Lighten up, she told herself.

Gabriel, who had let Case do all the talking, cupped his hands around his mouth and produced a strikingly good imitation of the call they'd just heard. Except he clipped the last hoot short.

They waited. Dusk expanded across the field like a black tide. And then the female's voice floated from the woods.

"Congratulations, Gabriel," Farley said. "You're in the barred owl dating game."

"Come on, you big flirt," Case said with a grin, pulling Gabriel off the porch by his sleeve. "Goodnight," he called over his shoulder.

"Goodnight."

Farley and Kate walked toward their studios, her cabin crouched below his larger blue cottage, both invisible in the darkness under the trees. The temperature had dropped sharply. The wind in the pines sounded like a train, and a few dry leaves skittered past them.

"This air is delicious," Farley said. He walked slowly, with a limp.

Kate was startled at how relaxed she felt, in a new place, with a new home, walking with a man she'd known for just a couple of hours. "That was a treat," she said. "That owl."

"Agreed. And it was pleasant to have a moment with those two young men. They're not the most sociable among us."

11

"No, they didn't say much at dinner," Kate said. But neither had she.

"Wait until it's dark and you see the stars. It's stunning how white the sky gets." After another few steps he said, "And it's so quiet here. It doesn't get more peaceful than this."

"Yes."

"Good for the soul. And good for doing art. As you'll soon see."

"Yes," she said again. And hoped he was right.

TWO

The next morning a car crunched up the road outside her cabin. Scrambling out of bed in her T-shirt, she pulled on jeans and looked out. A silver SUV skidded to a stop in front of Bobcat and a woman jumped out. Danni! She wasn't a new resident with luggage to unload, but if you're founder and director you get to break your own rules.

Kate opened the door. Danni was talking as she hit the porch. "Kate, you're here. Hooray! Get dressed, quick, you've got to come to our house for breakfast, Andy and FatCat are waiting. Oh, I'm so glad you're here."

She was about Kate's size but her hug was bigger. Kate felt her surprising warmth. She must have a metabolism as fast as a bird's.

"You poor baby," Danni said in her ear. Then she held her at arm's length. "You just wait. Mike will be sorry he let you go. I mean really sorry. Lonely, too. Because women know scum when they see it."

"Hey, Danni. It's great to see you, too. Let's not talk about Mike, okay?" Danni hadn't thought he was scum for the three years Kate had been with him. "I *am* dressed, just let me find my shoes." She pulled on a UMass sweatshirt and sat on the bed to put on her sneakers. She grinned up at her friend. "Bet I get dressed faster than you do."

Danni snorted. "Is that with or without makeup?"

* * *

"Andy and I live just a few miles from here," Danni said as she turned out of the FACEM lot. "We overlook Short Creek."

"I can't believe you live in a town this small," Kate said as the SUV whizzed up Farm Road. Mailboxes flagging driveways were widely separated, the houses hidden on wooded lots. "You used to call Amherst 'Hicksville,' and this isn't exactly Amherst. And you said there isn't even cell phone coverage up here?"

"Yeah, isn't that crazy? Sooner or later we'll get a cell tower and join the twenty-first century." Danni was driving too fast, as always. Kate closed her eyes. "It isn't like I'm stuck here, though. I go to meetings in fun places, like New York and DC and the other Portland, you know, about managing an arts nonprofit, or about fund-raising, stuff like that. So far Deep Pockets has sent me everywhere I've asked him to." Her speed mercifully dropped as the road climbed.

"Deep Pockets?"

"Yeah, isn't that great? Well, okay, that's just my name for him. He provides a huge amount of support for EMAC. But he's, like, anonymous. Talks to me through a lawyer in Bangor, who says he doesn't know who he is either."

At the top of the hill Danni cornered sharply into a driveway and stopped beside a black pick-up. "Ta da! Here it is, home sweet home."

Kate hadn't realized how far they'd climbed until she got out of the car. The view was splendid, a green ocean of treetops. Between the house and the town below, a pond breathed mist into the cool morning air. A great blue heron glided over the gray water.

"Pretty, isn't it?" Danni asked.

"It's gorgeous, Danni." But when she turned, Danni wasn't looking at the view. The house looked well-kept, two stories of cedar clapboard. Tidy plantings lined the brick walk. Kate swallowed hard, trying not to think of how homeless she felt. Danni was lucky, always had been. Her personality made luck out of thin air.

Andy came out of the house. "Hey, Kate," he said. "Been awhile. Welcome to Short Creek." His blond hair was shorter than the last time Kate had seen him, at his and Danni's wedding, but otherwise he looked the same: drop-dead gorgeous. He gave her a grin and a hug.

Light flowed into the living room through a big window with a view of distant hills. A fig tree in a terra cotta planter was making good use of the light, shadows of its leaves dappling the sand-colored couch.

A large striped cat woke up from a nap on a recliner and looked at her with amber eyes.

"Is this FatCat? The stray from Amherst?"

Danni laughed. "The same. He grew into his name, didn't he? He had such enormous paws, I knew it would happen."

"He's huge."

But Danni was in house-tour mode. "Andy made most of the furniture. The bookcases, this coffee table." Danni brushed the glossy surface, her red nails gleaming. "Look at the inlaid tile. Isn't that amazing?"

Andy wasn't around for the compliment; Kate heard him in the kitchen, whistling.

"You won't see much of Andy," Danni said. "That door in the kitchen goes to the garage, which he's taken over for a workshop. Threw my poor Subaru out on its ass."

A few small abstract paintings brightened the walls. The place looked so pleasant Kate had to admit to herself she was jealous. Then she turned a mental corner, and enjoyed the look of the place for itself, and was glad for her friend, who lived in a lovely house with a sweet man.

15

And with her sister. "You remember Harri? She's visiting, sort of," Danni said quietly.

Harri was younger than Danni by five or so years. When Kate and Danni were at UMass, Harri had run away from home a couple of times. Kate remembered the phone ringing in the middle of the night, Danni hunched over it for hours talking to her distraught parents or to an angry or lonely or frightened Harri.

And once Harri had hitchhiked to Amherst. They'd found her asleep on the floor when they got up in the morning. Kate remembered a rebellious fifteen-year-old with green eyes and a mass of curls.

"She got into heroin in Boston for a while, but she's really turned herself around. If she goes anywhere near drugs again she won't be able to stay here," Danni said. "She needs a little time to figure out what to do next. But it'll be easier now that she's clean. I'm really proud of her."

* * *

Andy turned out a masterful batch of pancakes—whole wheat with real (and local) maple syrup, and a plate of kiwi-fruit and banana slices on the side in deference to what he called Kate's "health-nut habits." She'd met him a few times before, back when he was boyfriend not husband, and she liked him a lot. He'd worked for a cabinetmaker then and made custom furniture. With his square, chiseled face and blond crewcut he looked younger than Danni, though she'd said he was few years older.

Only when breakfast was on the table did Danni call up the stairs. "Harri? Harri, honey, c'mon down and eat."

Oh, coffee. Kate could live on the stuff. She looked up to compliment Andy on his java when someone appeared at the far end of the dining room, moving silently in socks.

Kate tried not to show how shocked she was. Harri looked like Danni's older sister, not a younger one. Drugs hadn't done her face any favors. Compared to the kid who slept on the dorm room floor, this person was ancient.

"You remember Kate, don't you?" Danni asked.

"Hey, Harri," Kate said.

Harri didn't make eye contact but said "Hi" in Kate's direction and slipped into a chair.

Andy had spent more time cooking than he did eating—he went through a couple of cakes, gulped some coffee, and excused himself to work in the shop.

"Once a carpenter, always a carpenter," Danni said, shaking her head, and Andy smiled. Kate liked the chemistry between them.

Harri, who'd barely said a word, excused herself not long after Andy had.

The two women took their second mugs of coffee into the living room. FatCat saw Danni coming and abandoned the recliner, promptly but with dignity.

"He always knows where I'm going to sit," Danni said. "Mind reader."

"I bet it's your habits he reads." Kate sat at one end of the couch and FatCat jumped into her lap. "Ooof. I don't know if I'm flattered or flattened. I remember when you could hold this kitty in the palm of your hand. Back when he was an illegal dorm cat."

"He was so cute, what could I do? Throw him to the wolves?"

FatCat kneaded Kate's thighs with his paws. "Gosh, you've had him de-clawed?"

"Yeah," Danni said apologetically. "The furniture, you know?"

Kate would never do that to an animal, but it wasn't her cat. "Hey, big guy," she said, "you're sitting on my breakfast." She rubbed him behind his ears.

"He's one lazy ball of fur. Who does all the work around here?" Danni looked at FatCat fondly, but her mind had turned to

17

business. "This is EMAC's fifth year and the fund-raising campaigns are doing better. I apply for grants, state and NEA and all that, but the Center would just be a gleam in my eye without Deep Pockets. The best part is we're slowly building a reputation—some of our artists are getting shows."

Kate's lap was vibrating. "FatCat has the best purr." As soon as she said it, the tiger left her lap in favor of Danni's.

"Just like you, Kate—can't take a compliment," Danni said. She stroked the cat's glossy coat and Kate could hear him purr across the room.

"I'm going to talk Deep Pockets into letting me set up a storefront gallery next summer in Short Creek. It sure would change the place—can you imagine? Hank's Hardware, move over, Danni's in town!" She threw her arms wide, accidentally popping the recliner into its extended position with a thump. FatCat shot off her lap. The look on Danni's face as she found herself on her back cracked Kate up, and the two of them laughed themselves into hiccups.

"This stupid chair." Danni struggled upright in the flat recliner and sat at the end, bringing her closer to Kate. She wiped her eyes and her mood turned serious. "Hey, I know this is a hard time for you, Kate, but it's so good to have you here. And I hope you can do some work, too. You did some incredible stuff, back in the day. Remember that huge mural of jungle plants you did freshman year? The one they put up in the library? It was black and white— you used charcoal—but it was so real that everybody in the dorm swore it was green. I won a pizza on that bet."

This was the pep talk Kate both wanted and dreaded. "Of course I remember. I had a slice or two myself," she said. "But I haven't even thought about drawing for a couple of years now. It slowly dropped out of my life. You know, working and, and—I don't know what I've spent my time doing." Mike, she thought. Relationships are complete time sinks. But she didn't want to talk about him. "Funny, I'd always have a sketchbook in my daypack. Every now and then I'd work a little, kept thinking I'd get back to it in a bigger way."

"This is your chance. You haven't been able to work seriously because you had to work—I mean the other kind of work, at a job. Well, now you're free, at least for a month. Sometimes things just turn out right, you know?"

Things work out for you, Kate thought. But she felt a flicker of Danni's enthusiasm.

"The number of applications is going up, most of them from Boston and New York," Danni said. "I need to find more writers, though. I'm wicked busy now, fund-raising and getting the rest of the cabins fixed up. I used to have dinner at the Big House sometimes, chat with the artists. I miss that."

"You have a committee to help you run this place, don't you? An editor at the newspaper told me administration means being nibbled to death by mice."

"You're looking at it. Me, myself and I. Judging portfolios and deciding who comes here is the best part. I look at art all day, some days. I love it."

That was a job Kate wouldn't want, but Danni had greater confidence in her judgment.

"I used to see more of the residents after they got here, invited them up here sometimes." Danni sighed. "You're right, I'll have to get help. I just hate committees."

"Get some literary types. Then you can still make all the art decisions."

"That's a good idea." Danni brightened, then subsided. "For now, it's probably just as well I stay home for dinner. I travel a lot, and Andy doesn't like to eat alone."

* * *

19

It felt good to spend time with Danni. They'd shared so much in college—Harri's crises and those of Kate's mother, who had alcoholic episodes. After graduating they'd both gotten jobs in Massachusetts, Danni's a demanding one working for an arts organization, lobbying at the State House. They hadn't stayed in close touch, but they hadn't lost track of each other, either. Occasional phone calls, at Christmas, on birthdays. And of course she'd gone to Danni's wedding at that big church in Newton. Kate didn't know Andy well, but Danni was practically a sister.

"How's your Aunt Sarah?" Danni asked, as if catching Kate's family vibes.

"She knocks me out," Kate said. "She's organized a group of bird-watching friends for a trip to Costa Rica. "

When Kate was growing up in Tucson, Aunt Sarah had been a warm, supportive presence. Then she and Uncle Pete moved to Massachusetts when he got a tenure-track teaching job there. Funny name for a state, she'd written to Kate. Sounds like a sneeze. Aunt Sarah was the reason Kate had even considered going to college, and then had kept her from quitting. She'd applied only to UMass, not really expecting to get in, then felt lost in the leafy Berkshires. She didn't make friends quickly. Aunt Sarah, who lived nearby, talked her through the adjustment.

"Your self-esteem level stinks," she'd said. "Frankly, I'd like to wring your father's neck."

Kate's father had disappeared when she was eleven, and she'd missed him terribly. She pored over the newspaper every day: something as important as her father vanishing would of course be covered sooner or later.

"Don't be stupid," her mother said. "He just went fishing." She said it in a way that meant something other than fishing for fish. And then she canceled the newspaper subscription to save money.

All these years later, Kate still missed him. Unlike her mother and aunt, she didn't believe he'd simply turned his back on his children. Something must have happened to him.

Family is as family does. Since they'd met, Danni had treated her better than her own mother.

"You're such a great friend, Danni. I'm glad to be here, glad you thought of me."

"Of course I thought of you. I'm glad you're here for me, and for you. And I'm glad you're here for her." Her eyes flicked toward the ceiling and Kate knew she meant Harri. "She's dealing with a lot right now, but she knows you weathered some tough stuff and came out of it just fine. I'm hoping she'll get her act together enough to go back to school. She wants to be a geologist."

"Is she getting along with your parents any better?"

"God, I think they're two of her biggest problems. A wimp of a mother—no role model there—and a father who wanted boys and got girls."

Danni's father was a short, balding man who'd made a ton of money in real estate. "I didn't know your father was like that."

"Oh, he's sexist as hell. A throwback to the nineteenth century. When is civilization going to get over it? I'm sure glad I'm not a guy." She laughed. "Why do you think we have almost-boy names? I've never minded 'Danielle,' but Harri's always hated 'Harriet.' I'd probably be harder on him if he hadn't put a ton of money into EMAC when we started it up."

Sometimes she said "we" when she meant "I." Kate had the impression her friend's husband hadn't been thrilled about the EMAC idea. But maybe he'd warmed up to it.

Danni made another pot, and Andy came in just long enough to fill up his mug. "I'm a coffee psychic," he told Kate with a wink. "I can feel the vibrations when it's brewing."

"I'm glad he's cheered up," Danni said, rearranging herself, carefully, in the recliner she'd restored to the upright position.

21

"Why, has he been depressed or something?"

"Oh, heck, no, not Andy. But he was peeved at me a while back. Barely spoke for a few days. That's a big deal for him—he's usually as happy as a beach ball. I had one new cabin built, Peacock, to add to the ten around the Loop and the three in the woods in the middle."

"Peacock." Kate thought of the sweet blue studio behind Bobcat. "That's the one Farley's in?"

"Yeah." She shrugged. "Andy must've wanted to do it himself, but I thought he had enough projects already. He was down in Boston doing a custom kitchen, for heaven's sake. But so much of EMAC is mine—I must have stepped into what he considers his territory."

FatCat prowled back into the room and claimed a chair in full sun.

"You can see Peacock from Shady River Road—it's the only visible studio. That's why I put it there, and painted it blue—a perfect advertisement for EMAC. Andy came back and saw it, asked me what the hell was going on, then stomped back out to his truck and didn't come home until after I fell asleep that night."

"Wow." Kate reminded herself that nobody's life was perfect, no matter what it looked like from the outside.

Danni shook her head. "Men are from Mars," she said. "Even you, FatCat."

The big tiger blinked inscrutably.

"For a while we had trouble at the site. A bunch of lumber and a generator got stolen, then a fire got started one night. Thank goodness a guy driving past saw it and called the fire department."

"Wait, how could they get a truck up there?" The path past Bobcat was too narrow for anything but an ATV.

"There's an old road that runs along the edge of the property, outside all the cabins. Behind Peacock, it's right at the edge of that drop-off over the road and river," Danni said. "I make sure my

22

crew cuts the saplings to keep that road clear, especially since that fire almost happened."

She got up and paced in front of the big window. Its light brought out the auburn in her dark hair. "I'm glad that trouble's behind us. I wake up every morning now just so jazzed to make this place take off. I've got to pace myself, though—it takes years, decades really, to build the kind of reputation that will draw the best artists."

"You've got Farley."

"Yes, I'm thrilled about him." Danni beamed. "He's such a big name, I'm honestly surprised he's here. We met at a conference, and hit it off, but still. Hey, I'll tell you a secret, if you promise not to tell anyone."

Kate nodded.

"He didn't apply. He just called me up, and I said sure, you're in."

"I'm glad he's here. He's great to talk to."

"And he's a five-star artist," Danni said.

"What about Reggie Blair? He's a big deal too, isn't he?"

"Oh, him. He's not nearly as big as he thinks he is. I'm sorry I let him in." She threw herself on the other end of the couch from Kate. "He was mean to a waitress in the café downtown. He's never coming back."

They sat for a bit. The whine of a saw reached them faintly from Andy's workshop.

"Do the townspeople like having an arts center here?" Kate asked.

Danni didn't answer right away. "Some of them think art is frivolous—you know, a hobby for rich people. The business community came on board first, when they figured out my artists were dropping a decent amount of cash in Short Creek. Used to be just a few hunters who came around in the fall. Or bird-watchers."

"You must hire local people, to rehab the cabins. Aren't they happy about the jobs?"

"Yeah, the electrical work, plumbing, landscaping, painting—all that goes to locals. Only one full-timer, though. Ryan. He's our contractor, plus he runs his own trucking company. Have you seen him around? He's a big guy, always wears a red bandana tied at the back, like an hippie biker." She giggled. "I think he's bald."

"Nope, haven't seen him yet."

"The Big House is so old, something's always coming up. Pipes leak and wires break. Ryan's guys are great about taking care of stuff—nights, weekends, whenever. He and Andy spend a lot of time together." Danni played with her cup. "I'm glad Andy finally has a good friend up here. He felt a little lost right after we moved. I had a new identity, running EMAC, and he'd given up his cabinetmaking job."

"Yes, friends are a big deal. They can change your life," Kate said. "Andy's okay now?"

"I think so. I travel a lot, though, and he sometimes gets work in Boston for a couple of weeks, from his old boss. Wish we had more time together. "

Kate swallowed hard again, thinking of Mike, her jealousy reasserting itself. Like the Loch Ness monster, it was always lurking. She never knew when it would stick its ugly head out of the black water.

* * *

Walking the mile back to EMAC, Kate was glad of the exercise. She kept her pace fast and searched her mind for the last time she'd done any serious drawing. What had inspired her?

Oh, heck, it didn't matter. She had to find inspiration here, now.

Preoccupied, she stopped at the Big House to check her cubbyhole for mail. Not that snail mail amounted to much these days.

She went up the porch steps two at a time. The front door was open to the pleasant weather; the screen door bumped shut behind her. She crossed the vast lounge, its wooden floor creaking until she got to the hearth area, with its rug and heavy leather furniture.

Leaving the glass doors to the dining room open, she went around the corner to the mail slots.

Oh, wait, today was Sunday—no snail mail. But every box was brightened by a memo from Danni on lime-green paper, a reminder about the upcoming Open Studios event and how important it was to have work ready to show the public. Some kind of oral presentation would be useful too. Danni liked exclamation points. "All in the interest of making us friends in the community of Short Creek! in northeastern Maine! And on the national arts scene!"

Oh, great. Well, maybe she'd let Kate off the hook because she'd barely settled in.

The screen door slapped shut, and she found herself half-listening to hesitant footsteps. A new arrival? The memo went on with instructions for the big day, but she slipped it back into her box. Later.

At the glass doors, she was readying a welcome, one newbie to another—

A tall figure whirled and fled, the screen door slamming shut. What the heck?

She dashed across the main room and out the door. Nobody in sight in the parking lot. Ran to the road, looked in both directions. Someone was running to her right, down the hill toward the river. He had too much of a head start: she'd never catch up. Whoever it was, he was a strong runner, with a bounding stride and great form. He was really covering ground.

Probably some townie. A kid curious about the bunch of artists on the hill.

She turned toward Bobcat, wishing she'd gotten a better look at the guy. All she had, really, was an impression—slender, taller than her five-seven. On foot, so probably a local. With the movement of a trained runner.

High-school track athlete, bored and curious on an August afternoon?

Or an adult? Curiosity doesn't get erased by a high-school diploma.

But was that really his motive for going into the Big House? If so, he would have asked questions rather than fleeing.

What would he have done if she hadn't been there to scare him away?

Sunlight flooded the Loop as she walked to Bobcat. She thought of the fire meant to destroy Peacock, and shivered.

THREE

The first few days were hard. Even though she woke early, Kate had trouble getting out of bed. Drawing was the first thing on her mind, but she didn't know where to start. She willed herself back to sleep, or something like sleep, and then it was nine-thirty or ten o'clock and the day already a failure.

She forced herself up. She'd found coffee in the kitchen, along with filters and a plastic holder for them. The kettle whistled. She poured steaming water over the grounds and watched it drain. Took the cup to the front window and looked at the birch trees across the dirt road, radiant against dark pines. She waited for an impulse to draw them, their delicacy and resilience, but it didn't come. Instead of lifting her spirits, their beauty made her feel inadequate.

Breakfast with the group at the Big House wasn't going to happen with her mood this bleak. She liked most of the other artists, but she wasn't really social enough for two meals' worth of conversation a day.

Okay, she was depressed. The best medicine for that was exercise. And so she walked or rode her bike, even though it felt half-hearted, even though she didn't push herself. At least she was moving.

By the time she got back most days, someone had gone around to the studios and left a lunch basket at each door. What a privilege it was to be here. It made her feel like a fraud.

She stopped waiting for any sort of impulse and waited instead for something sad and heavy to slide away. She walked. The cabins along the Loop were occupied, and she didn't like the fact that she might be watched. A trail cut across the middle of the property and she explored that, checking out the three cabins Danni hadn't had fixed up yet. They were unlocked, and she took a look inside one. Rough-finished, but sound; Danni had made a smart investment.

Other trails led away from the Loop, some of them old, made by deer and their hunters.

She walked, and worked to forget who she had been yesterday or last year and who she might be tomorrow or a month from now.

Just be a person walking, she told herself. Better yet, just be walking.

Just be.

She decided what she was doing was moving meditation. Yoga to go.

After a few days on the EMAC property, Kate followed Farm Road to Shady River Road and explored the area below Peacock. Four abandoned, industrial buildings along the river suggested the site had been a mill once. Kate loved old buildings. Growing up, she'd spent hours happily poking around lost homesteads she and her father found on hikes in the desert.

Some little girls liked dollhouses; Kate preferred ghost towns. Her sister Vickie, three years older, stayed in town on weekends and went to movies with her friends; her brother Cam, six years older, worked on his motorcycle in the yard in front of their trailer. Kate loved those trips with just her father. She'd had him at his best, relaxed, pointing out javelina tracks or the blue patches on the back of road runners' heads that looked like a second pair of eyes.

When she went out with him at dawn, the world was cold and the sky huge. Its light had a softness that wore away. In

28

a few hours the desert became the scratchy, brittle, bitey place that most people knew.

She was sure she missed her father more than Vickie or Cam did.

* * *

The buildings along the Shady River were much larger than anything she and her father had found. Mostly brick, three stories high, they looked like a tenement for ghosts. Many of the windows were broken, and a few doors were boarded up with plywood.

Sometimes when people move out, wildlife moves in, so Kate had a look inside wherever she could. She was hoping to see a barn owl roosting on a rafter or a family of raccoons curled up after a night of foraging, but all she found were rusted machines with huge gears, a ruined scale at what must have been a loading dock, and a metal shed with a smokestack out the top. Tire tracks in the open space between the buildings and the road told her the place still got some use, probably local fishermen or hunters.

A trail that ran past the back of the site promised good hiking farther along the Shady. And maybe she'd get her kayak into the water. That would be a treat.

* * *

She laid out her art supplies on the work table. After a walk she sat there sometimes, picking up a pencil or pastel crayon for a minute. Her mind wandered. She'd lose herself in her past and then come back to the present with a start. The object in her hand could have been a fork or flare.

She'd known it would be hard, but not this hard.

* * *

Everything had happened so fast. She'd been such a fool not to see it coming. Friends said, What's up with Mike? Then they said, Kate, listen to me, he's seeing someone else.

She hadn't believed it, not for a second. She and Mike had been together three years. Sure he'd been quiet, spent more time at the lab, had dinner with his buddies sometimes. But he always called to let her know if he'd be home late. If she'd thought anything, it was that they were well-matched in terms of independence and trust, neither one of them possessively checking up on the other all the time like some couples. He'd had a lot of grants to write—he'd complained about how much time that took from his research. But he had to write them, sometimes alone, sometimes with other postdocs. Grants—from the National Institutes of Health or the National Science Foundation or the American Cancer Society—brought in the money that paid his salary. Soft money, it was called; hard money was salary provided by the university, but that was only available to the head of the lab, who had a faculty position. Mike burned to have his own lab some day.

She had dinner with friends, too, didn't she? And sometimes she was the one who brought work home. She'd thought things were pretty good with Mike. Oh, they'd had a few arguments—everybody does. He wanted her to dress up more; she wanted the two of them to have some time together doing the fun outdoor things they used to do. Kayaking on the Deerfield River when recreational dam releases gave it enough water. Hiking up Mt. Washington, even though it was a three-hour drive to to Pinkham Notch. Biking on back roads in the Berkshires.

The dress code at the newspaper was great—there wasn't one. She wore jeans and boots or sneakers, and the same fleece jacket just about every day. But after Mike complained, she went clothes shopping with her friend Marjorie and got a pair of slacks and some blouses. And he promised they'd go cross-country skiing right after the holidays. Things weren't perfect but they were good; she'd even thought they were getting better. A Christmas ski trip with Mike would be the best present ever.

* * *

She'd walked home that Friday feeling good. She'd gone to the gym after work, talked to a woman on the stationary bike next to hers who'd gained 25 pounds after breaking a bone in her foot and being inactive for three months. Kate felt lucky to be healthy and to have only a couple of pounds to lose before she spent a week at a cabin in Waterville Valley, skiing every day. She hoped Mike wouldn't bring too much work on the trip. She promised herself she wasn't going to bring any.

His aging Volvo wasn't parked out front. Odd—it was after six, and he was usually a bear for dinner. She flung her jacket at the coat-rack and headed for the kitchen, singing an old Beatles song. *Blackbird singing in the dead of night. . . .* They had some hummus left over from last night, didn't they? She'd have a snack before she fixed dinner.

A note flapped on the fridge door when she opened it. Were they out of wine, or did he want his favorite curry tonight? She tore off a piece of pita and scooped some hummus before she read it.

Swallowing hard, she read it again. *Kate, I didn't know how to say this, I don't want to hurt you but I want out, I'm seeing Becka and hoping you'll be reasonable. I didn't mean for this to happen but it's happened and here's the thing, do you think you could find another place by the end of the month. I'm staying with her please don't call, but you could just leave voice-mail at the lab, let me know you're out, okay? You'll be fine, you'll be better off with someone else.*

31

Don't call? Like she even knew Becka's number—she barely knew there was a Becka.

At the bottom he'd added a drawing of a smiley-face with a turned-down mouth, colored in with a yellow high-lighter. *Friends?*

Red roses for love, she'd read somewhere. Yellow for friendship.

Yellow was the color of something else, too. Cowardice.

* * *

It hadn't taken her long to pack. She didn't have much stuff, and as soon as she read that note she wanted to be out of there.

She jammed a bunch of clothes—jeans and turtlenecks and handfuls of underwear—into the big Kelty frame pack and threw it into the camper on the truck. Her bicycle came off the porch and went on board, too. She had a rack in the hitch but didn't like to leave the bike out in the weather.

She walked around the apartment and tossed items into her daypack. The tablet, its charger and the one for her cell phone. A journal and an old sketchbook—she didn't want to leave those for Mike to nose around in. Binoculars, a solar-charged clock-radio. What else? A nice set of oil pastels she'd bought with good intentions a couple of years ago and barely used. New sketchbooks, ditto.

In the basement she grabbed her paddle, PFD and the waterproof bag full of other boating gear. Thank goodness her kayak was already on top of the camper, strapped down and locked. The apartment's hallway had room for only one, and it was Mike's. He'd never gotten around to making the promised wall rack so she could put hers inside, too. After a while she'd mentally shrugged and gotten a good cover for her boat.

Anything else?

Oh, right, Mike's Christmas present. She went back inside, found the package at the back of the closet: a luxurious set of long underwear from L. L. Bean. They'd fit her just fine.

TGIF had a different meaning that week. She was glad she didn't have to talk to anyone for two days. Dinner was a sandwich to go, and then she parked on a side street and crawled into her sleeping bag in the bunk over the cab. She'd need to start dealing with her new circumstances and all the problems they would bring, but not tonight.

At least she was out of there.

On Saturday she called Marjorie, who blessedly didn't say I told you so. They'd met when Kate had interviewed her for a feature article on the Danvers school system, where Marjorie taught fifth grade. She was taking courses toward a Master's degree in psychology and sounded like a shrink wanna-be sometimes, which could be annoying, but she was supportive and smart. She had an ex-husband now and two small children.

She offered Kate a cot on her sun-porch, with a space heater, which Kate declined. She also offered coffee and "a good talk," which Kate accepted gratefully.

When she got to her friend's house in Somerville, Marjorie gave her a long hug and then led her to the kitchen. The baby was down for a nap and the little boy was playing with trucks on the linoleum floor. Sunlight flooded the place, along with the smell of cinnamon. Marjorie's curly hair shone gold like a halo.

Kate told her about the note, and Marjorie didn't say How does that make you feel? Kate knew it was written all over her face.

"You moved out awful fast" is what she did say.

"There wasn't a lot to move. And it's a big motivator, knowing you're not wanted."

"You're welcome here for as long as you need to stay, you know."

"Thanks." Kate tried to keep her voice from going wobbly. "I can't really believe this has happened. I'll have to find a place. I guess I should look around Danvers, so I'll be close to work. Or maybe one of the smaller towns. I want someplace where I won't be running into Mike at the grocery store."

They sat for a bit. Kate watched the boy push the truck in circles, making *vroom vroom* noises. She'd never wanted kids of her own, but other people's could be fun. He waved the truck in the air, smiled at her. More *vrooms*.

If trucks could fly.

"I'm not calling to let him know I've left, like he asked me to. Like the note asked me to. He can figure it out." She took a good swallow of Marjorie's strong coffee. "I left the note on the kitchen floor with a big old bootprint on it."

"You'll need someplace to stay besides your camper."

"Eventually." She'd gotten used to her friends not understanding how comfortable the camper was, with its propane heater and stove, and bathroom, and double bed up over the cab. "One day at a time," she said, "just like AA." Kate knew the slogans from her mother.

"As far as I'm concerned," Marjorie was saying, "you have your life back, free from someone who couldn't accept you for who you are. It's really good news disguised as bad. You're free."

* * *

Someone had once described a serious California earthquake to her: solid ground rolled like ocean swells. If Mike's throwing her out felt like that, what happened a few months later felt like the collapse of a building that had appeared to survive the quake.

As soon as she walked into the newsroom that day, the editor said "Kate! Need to see you in here."

Somehow she knew.

She'd been in Bob's office only once before, when he'd hired her. She'd thought at the time that he looked like a caricature—his fat stuffed into a suit, face red, cigarette in hand. He'd glanced at her resume and asked two questions: Had she worked for her college paper? Had she worked for her high school paper? The answer to both was No.

When he said, "Come in on Monday," she'd been stunned.

That had been three years earlier, and in that time he had quit smoking, lost considerable weight, and shown he had a sharp mind and an amazing vocabulary.

That day he looked grim. He sat on the front of his desk and didn't invite her to sit down. "Thing is, Kate, the *News* is being bought. Big chain made an offer, the owner wants to go with it."

"Oh."

"And—" he heaved a sigh—"we have to cut staff big-time. Fifty percent. They want to bring in some of their own." He was looking at the floor.

"Makes sense. I guess."

"Doubt I'll have a job here myself much longer." He looked up. "It's a rotten break, Kate, and I'm sorry."

"When you hired me I didn't have a scrap of experience. You took a chance on me, Bob, and I really appreciate it."

"Worked out pretty well for both of us. You picked things up fast, and you got 'em right. " He gave her a sad smile. "Wish you the best, Kate."

"Best job I've ever had," she managed to say, and then got the heck out of there.

* * *

Danni's call had been a shock too, but at least a pleasant one.

As roommates at UMass Amherst they'd joked about how they were totally incompatible. Danni was gorgeous, fun-loving, into fancy clothes and parties. She was shocked to find that Kate actually liked to read, while for her it was like washing the dishes. "You read one book and then you just have to read another one," she said. "It takes forever. Don't these profs have lives?"

Kate was often in, Danni was always out and about. Kate liked the combination of solitude and company. She suspected Danni liked having her around as a foil, Kate being the dull piece of cloth against which the jewel shone. But that was okay—she knew she wasn't any jewel.

* * *

So long ago; so much had changed. Sitting at the work table in Bobcat, Kate tried not to compare herself to Danni, with her husband and lovely house, her state-wide connections and grand new arts-center project. Stop thinking about Danni, she told herself. Stop thinking about Mike. Think about you.

Maybe she didn't want to.

* * *

The rule at EMAC was that you never visit someone's studio without an invitation. You don't drop in on artists who have left busy lives behind in order to have uninterrupted work time. Kate was startled one afternoon when someone tapped at her door.

She was lying on her bed, hands folded behind her head, staring at the ceiling. It was a warm day and she'd opened the inner door. Birdsong and a soft, piney breeze drifted through the screen door. And now a figure stood on the porch, peering in.

Feeling vulnerable, she sprang to her feet.

"Hey." The voice was gentle. Farley.

"Hi!" The energy in her voice surprised her. "Come in."

"Thanks, but not now. Don't want to disturb you—I'm already breaking the rules. But the thing is—" He laughed a little. "The thing is, I love interruptions. I just want to say that you're welcome to come up to my studio any time." Even through the screen, his eyes were bright.

"Really? What about working? Don't you—?"

"It sounds absurd, but I think it's too darn quiet around here. At night, that's fine, I sleep like the dead, but during the day—well, hey. I saw your door open and told myself I'd just let you know you're welcome. Your studio's closest to mine, and I'm getting plenty of work done. Too much."

She cocked her head. "That's not possible."

"Use the back door—the front steps are scary. Come on up, any time. Bye for now."

Kate lay back and thought about it. Getting too much work done? Maybe she could learn a thing or two from Farland McQuay.

* * *

She visited him the next day. The trail up to Peacock was wide, the two cabins only a couple of hundred feet apart. Maple trees hung a loose screen of leaves between them.

All the other studios had unpainted siding, done with cedar shakes that would weather in a few years to a pretty silver gray. Farley's had clapboards like a house, painted vivid blue with crisp white trim. Kate had seen it from the road below, and it stood out like a lighthouse. Danni knew what she was doing: Peacock was EMAC's flagship studio, with an advertising function.

A steep stairway rose to the front porch, but Kate went past the flagstone path that led to it. At the top of the hill she found the perimeter road Danni had mentioned. It was passable but weedy; she'd never have guessed a fire truck had used it earlier in the summer.

Farley was sitting in a wicker rocking chair on the big back deck. An easel in front of him held a half-finished painting. He saw her and smiled. "Hello, my young friend," he said. "Good to see you."

The other chairs were Adirondack style. Kate sat on the front edge of one and enjoyed the view: clouds of maple leaves above and the Shady River below, its water reflecting the foliage in shivery green ripples. "What a great perch," she said. "You must feel like a bird on a branch."

"You're right," he said. "Though I hadn't thought of it that way." He took a closer look at her. "You're staying more than a minute, I hope? You don't look quite settled."

"Oh, I've never gotten along with this kind of chair," Kate said. "Sitting down is like falling into a ditch."

He laughed. "I know what you mean. Adirondack chairs require commitment. It would take me a month to get out of one. Want some coffee?"

They went inside. The odor of oil paint and mineral spirits greeted Kate like an old friend.

"David came by yesterday," Farley said from the kitchen. "He said those chairs are in italics. Isn't that marvelous?"

It took her a few seconds. "Oh, I get it," she said. "The backs are slanted, and the seats tilt."

"Right. Leave it to a writer to find real-world, tangible italics."

Peacock looked much like Kate's cabin inside, the only difference being a loft. The front window looked over Bobcat's roof, out to the field behind the Big House and to the woods of the rest of the EMAC land.

"David's place has a loft, too, and he sleeps in his. Says not having a bed in his day space prevents procrastinating naps. But I spend a lot of time on the deck, so my day-space is outdoors," Farley said.

She looked around. No bed. "You sleep on the couch?" It didn't look wide enough.

"Sofa-bed," he said. "It's perfectly comfortable." He looked around, obviously pleased. "Of course, the place is a little cluttered right now."

Near the front window, an easel held a canvas in progress: a blue cityscape, abstract enough to be either a pueblo or Manhattan. Three smaller paintings leaned against the wall below it. The one on the deck made five.

"Yikes," she said. "You have been busy."

"I've done some drawings, too. I'm very happy."

"You look like a cat that's swallowed a couple dozen canaries."

Outside, Farley's rocker creaked as he settled back into it, and Kate slid into one of the Adirondacks she'd maligned. At least it had a wide arm for her cup. She watched Farley as he added some brush strokes to his painting. It was an abstract using shades of orange and rust, but its intricate shapes looked looked organic, like a close-up of some exotic bird's feathers.

"It's so quiet here," she said after a while.

"Mostly it is. Now and then there's some truck action down there, late at night. But I'd still call it quiet compared to where I'm from." He looked at her. "You're a study in earth tones. If you went for a walk in the forest, would you be invisible?"

She looked down at her clothes. Boots, brown cargo pants, a black turtleneck. "Animals would smell me."

He lifted an eyebrow. "Really?"

"Wait, I'm not smelly in human terms," she said. "I take showers. But to a coyote or a bobcat, I reek. We all do.

Shampoo, so-called deodorant, sunblock, even the laundry-scent of our clothes, all that adds up to quite a wallop for noses that are hundreds of times more sensitive than ours."

"I had no idea."

"Birds, though, birds can't smell well at all. Except vultures, of course."

Farley laughed. "I'm not sure I've ever seen a vulture." He held up a hand. "Don't describe them. There are some things about which I prefer to remain ignorant."

"They wouldn't win any beauty contests."

She watched time pass in the form of light changing on the leaves overhead. They talked, and he made occasional adjustments to his painting, refolding tinfoil around the brush each time so the paint didn't dry. He told her he'd been in a car accident that shattered one leg and that rehab and physical therapy had taken almost a year. "It's wonderful just to walk again, even though I can't go nearly as fast as I used to. Nor as far. I spend more time in the Frick and smaller galleries now. You have to walk miles in the Met."

Kate told him a little about her life—losing Mike, the subdued Christmas spent with Marjorie, getting laid off at the newspaper, then the serendipitous timing of Danni's invitation.

She was surprised at how soon she spilled the uneasy truth about having trouble focusing, reviving her ability to work. Telling him felt good. Such a peculiar position: the luxury of time to create in a beautiful place, and yet she felt more scared than grateful.

"Wait a minute," she said. "I shouldn't be telling this to Mr. Productive."

He didn't seem to hear the compliment. "I start small," he said. "Use my sketchbook as a place to put things that might interest me in a bigger way. I'd be lost without it. If I could take one thing from a burning house, that would be it.

Not the finished stuff—that's a done deal, old news. The notebook is where my life is."

She liked that he didn't judge her or lecture her about wasted opportunity.

The rocker creaked as he lit a pipe. Cherry tobacco, sweet. She felt comfortable, as if they'd been friends for years.

"The sketchbook—that's what gets me jazzed. But you've worked before, you'll find your way. You'll know it, that way of seeing that gives you so much pleasure you have to reach out to touch it, capture it it, put it down on paper. That's really it—just teaching yourself to see again. Or feel."

"I know what you mean," she said. "Or rather I remember what you mean. I always have a sketchbook in my daypack. Funny habit, since I haven't worked in quite a while."

"You'll find your way back."

Find her way. Like the deer in the woods that made all those trails. Or like Marjorie's boy in kitchen sunshine, back in Massachusetts, zooming his truck through the air. Trucks *could* fly—you just had to hold them the right way.

They talked for a long time. Now and then he hoisted himself up, limped a few steps and looked out over the river. He kept talking while he did it, telling Kate stories about growing up in "the City," by which he meant New York, a place that Kate found intimidating. She enjoyed hearing it demystified by a native, and someone so unlike her clichéd image of an egocentric New Yorker.

* * *

"Well, my dear neighbor, shall we go to dinner? It's almost six."

She didn't flinch at "dear" this time. She knew him better, knew his manner; also, she was a bit tipsy. When it had gotten cool on the deck they'd gone inside, and Farley had started pouring wine instead of coffee. She felt more relaxed than she had in ages. What a pleasure it was to hang out with a fellow artist. And yes, she was hungry.

"Sure, let's go." She stood, set her glass on the counter. And froze.

The sound was indescribable. It wrenched her brain into red alert, heart racing.

Farley was staring at her, eyes wide. "What on earth was *that?*"

"God, Farley. I have no idea."

It came again. Even though it was probably less than ten seconds long, it reached into whatever part of her brain controlled anxiety and turned on all the lights. It was a garbled noise that ended in something like a hoarse cough. Some large animal must be prowling around outside. Maybe her cabin was named Bobcat for a reason.

No, bobcats don't make noises like that. She'd grown up with them, had fond memories of seeing them occasionally when she'd hiked with her father. The only sound she'd ever heard one make was a hiss like a house cat's.

"It sounds like something quite large," Farley said carefully.

"I've never heard anything like it. It's not a fox, or a coyote. They can be noisy, but not like that."

"A friend insisted I bring bear spray," Farley said. "Let's see if I can find it." He opened a drawer under the kitchen counter and rummaged.

Kate stopped herself from saying the noise wasn't made by a bear. It wouldn't hurt to have some defense against whatever it was.

She slipped onto the back porch a few steps ahead of Farley and did a quick scan behind the cabin and to each side. Then a slower look. Nothing but trees.

She went to the corner of the cabin and looked down the trail. "I don't see anything," she said. She'd almost said "anybody," because it might not be an animal. Maybe it was a person imitating an animal, intending to scare them. The intruder who'd run from the Big House lounge? But she hadn't told Farley about the incident, and she didn't want to alarm him now with that dreadful noise fresh in his mind.

They both looked over their shoulders more than once as they moved down the trail past Bobcat. Farley held the canister of bear spray slightly ahead of him, his finger riding on the button, even after they reached the openness of the Loop and the field beside it. Kate sneaked a look. Yes, he had the spray nozzle pointed away from himself.

They walked without speaking The sun, just over the trees, threw lances of light in their eyes, blinding them. Kate was tense. Farley's breathing was fast, though the pace felt slow to her, even slower than when they'd walked in the other direction after dinner the night before. The man is not well, she thought. He doesn't need this kind of stress.

At the door to the Big House, he dropped the bear spray into a pocket and smiled ruefully at her. "Dinner. Safe from lions and tigers and bears. After dinner, let's walk back together."

"You bet," she said. Whatever the creature was, she didn't want Farley to face it alone. And she didn't mind having his bear spray at the ready, either.

* * *

She slipped out of her jeans and into bed, willing her mind to focus on hope. Farley had said such helpful things about how to break through what he called droughts. She would just have to keep trying until she found her way back to art. Danni had faith in her, and now Farley did too. She couldn't let them down.

Despite her efforts, the frightening call she'd heard with Farley echoed in her mind. They'd described it at dinner, but nobody had had any good ideas about what it might have been. The description had suffered from Farley's narrative style: he'd presented it as an amusing dinner-time anecdote.

He hadn't thought it was funny at the time. They'd both been scared silly.

As she drifted off to sleep she wondered whether an animal had made it or whether some human, some practical joker, was prowling the EMAC grounds.

Why would someone want to scare Farley? Or her?

FOUR

Kate leaned against the fender, waiting for Joy and Nava. Neither had a car, so they were all going to town in Kate's truck.

"Girls' day off," Joy called from the Big House steps. "Yay!" As she and Nava joined Kate, an ATV rolled into the parking lot from the Loop. The well-muscled rider, a man in his forties with a red bandana above mirrored sunglasses, came to a stop and nodded at them.

"Hi, Joy. Hi, Nava," he said. "And you must be Danni's friend Kate?" He stuck out a hand.

It was rough, calloused. A tradesman, or outdoorsman. Or both. "Yes."

"Welcome to EMAC. I'm Ryan, and I handle everything Danni can't. She does the paperwork and PR, and I do the physical stuff. All the work that goes into keeping the cabins—excuse me, studios—up to snuff."

"Thanks for everything you do, Ryan. You work with Andy, don't you?" Danni had said the two men were friends.

"Oh, I have lots of help. You've seen guys on four-wheeler like this one? They do tons more than deliver lunch baskets. Only difference with Andy is I don't have to pay him." He laughed. "Me and my crew, we get stuff done. But if you want it done sooner and better, talk to me." He gave the throttle a quick twist, revving the engine.

The women looked at each other, unsure what to say.

"So if you have a stopped-up sink, or a latch that won't catch, flag me down or leave a note in my mailbox," he said.

"It's the last one in the bottom row of cubbies in the Big House. Marked 'Staff.'"

"Thanks, Ryan," Joy said.

"You ladies have a fine day." He gave his ride a little too much gas as he left, spraying gravel over their shoes.

Nava watched the ATV turn back toward the Loop. "He always wears those mirrored sunglasses," she said. "They make me uncomfortable."

Joy, being petite, got the middle position on the bench seat. She giggled as Kate drove down the Farm Road switchbacks to Short Creek. "I've never been in such a big truck," she said.

"This isn't big," Kate said. "It's just an ordinary pick-up, three-quarter-ton. You New Yorkers. Where I grew up, everybody drove these things." She smiled but kept her eyes on the road. "Out West, most cars are trucks."

They all wanted to check their email, but according to Danni the library had only one computer and they'd have to take turns. Nava wanted to get some snacks at the IGA to help manage her blood sugar between meals, Kate wanted to check out the bookshop and the outdoor store, and Joy was going to scout the Bear Pause general store for art supplies. The plan was they'd meet at the Crazy Cat Café for lunch after their errands. Kate had left a note in the kitchen cancelling their doorstep baskets.

In the small lobby of the brick Civic Center, doors marked *Library* and *Police* faced each other. Kate exchanged smiles with a young librarian and settled at the computer. An email from Marjorie asked how the work was going. What a supportive friend she'd been through Kate's double disaster of losing Mike and, a few months later, her job. Kate had finally moved from her camper to Marjorie's enclosed back porch for a few months. The quiet Christmas they'd spent together—well, quiet after the children went to sleep—had been a blessing.

Kate's return email didn't say anything about her trouble working, just that she was fine and settling in and it was pretty in Maine. A quick search on the Internet turned up a cartoon dinosaur, which she attached to her message, for Marjorie's son. Then she went down the street to check out the used bookstore. Although she read mostly on her tablet these days, she still liked physical books.

Books, Ink was small but well-stocked. Kate found a used copy of a Barbara Kingsolver novel she hadn't read. She was tempted to browse further but reminded herself she wasn't working—no paycheck from the *Danvers Daily News*. So she bought the Kingsolver (a steal at three bucks) and told herself she could have another book as a reward when she'd finished a drawing. Or two or three.

She didn't want to keep the others waiting, so her camping store visit was quick. A lot of its stock was Army surplus, which meant good, cheap equipment even if it didn't have the sleek look and trendy colors of L.L. Bean's.

She hurried down the sidewalk. The day was cloudy and cool, but dry. At the café, Joy waved from a table. She was laughing before Kate sat down. "God, I can't believe the names of the shops around here. Crazy Cat Café? Bear Pause? Sew What? They'd get laughed right out of the City." She took a breath. "Lots of art supplies at Bear Pause, though. Oils, acrylics, gesso, canvas, paper, you name it. Happy day."

"Not bad for a one-stoplight town at the east end of nowhere," Kate said. She took the wooden chair opposite Joy and looked around. They were surrounded by cute kitty pictures, on the walls, on the paper placemats, on the menu. Even on the napkins.

"This place does make me miss my cats, though," Joy said.

"I like cats. How many do you have?"

"Just two. My boyfriend's taking care of them but he doesn't let them snuggle the way I do. He's always on his laptop, and he says there's not enough room."

"Cats are the original laptops. Tell him they got there first."

"He's not a cat person. I had to tell him 'Love me, love my kitties.'"

The place wasn't busy, but it was early for lunch. Two men near the door who looked like they worked outdoors wolfed sandwiches. At another table a woman sat next to her little boy, both of them laughing as she flew French fries toward him one by one, edible airplanes swooping into the hangar of his mouth.

The waitress looked really young. Shouldn't she be in school? She had rings piercing her eyebrows. Ouch. I must be getting old, Kate thought. She and Joy both got coffee while they waited for Nava.

"They sleep with me when he doesn't." *What?* Oh, Joy was talking about her cats. "When he's on a trip or off visiting his mother. They don't sleep with him, though, when I'm gone. They'll be all over me like Velcro when I get back. Oh, here's Nava." Joy leaned across the table and lowered her voice. "She is *so* nice. And she's doing well, even though she's only been working in oils for a couple of years. She told me she used to be in Army intelligence. Isn't that amazing?!"

Kate couldn't imagine Nava in the Army. That must have been ages ago. The woman had to be on the far side of 80.

Joy seemed to inspire people to tell her important things about themselves. Kate looked at her face, her huge eyes, the smile creases on each side of her mouth like parentheses, and an expression of complete interest in what was going on around her. Kate knew her own face didn't look nearly that open.

The older woman paused just inside the door, probably waiting for her eyes to adjust. When she started moving she tripped a little on the edge of the mat. Both Kate and Joy half-rose, but Nava caught herself with her cane and joined them, putting a paper grocery bag on the fourth chair.

"I hope you girls haven't been here long." Her voice was high, fluty. "Don't worry about my tripping. I've got some very simple surgery scheduled in a few weeks to deal with these eyelids. They've lost their elasticity so they're lower than they should be. It's like living under an umbrella or an awning all the time. Like not being able to roll the window shades up. Or the blinds. Ah, that's why they're called blinds." She laughed. "I think it affects my work, my sense of color, and I'm really looking forward to that surgery. It's much simpler than the cataract surgery I had ten years ago. Of course that was a breeze. For me. I bet this one will be simpler for the surgeons." She looked back and forth between them. "Oh, I am running on a bit, aren't I?"

Kate and Joy protested. But as it turned out, both Joy and Nava loved to talk, and they loved to talk about other people, and much of the conversation for the next hour or so was about their fellow EMAC artists. Kate wondered what they would be saying about her if she weren't there.

She remembered how glad she'd been when Joy had stopped Hallsy and David from taking pot shots at Reggie that first night. And now listen to her. Maybe if gossiping needed to be done Joy wanted to be the one doing it.

Reggie, of course, came in for criticism of both his ego and his cigar. "I can smell that horrible smoke all over him, even when he isn't carrying the thing," Nava complained. "Even that woman of his—Sherri? smells nasty. I think it gets in her hair." The two agreed that Hallsy was almost as loud as Reggie but was otherwise not at all like him. "Hallsy has a generous heart," Nava said. "He'd give you the shirt off his back."

"Or the canvas off his easel," Joy agreed. "I get great vibes from him."

"And David is very kind, too," Nava said. "He helped me move the table in my studio over to the window. I do love natural light, don't you? I need it, especially now. Oh, I shouldn't say he helped me—he was the one who moved the table. I helped by telling him where I wanted it." She laughed again. She laughs a lot, Kate thought. With her high voice it sounded like birdsong.

"That Danielle has done a wonderful thing," Nava said. "Bringing us all together."

"I don't know how she does it," Joy said. "Out here, so far from anything else. No museums or galleries. I mean, that library has about a dozen books, none of them about art."

"That's the point, isn't it? No distractions? For us anyway." Nava said. "Thank goodness for e-books."

"Well, you keep up," Kate put in. It was the first thing she'd said in ten minutes.

"We have to, don't we? Yes, this old lady is all over the Internet. When it's available."

Kate started to take a bite from the second half of her BLT and noticed the salads on the other two plates looked barely touched. At the rate they were going they'd close the place down. She made her bite a small one.

"Danni has sacrificed a cosmopolitan lifestyle. I suppose we all sacrifice something, at least temporarily, to work here," Nava said. "Life isn't easy for anyone. David was telling me how bad he felt about his divorce—not about his ex-wife, he's happy to be rid of her, but for his son, who's fifteen and is suddenly getting into trouble all the time. Some kind of theft, that was the last thing. His wife is blaming it all on him, and he kind of agrees. Thinks he should have maybe waited, but he just couldn't stand it, stand her, anymore.

"And that nice young photographer, Kim, he told me all about his immigration status. Worried about being deported. I feel so sorry for him."

Amazing how much Nava, too, knew about everyone. Maybe Kate could imagine her in the intelligence game, after all. The older woman had been at the Center only a few more days than Kate, but the other artists seemed to be falling all over themselves to tell Nava their troubles. As a reporter, Kate's job had been to get information from sources, but that was different. Referendum results, unemployment rates, zoning board appeals—it could be complicated, but it wasn't personal. Nobody told her their life story.

Marjorie had explained to her once that some people get energized by talking to others and some people get depleted. Kate had put herself in the latter category, but clearly her two new friends found conversation invigorating.

She should be careful what she said to Joy or Nava. Talking to them might be a form of broadcasting. The town criers of EMAC.

And then she thought of all the things she'd told Farley. She hoped he wasn't letting the other artists know about her trouble working. She didn't think so, but maybe she'd ask him.

Her ears perked up at a familiar name. Nava was talking about Andy. "He came over to replace the light bulb in my kitchen—had to use a ladder to get up there. He was so funny and friendly. He doesn't seem to have a problem living way out here."

"I love living here, but only for a month, with a project to work on," Joy said. "And Danni, she's a city rat, like me. She must get crazy hanging around with a bunch of pine trees."

"She's gone a lot," Nava said, "fund-raising and conferences, that sort of thing. I would think that'd be difficult for Andy, but he didn't say so. Said he'd gotten used to being stuck in the sticks." Her laugh at the pun sounded like ice tinkling in a glass.

Kate kept her head down. These two didn't know she was good friends with Danni.

Or maybe they did know. It was quiet for a bit. They were actually eating.

* * *

Kate drove up the switchbacks to the arts center, then gave Joy and Nava a tour of her camper. Joy got on board; Nava stood at the door and looked in as Kate pointed out the three-burner propane stove, fridge, and the little furnace tucked under a settee. She told them she'd had an extra battery installed and put LED bulbs in all the light fixtures. "They hardly use any juice," she said. "I can camp anywhere I want, not just at an RV park with electricity."

Both of her friends said she was nuts. Kate had heard that before.

"I've got 30 gallons of water. Air conditioning and a microwave when I run the generator. A water heater. A queen bed. What's not to like?"

"I don't know how you can live in such a small space," Joy said. "What if you want to dance?"

"I go outside. Being outdoors is what makes me want to dance."

* * *

She walked the Loop, then went back to the Big House to check her mailbox. Erik was leaning on the porch rail. She gave him a smile on her way in.

"Hiya." His wild brown hair stuck out in all directions, and stubble on his face said he hadn't shaved today. Or yesterday.

Her mail was a lonely postcard; she read it as she stepped back out.

"Something from your boyfriend?"

She glanced up. "My mother," she said. "She doesn't do letters, says they're too much work. Her cards usually say 'Hi! How are you? Love, Ma.' It means I should call her." Her mother must have gotten the EMAC address from Kate's sister in Colorado. "Hey, you're here kind of early for dinner. And kind of late for breakfast. Don't you get any time off?"

"I live here."

"Oh? In one of the studios?"

"Heck, no, not one of her precious studios. I live in a closet."

"What? No. You're pulling my leg."

"I don't mind. It's a large closet. The second floor has a bunch of storerooms, and Danni renovated one of them into a pretty nice living space. Skylight, even."

Kate shook her head. "She's amazing."

"Cheap way to get live-in help," Erik said. "But no worries. Free rent. And I'll let you hang out on my porch. What do they say where you come from? Mi casa es su casa?"

Funny he knew she'd grown up in Tucson, but word gets around, she supposed. Would Farley have mentioned it? She joined him at the rail, and neither of them spoke for a minute. They looked across the field to the woods. The light was long and slanted, the day still.

"Hey, you smell like garlic," Kate said.

"Yep. Always do. Cook's perfume."

Insect noise. The firmness of the warm boards under her feet. A shiver as cloud-shadow passed over them, spread across the field.

She whispered. "Look, Erik."

A fox was hunting in the grass. It took a few steps, and stopped, and cocked its head to listen. Took a few more steps. Kate watched it with that rush of joy that seeing wildlife always gave her. This time she wasn't just seeing the fox, she was seeing how it lived its life.

The fox froze, head down. Held the position for long seconds. Then rose up into an arc and came down with its front paws together.

Erik laughed.

The fox put its nose into the grass and came up with something small and limp dangling from its mouth. It turned and trotted toward the woods.

"I was hoping I'd see one," Erik said. "They don't come every day. " He turned his back to the field, put his palms behind him on the rail and lifted himself up to sit on it.

Strong arms. The guy was fit. Was he showing off for her?

"I sure do like living in this part of the world," he said. "I was a Coast Guard brat and my father got stationed in Jonesport. So I grew up not far from here, ran around in the woods as a kid."

Great, an outdoorsy guy who knew the area. Kate thought he'd been busy in the kitchen during the dinner conversation about the strange noise she and Farley had heard. She told Erik about it now, how frightening it had been. "Do you know any kind of animal that would make a sound like that? Like a horse with a bad cough?"

He snorted. "A horse with a cold? A hoarse horse?" He thought for a bit. "You heard it twice. Was it exactly the same each time?"

She thought back. "Yes, I think so."

"Then it's probably one of them barred owls. They can make some hellacious noises. Curdle your blood."

"But no, wait, we heard a barred owl, a few of us, on the porch the first night. It was sweet."

"That's their mating call," Erik said. "You know, like when you date a girl and she's all lovey-dovey and then it

54

turns out—" He took a deep breath. "They have other calls, weird ones, really chill your bones. To scare up prey, maybe."

A few minutes later, walking to Bobcat, she focused on the fox, running the memory of its pounce through her mind a couple of times. What a gorgeous animal. The sun on its fur washed the uneasiness about that crazy call out of her mind.

An owl? Really? The next time she was in Short Creek she'd do an online search on the bird, maybe find an audio of their calls.

Erik sounded like he knew what he was talking about, though. Just a bird. Her tension eased.

* * *

She was reading in bed and had almost nodded off when a sharp thump jerked her awake. Something had hit Bobcat, hard.

Dammit, somebody *was* trying to scare her. Some ten-year-old townie twit whose parents thought artists were fragile, impractical people who didn't know how to use a screwdriver or boil water. Kate yanked on jeans and jammed her feet into sneakers. She grabbed a flashlight on her way out the door.

No flashlight needed. The moon was full and high, flooding the Loop with silver light. She looked left and right. Nobody.

Ahead of her, moonlight highlighted the birches along the road but didn't penetrate the dark mass of forest behind them. Was someone hiding in there?

Faint noise of an engine starting up, down by the Big House. An ATV came into view, puttering across the parking lot. As it turned onto Farm Road, the spotlight above the EMAC sign lit the rider's blue and white checked shirt.

Kate sighed. That guy could be the cabin-thumping culprit or a just a worker fixing something that couldn't wait, like a plumbing leak. She hadn't been fast enough to know.

She went around the corner to the window nearest her bed. A smear on the glass turned dark red in the flashlight beam, and on the ground below sprawled a huge black bird, a raven. She prodded it with her boot. The body was practically in shreds, as if it had been hit with a shotgun blast.

Why her? Why now? Was this random vandalism? Some small-town kid gone bonkers? She couldn't think of anyone she'd pissed off with a news story, and even if such a person existed she doubted he would know where to find her.

No, if it wasn't aimed at her then it must have to do with EMAC. Someone who hated the place. Or hated Danni. She'd have to find out if other artists were being harassed. Were dead birds showing up at Danni and Andy's house?

She had a lot of questions, but one thing was for sure. Ravens don't fly at night.

FIVE

She taped the list to the fridge door. Only four items, much shorter than her to-do lists when she'd worked at the newspaper.

1. Make art
2. Bike or walk
3. Read
4. Talk to somebody.

Then she took it down and wrote at the top: "Don't Think about It, Do It." One of each, every day. The list was a prescription to prevent naps, the kind of naps that lasted all day. It would fight depression, that sneak-thief of time and energy.

All right, she had a job, daily tasks. She was no longer unemployed.

Finding somebody to talk to wasn't a problem. Farley, Joy and Nava had all invited her to drop into their studios. "If I don't answer the door, I'm thinking too hard," Nava said, "but nine times out of ten I'm happy when a fellow artist visits." Dinner was a daily opportunity. She didn't necessarily look forward to it—socializing with that many people was an effort—but she always went.

She had some unread books on her tablet, and she'd found a shelf in the Big House where former residents donated books they didn't want to take home.

Biking or walking? Easy. So many roads and trails to choose from. Inside Bobcat, her bicycle leaned against the wall, ready to go. She'd found a twenty-mile bike route she liked, uphill going out, downhill coming back. She told herself, floating down the hill on her Trek, how lucky she was to have the time to do this.

Art. That was the hard part.

She liked having it on a list. Just another thing to do. She made herself sit at the table for an hour. Sometimes she even doodled. But nothing interested her. Nothing happened in her head.

She'd been at EMAC a week. Danni believed in her and Farley believed in her, but even geniuses make mistakes. Kate would give herself a few days after the Open Studio event, and if she couldn't produce something she'd leave.

Anxiety hung around her like a cloud of mosquitos as she walked down the road to the abandoned mill. Even the sound of the river wasn't soothing today. Was the raven incident unnerving her? The man running from the Big House lounge? Were they part of the reason she had nothing to say with her pencil?

* * *

That night's dinner was the first meal at EMAC that was less than stellar. Joy, who always knew everything, told the group in the lounge Erik was angry because he'd found an entire sheet apple pie gone, eaten right out of the pan, the glutton's fork left among the crumbs like a metallic middle finger.

Worse, when whoever had been in the kitchen turned off the lights on the way out, he hit the adjacent switch that controlled electricity to the stoves. So the ovens went off and the four marinated chickens not only didn't cook, they had to be thrown out.

It was pretty clear the "perp" was Reggie, Erik had told Joy, because the kitchen smelled like a "cat-piss cigar."

"Erik said the bozo just swiped his paw down the row of switches, didn't notice one of them was red," Joy said. "Goodbye dinner. What a jerk." She might not have said that to Reggie's face, but he and Sherri always came in around seven, skipping the social hour.

That night they were even later. Erik rang the bell, and the rest of them settled around the table. Rolls and salad made the rounds.

"Hey! Spinach salad. All right, I'm Popeye, you're Olive. No, you're not ugly enough," Hallsy said to Joy, adding "You neither" to Kate.

"The Olive Oyls of the world unite to smack you in the face with a salmon-colored cloth napkin," Joy said, doing so.

Reggie and Sherri swept in like royalty. Nobody greeted them.

Erik must have been watching, because within seconds he set a steaming casserole dish next to Reggie, who immediately helped himself. He took a bite and made a face. "Not so great," he said to Sherri, who put back some of what she'd served herself. "Way too salty."

"How about a second opinion?" Farley asked. Reggie didn't respond. Was he deaf, or just inconsiderate?

"Do pass it along, won't you?" Farley said, louder.

Reggie ignored him. Sherri reached around him and slid the dish along the table.

"Speaking of opinions," Reggie said, "I got a personal note from my pal at the Whitney today. I was the most qualified candidate for the Bucksbaum they've ever seen. But I didn't get the prize."

A short silence. Next to Kate, Farley said "Condolences."

Reggie slammed his fist on the table so hard the silverware jumped. Kate jumped too. "Don't give me that crap, Farley. I know you're tight with that family. You have a say in what goes on."

"I have absolutely no influence over—"

"That's a hundred thousand bucks out the window," Reggie shouted. "You're set for life, you pompous ass, but I sure could've used that money." His face was red, and spittle flew from his lips.

Kate looked at Farley. His mouth was a thin line. His hands were in his lap, and she put her own hand over them for a moment. He gave her a look of appreciation.

"Wow, Reggie is actually right," Hallsy said. "Erik struck out this time. Who'd have thunk it possible?"

"Major ingredient is cream of mushroom soup, from a can," Joy said. "Takes me right back to my childhood."

Bless Hallsy and Joy for ignoring Reggie, Kate thought. That said plainer than words his tirade wasn't worth a response.

In a voice loud enough to carry to the kitchen, Reggie said, "What is this garbage? Looks like something I had to eat in my high-school cafeteria, but in those days I wasn't smart enough to complain. Danni pays that schmo back there enough to do better than this."

Sherri usually supported everything Reggie said. This time she looked embarrassed and said "Reggie, honey," in a low voice.

"Shut up, Reggie," Hallsy said cheerfully. "Erik isn't bigger than you are, but he's a whole lot stronger."

Kim said, "Is it a saying you have about breaking the hand that feed you?"

"Stupid son of a bitch ought to be fired," Reggie said.

David said quietly, "How about we all take a deep breath? I don't know about the rest of you, but I'd really hate cooking for myself."

"Better you than me," Hallsy said. "I live on boiled pork chops at home. And beer."

"Wine for me," Nava said, and smiled.

"The saying is about *biting* the hand that feeds you, Kim," David said. "Like a dog might."

"We're lucky to have Erik, you know," Joy said. "He was in the Navy for a couple of years but he wasn't just a regular mess cook for long. He has a flair, got himself promoted to doing banquets for big brass, admirals and—" she apparently couldn't think of another naval rank. "And the other top dudes. Pretty cool for a guy from the sticks of Maine."

Reggie looked at her. "And just how, exactly, do you know all this?" His face was still red, but at least he wasn't shouting at Farley.

"I talk with him. You know? Talk with, not at."

"You could talk the socks off a snake, Joy," Nava said.

Kate stifled a yawn. It's a bad sign when even a fight among your dinner partners can't keep you awake, but she hadn't been sleeping well.

She took her plate to the kitchen pass-through. Her weight was coming down a little and the last thing she needed was dessert. Too bad Bobcat didn't have a scale.

Erik came out of the kitchen carrying a baking pan. "Hey," Kate said. "That casserole was just fine. Reminded both me and Joy of home. Don't let the buzzard get you down."

Without a glance, he walked past her and put the pan down on the table right in front of Reggie.

Kate had gotten in the habit of getting coffee for herself and Farley. She took two cups off the rack and was filling them from the electric urn when Joy said, "Oh, ugh. What *is* this?"

On the way back to her seat, Kate checked out the dessert. The main layer looked like it was made of oatmeal, a tan, granular stuff. On top lay some dark shapes the size of mice. Some of them had tan flakes stuck to them. In the middle Erik had placed a small plastic cat.

Reggie looked furious, his hands clenched on the table, his arms rigid.

"What we have here," David said in his calm way, "appears to be a cat's litter box. In active use."

"The man is pissed," Hallsy said. "So to speak."

Reggie got slowly to his feet. "I'll be talking to Danni about this," he shouted toward the kitchen. Then he slammed his chair into the table so hard all the silverware jumped again.

"Oh, lighten up." Joy had recovered. She even giggled.

Sherri said, "It's funny, Reggie."

He glared at her.

Erik's voice sailed out of the kitchen. "Apricot crumble with chocolate medallions."

"Sounds good to me." Hallsy was the first to take a serving, and it wasn't a small one.

"I don't even want to look at it," Reggie said. "And I don't have to put up with this crap."

Joy giggled again. "Cool pun."

Reggie ignored her. He looked down at Sherri. "Are you coming?"

She hesitated, then stood up.

"Man's asking for trouble and I'm going to give it to him. Practical jokes are for kids in middle school. Or the Army," Reggie said, looking at Joy.

"Navy," she said.

"You're easily offended, big guy," Hallsy said. "And watch what you say about the Army. I'm a vet." His voice changed. "Hey! This stuff's great. Pass it along."

"So am I," Nava said. "I mean, I'm also a vet. Not I'm great." Her melodious laugh didn't change the scowl on Reggie's face.

"You're right, Hallsy, this is yummy," David said. "Creative use of anger."

"I think you're pretty great, Nava," Joy said.

"Is there a word 'prant'?" Kim asked. "A joke that someone does?"

"Prank," David said. "With a 'k.'"

Reggie stalked out. Sherri turned and gave the room a sad look before she followed him.

"Poor girl," Nava said.

"She's got a spine," Hallsy said. "She just has to figure out what it's for."

* * *

After dinner Kate and Farley walked back toward their cabins together.

"Glass of wine?" he asked, as they approached Bobcat.

"Thanks," she said. "I'd like that. It'd be nice to unwind from Reggie's tantrum."

"He's a pretty good artist, but he thinks he's even better. I didn't have anything to do with his not getting that prize. It's another example of his hyperbolic thinking. He's good, so he's a genius. I'm influential, so I decide everything."

"He's crazy."

"I just hope he doesn't go over the edge."

"How would we know?" Kate asked, but Farley didn't laugh.

Should she suspect Reggie as the slinger of dead ravens at her window? No, whoever did that had been able to move quickly enough afterwards that she hadn't caught sight of him. Reggie was ponderous and slow.

Careful with her glass of Pinot Noir, Kate slid into an Adirondack chair. She took a sip and sighed. "You know, I've told you a lot of stuff about myself. My mother's an alcoholic, my father left us, I lost my job and my boyfriend, a whole lot of stuff like that. And how worried I am about getting myself back to work as an artist. And I'm wondering—"

"If I tell other people. No, Kate, I don't." He took a sip of his wine, set it down on the deck beside his rocker. "Sherri comes up here and talks to me, and Joy. Have I told you any of their confidences?"

"No." She was already kicking herself for having to ask, for not trusting him. The word "confidences" was so Farley—old-fashioned but perfectly accurate, an older and wiser version of her own "I've told you a lot of stuff." His word sounded a little shrink-like, but not in that annoying way Marjorie sometimes had. This was a man she could trust. Sherri and Joy apparently thought so too. Interesting that it would mostly be the women who came to talk to him. Although she'd seen David going up the path to Peacock a couple of times. Hallsy, too, once.

"Well, then. You're safe here."

The hoot of a great-horned owl came faintly from behind them. Somewhere on the EMAC property silent wings were opening, talons reaching—

Much closer, an engine in low gear grumbled along the river road and went silent. Kate stood and looked down toward the Shady, but didn't see any lights.

She paced the deck, restless. "You know, Farley, I think somebody's trying to scare me." She told him about the dead raven. "Why would anyone want to spook me? Or us? Nobody else is getting messed with like this. I checked with Joy and Nava, and Danni."

"I can think of a few people who don't like me, but I doubt they'd follow me up here from Manhattan. You know anybody in Massachusetts who'd come up here to kill you a personal raven?"

"No way. It must be somebody local."

He picked up his wine, swirled it in the glass. "Short Creek has changed a lot in the past few years. Sometimes people don't like change."

"But if EMAC's the target, why not throw dead ravens at Danni's house, not mine?"

"A good question. I'm afraid I don't have the answer." He stood and turned on the light outside Peacock's back door, then regarded the nearly finished canvas on the easel. "Let's think about it."

* * *

It was fully dark when Kate left Farley's. She felt jumpy. She didn't want to see another dead bird, or anybody around her cabin. She aimed her flashlight beam along the trees at the side of the trail, across the back and side of Bobcat.

She'd come to the Center with such good intentions, such hope. Marjorie had told her she was free. Farley was telling her she was safe. So why couldn't she work? Was she going to let a couple of stupid pranks disrupt her life?

The door to her cabin was wide open.

She was sure she hadn't left it like that, sure she would have noticed if it had been open after dinner when she and Farley walked past Bobcat on their way to Peacock. Somebody had gone in while she and Farley were talking. From now on, she'd lock the cabin.

She was glad she had on sneakers. She crept onto the porch and reached inside the screen door, flipped on the light.

Only the one room, and nobody in it. The bathroom door was half-open; she looked in. Empty.

Rolling her shoulders to relax, she locked the door and turned around. That's when she saw it.

At its thickest, the snake was as big around as her forearm. Loosely coiled on her bed, gleaming black, it blended enough with the dark green spread that she hadn't noticed it right away. She'd been about to sit next to it to take off her sneakers.

Its eyes were bright and its black tongue flickered, tasting the air. Kate wasn't up on her snakes, but at least it didn't have rattles at the end of its tail.

She'd been startled, but she was calming down. Snakes weren't so bad. She'd take a snake any day over a hairy spider or a cockroach. But she didn't want to sleep with one.

She flipped the bottom of the bedspread over the snake. It didn't move. She flipped the top of the bedspread down, and folded the sides together.

Origami. One snake to go.

She unlocked the door, grabbed the folded-up spread by its corners and eased the whole package onto the porch. Looking into the moonlit night, she wondered if whoever had parked the reptile in her cabin was still out there, watching.

Why was he—or they, or she, for all Kate knew—trying to scare her? The big snake didn't bother her, but the person who'd made the delivery did.

She closed the door and locked it.

Tablet and books and clothes were all undisturbed. Even the cell phone, in plain sight on the bedside table where she kept it charging and occasionally used as a nightlight. Nothing was missing.

Even so, it took her a long time to get to sleep.

SIX

The morning was splendid, sun filtering through the pines and the air warming quickly. Halfway up the hill, Kate watched Erik pump along Farm Road above her. He was an experienced rider, knew to shift up and keep spinning instead of straining his knees.

Fifteen minutes ago, when she'd headed out for her daily exercise, he'd been leaning on the patio railing behind the Big House. She waved; he raised a hand. His wild hair was shorter, and ragged. Maybe he'd cut it himself.

"Nice bike," he'd said.

"Thanks," she said, braking to a stop next to the patio. "Do you like to ride?"

"Those are my wheels over there," he said, pointing to the red Specialized at the end of the rack. Kate had noticed it her first day here because it put the gaggle of decrepit EMAC bikes to shame. "Feel like company?"

Kate shrugged. "Fine with me."

He vaulted over the railing, landing gracefully. "Where're you going?"

"Up. Down. You know these roads. Why don't you take us for a ride?"

"I might do that. Hang on, I'll get my helmet."

Kate followed him inside. While he went upstairs, she lifted the second key off the Bobcat hook. The Big House was always unlocked; anyone could borrow a key. Copy it, even. She didn't want any more snakes in her bed. Or anything worse.

Before rolling her bike out of the cabin, she'd gone out to the porch and tugged a corner of the bedspread. It moved easily, so she shook it out and put it back on the bed. The wise snake had opted for more natural haunts.

* * *

Erik was honking up the long grade, the bike rocking slightly as he stood over the saddle, his weight shifting back and forth between the pedals. He was a lot stronger rider than Kate.

In her mirror a red pick-up truck rounded the curve behind them, going a little too fast. When you're on a bike just about anything with an engine looks like it's going too fast. The truck slowed as it passed her, then slowed even more as it came alongside Erik, the passenger leaning out the window. Then his arm came up, and with a glint of metal something arced through the air, hit Erik's shoulder and clattered onto the road.

Erik had stopped and was wiping his face against his sleeve when she got to him. "Are you okay? What a punk."

"Ah, crap. Some people don't like artists. I should wear a T-shirt that says Don't Shoot Me, I'm Only the Cook."

The blue-and-silver can at the edge of the road dribbled beer. Kate set it upright, stomped it flat and tucked it in her jersey pocket. She hated litter. "Huh. Now you smell like garlic and beer. Want to go back?"

"Nope. Screw the creeps."

So they went on, up the hill past Danni's house and left on Quail Ridge Road. She'd biked it before—a pleasant, curvy road running above the valley where Short Creek nestled. Quiet, with pretty views, and a dirt shoulder available in case a car came along.

Biking heaven. A good workout.

Then another left on Fisherman's Run, and its long grade downhill. Running north-south, parallel to Farm Road, it was less steep and a lot straighter.

Ahead of her, Erik stopped, dismounted and disappeared. Puzzled, she stopped where he had. He'd walked his bike down a trail into the woods and was leaning it against a tree. She did the same, but he looked back and called, "No, don't leave it so close to the road."

Sensible guy. He was probably thinking of the red truck, how easy it would be to toss a bike into the bed and take off with it. Or worse, follow them in here.

But they were punks, not ax murderers. Her mother had always loved mystery stories, and Kate had read too many of them when she was in junior high. She'd scared herself, but had later come to believe that real people weren't often violent.

She walked her Trek farther in. Erik lifted his bike, then hers, over a big log beside the trail. His arms, triceps and biceps, were impressive. No bat-wings on this guy.

They followed the path for a few minutes. While the EMAC land hosted many pines, the woods here were mixed. Beech and maple, and some yellow birch, joined their darker coniferous cousins. The friendly calls of chickadees percolated through leaves and needles.

A flick of movement on a large hemlock stopped Kate. Difficult to see in the shadows, a brown creeper hitched its way upward in zigs and zags, picking at the bark with its down-curved beak that made her think of a dental tool. She loved these tiny birds, mottled backs blending with the bark they obsess about, gray feet looking enormous for their body size. The original tree huggers. She hadn't come across one in several years, and this little guy erased the grim mood she'd fallen into after the yahoo in the truck threw a beer can at Erik.

"Thank you, sweetie," she said out loud. And trotted to catch up to her guide.

She found him in a grassy clearing, a dark rock wall casting him in shadow.

"What's this? Some kind of old quarry?"

"Nope. Igneous rock all messed up by a glacier. Fire and ice, girl." He slapped the wall the way someone might slap a good horse, affectionately. "C'mon, let's go." He disappeared behind a huge slab of stone.

Kate peered after him. She wouldn't call it a trail. Only a series of opportunities among boulders. Spaces over, between, and sometimes under granite hulks the size of houses. Or bigger, so big you couldn't tell where they began or ended.

Yikes. Erik's sneakers, moving from foothold to foothold, were going up fast. He knew these rocks.

Following him took muscle but not strategy: worn places were obvious, clear signals for where to put her hands and feet. She took a breather partway up, on a flat area the size of a phone booth, surrounded by shoulder-high rocks. Her younger, tomboy self would have called the place a fort, with its commanding view of the end of the trail.

When she started up again, Erik was out of sight. It took her ten steady minutes to join him at the top, where a trail ran along the edge of a drop-off. Her quads and shoulders tingled from the work, and she was sweating lightly.

"What took you so long?" He flashed her a smile.

She took in the view. Rapids in the Shady River purled white; the road beyond it flashed with an occasional vehicle. Then the woods of EMAC and the field behind the Big House where they'd seen the fox. Off to the right Peacock's white trim gleamed among evergreens.

Above it all, the vast blue fanfare of sky. She stepped back from the edge.

"My favorite place to get some perspective," Erik said. "The life kind, not the artsy kind." Amid the clutter of boulders across the trail from the cliff, he sat on two rocks that were wedged at an angle to make a rough chair. "I call this my Stone Throne."

"What a cool place, Erik. Thanks for bringing me here." She found a flat rock near him.

"Kind of hazy today. Sometimes you can see the ocean, just a sliver of it, the harbor down by Machiasport."

They sat for a few minutes. A crow glided past, low, its head swiveling for a look at them, its eye bright and curious. Warmth from the sun balanced the stony coolness beneath her. She could smell the rocks, or maybe the damp soil beneath them.

"You've got such great places to explore around here," she said. "I've been meaning to get my kayak into the Shady. Do you paddle?"

Erik was leaning back, arms behind his head. "Nope."

"So many trails I want to take. There are some along the river, below Peacock."

He looked at her sharply.

"What?"

"I wouldn't go near those old buildings."

"Why not?"

"Just wouldn't be smart."

She was a little insulted. "I can take care of myself."

"You don't hunt, do you?"

What did that have to do with the buildings? "Haven't in a while."

"Like all of your life?" He was breaking a twig into small pieces and tossing them at nothing.

"I used to hunt growing up. In Arizona. Rabbits, mostly. Sometimes doves, quail."

"No shit."

"That's right." What was he getting at?

"And to think I took you for a city slicker. Faint at the sight of blood."

"Well, Tucson's a city. But cities in the West are different." She resisted the impulse to find a stick to play with, too. "And I wouldn't have been much use on an ambulance if I'd gotten faint at the sight of blood."

His silence made her feel she'd been bragging. But after a minute all he said was, "I hope I get me a good buck this fall."

"Of course. Good luck."

"Kinda messy, cleaning them. Not like a rabbit. Guts all over the place."

She thought he'd been needling her, but now she was sure. "Look, Erik, I don't know why some guys think it's funny to try to gross women out, but I'm gross-proof, okay? I've cut up rabbits, cats, chickens, a pig once, I've put a broken femur in traction and kept pressure on a guy's jugular all the way to the hospital after he cut it walking into a plate glass door. So lay off with the gross. Only eight-year-olds think it's funny."

He stared at her for a second and then roared with laughter. He slapped a knee and nearly fell off his rock.

At first she was pissed. Then his laughter got to her, and she couldn't help smiling. After he quieted down she said, "You want to talk blood?" And she told him about being the lab tech when she was a senior at UMass, driving out to a farmer's to pick up ten Rhode Island Reds for the anatomy lab. How the farmer killed the chickens by holding their necks and shaking them.

"Hell, it looked so easy. I threw 'em in the truck and I got back to the lab with this crate full of limp chickens and then one of them starts squawking and isn't dead. So I figure I'll knock it off the professional way and I grab it by the neck and shake. And its head comes off. I'm holding the head and the rest of it's running around the lab squirting blood like a

72

fire hydrant on speed. I mean, you want to talk mess. Beats a buck. Sprayed the lab, sprayed me—blood all over me, in my hair, up my nose. And I had less than an hour to get me and the lab cleaned up for class."

He smiled. "Okay, you win. Badder than a buck."

She felt like she'd passed some kind of a test, but wasn't sure what he'd been looking for. Erik was a puzzling guy.

They were quiet again for a while. Kate liked to be with people who didn't need to talk all the time, especially outdoors. She liked to open herself to where she was. This moment's gift was the vast arena of pure space that made her feel as if she were flying herself, like the crow that had cruised past a few minutes earlier. She didn't get many opportunities to make eye contact with a bird on the wing.

Turkey vultures coasted the thermals, their different apparent sizes giving the blank air depth.

She didn't understand Erik, but this was a special place she never would have found on her own.

As if reading her mind, he said, "Knew you'd appreciate it. Knew you were one of those outdoorsy types. I was just kidding about you being a city mouse."

This guy was full of tricks. "Why should I believe that? You didn't sound like you were kidding." She fished in her back jersey pocket for a protein bar.

"Easy." He tossed a bit of stick off the edge. "I read your file."

Her head snapped up. "What? No way."

"Key to the offices in the Big House, it's the same as the key to my room. I know quite a bit about all my—diners." He smiled. "So, girl, have I rocked your socks?"

She was indeed rocked. "Erik, that's pretty slimy."

"Have to say, I was surprised when you showed up. Thought you'd be in your fifties or sixties. Not many artists make it big at your age."

"That's not funny, Erik."

He looked startled. "But you didn't have to apply. You and Farley. No photos of work, no letters from people saying you're the biggest thing since Picasso. Which means you're the biggest thing since Picasso."

She didn't want to explain. "Danni must have taken the rest of my file home. I'm not big, Erik." She found a stick, and broke it in half.

* * *

As they stood to leave, Kate noticed a couple of paw prints at the edge of the trail. "Look, a coyote," she said. "We're not the only ones who like this place." She looked around. "How the heck did he get up here? Don't tell me the same way we did."

"Coyotes, they're full of tricks."

"Just wondering if there's another way out of here."

He didn't answer. Coyote wasn't the only mysterious one. I'd like to read Erik's file, Kate thought.

Going down through the chute of rocks was easier than climbing up had been. And faster.

"You know, that place at the top would be a good place to hide," Erik said as she followed him back along the trail toward the bikes. "If you needed a place."

Had she heard him right? "Why on earth would I need a place to hide?"

He glanced over his shoulder, his face serious. "Just saying."

"Erik, you're scaring me. Why would I need a place to hide?"

He didn't answer.

* * *

They got the bikes back on the road, turned east along the river. Kate found herself tensing when she heard vehicles

74

coming up from behind, and she told herself to relax. Just a couple of teenagers with nothing better to do. They were long gone.

And when, just a few minutes from EMAC, a red truck showed in her mirror, she told herself there was probably more than one red pick-up in the county.

The engine whined as the driver downshifted. She glanced to her left and saw the muzzle of a gun poking out the passenger window as the truck passed her and pulled even with Erik. Something bright burst from the window, his bike wobbled, and the truck roared away, tires squealing on the curve. Erik was down.

She sprinted to him.

"Jesus, Erik—"

He'd gotten up fast, taken off his helmet off. He wiped his face with the bottom of his T-shirt, let it fall. His face was calm. "Super-Soaker. Remember squirt-guns? This is the assault rifle version." Droplets in his hair sparkled as the sun hit them. "You can get one at Walmart if you've a mind to shoot back."

"Erik, this stinks. They must have been waiting, watching for us."

"Hey, it's how life's lived in the sticks. No big deal. I'm waterproof."

"It is too a big deal. You could have crashed into a tree and gotten hurt."

"Yeah. Well, I didn't."

"You know them?" It struck her that he probably did. This was a small town. He must know them, the boys who weren't satisfied with spontaneous beer cans, who came back to find them with a better weapon. "I wished I'd gotten their plate number."

"Forget it, will you?" He had his bike up, checked it quickly, and rolled away. He didn't turn in at EMAC lot but forged past it up the hill on Farm Road again. Kate groaned. Erik was one fit dude.

He went through town to the Gas N Go, leaned his bike against the building and dropped quarters into the soda machine. Still sweating from the hill climb, Kate did the same. They sat on a bench and drank. Smell of engine oil, of bricks in the sun, of the garlic that must be imbedded in Erik's hands.

A young beagle trotted over and sniffed their shoes.

"Nothing here for you, old boy," Erik said. "Kate's drinking that diet crap."

"He's drinking that sugar-water," she told the dog, who wagged his tail in response.

"So have you passed Buster's sniff test?" A thin guy in baggy pants had come from under the aging Ford hatchback on the lift, his hands oily. He wiped them on his pants and wiped his nose on his sleeve. "Wow. You been cranking those things. You're soaked, and it ain't even that hot."

"This-here's Kate, Billy. From the arts place."

"Hi, Billy," she said. "It's hot if you just biked up Farm Hill. Twice."

"This woman's a slave-driver when it comes to exercise," Erik said, and laughed.

Billy snorted. Then he went inside the bay and came back with a grease-smudged thermos and sat on the bench with them. That was one of the things she liked about small towns—people weren't always in a hurry. What mechanic in Boston would pass the time of day with you, even if he had only one ailing vehicle to work on?

Billy asked Kate if she was really an artist and what kind. When she said she'd been a reporter until a few months ago, he said his brother Joe worked at the *Washington County Watch,* wrote a lot of sports and some news and the notices about people who died.

Joe was a lot smarter than he was, Billy said, but he'd rather work at the garage any day. "Joe's got brains. I'm happier. Joe's boss is always crabbing about how much he has to pay him, or how the town's full of low-life Luddites and back-sliders. And I've never heard of a Luddite church around here."

That got him started about the town businesses, about the people who owned or ran them and whether they were good to work for or not. He and Joy would make a good pair. He'd been through the café, the dentist, and the hardware store when Erik got up and stretched.

"Got to get these bones rolling down the road, Billy."

"Okay, then, Erik." Greasy fingers spun the cap back on the thermos.

"Poor kid's so lonely even his dog's lonely," Erik said as they turned onto the road. "But having a brother on the paper, he knows everything that moves in this town. Right down to the number of fleas on the mayor's cat."

On a straight stretch of road they rode double.

"I wouldn't take my truck to Billy, if I were you," Erik said.

"Really? Why not?"

Erik managed to shrug without taking his hands off the bars. "Don't trust him."

"Really? You guys sounded like you were friends."

"Sometimes you're friends with people so you can keep an eye on them." He cranked harder, pulling ahead of her. "Do you trust all your friends?"

Following him, Kate wondered what kind of a person made friends like that.

* * *

Danni's sister Harri came to dinner at the Big House, slipping into a chair after the bell had rung. She wore jeans

77

and a flannel shirt with bright-colored patches. Making a fashion statement out of a necessity, Kate guessed. A political statement, too: peace signs had been drawn with thick felt pens on some of the patches. Kate sat next to her and introduced her around the table.

Farley, who usually sat with Kate, had been snagged as a dinner partner by David, across the table, who wanted some advice on his novel.

"I don't know a darn thing about literature," Farley had said. "Don't you know painters don't read?"

"That's okay, Farley," David said. "We'll just pretend my plot isn't written. It's real, okay? One of my characters—I mean, this guy I know would like your help."

Reggie and Sherri were mercifully absent. They'd been going out to dinner several times a week ever since Erik served the dessert that looked like a cat's litter box.

"Hey, Harri, what's up?" Kate said. "Nice to see you."

"Nothing's up. Just thought I'd spend some time over here with the arts crowd. Not that I'm an artist. But Erik said it was cool with him if I hang out."

Had Harri slipped? Her being here could be bad news. Had she been told to leave Danni's house? If so, she'd used her wits: this was the best free meal in the state.

"I used to think I was an artist, but that was stupid. My high school teacher told me I could maybe do commercial art but I didn't have—" she looked around the room for the phrase—"I dunno, something in some other language, something you have to have to be a real artist."

Great, a teacher like a door slammed in the kid's face. Kate leaned a little closer to catch Harri's attention. "He sounds like a crummy teacher. The only way you can find out if you have what it takes is to do it, try it out, play around." She was working to keep her face and voice on the earnest side. No need for Harri to know Kate wasn't sure if she was any kind of artist herself.

Harri looked up. Her eyes were dull. "Yeah, well, that's what I said, screw him. But then, I don't know, it's just too hard, you know? Like what the hell, anyway." She played with the ends of her long hair.

Erik brought out salad, then platters of broccoli and squash, and then a casserole dish full of garlic-sesame chicken. He nodded to Harri, gave her a smile, but she didn't seem to notice.

She filled her plate with broccoli and squash and passed the chicken on to Kate, who passed it on to Case. Harri looked at Kate's plate and then at her face, with a quick smile that made her look younger for a second. "Good, another vegetarian. We're like an endangered species, you know." And then the smile was gone. "Especially now."

"What do you mean?"

Harri glanced around and dropped her voice. "Well, what the hey, this place gives me the creeps. I dunno, I should probably get out of here. I'm calling some friends in Boston but it takes a while to set something up."

"Has anything happened? Are you okay?"

Harri ate a few bites. Was she sweating? "Nothing, like, really bad. Danni and Andy, I don't know, they aren't on the same wavelength anymore. It's just so confusing to see them this way."

She drank almost all of her glass of water, and Kate searched her brain about whether thirst was a sign of drug use. She wasn't sure. Diabetes, yes, but she wasn't concerned about the condition of Harri's pancreas. She wondered if Danni knew her sister was eating on EMAC's dime, with or without Erik's permission.

"Danni probably didn't mention this, but I'm a pretty good rough carpenter," Harri said. "I helped do some work on the cabins you all are living in. When Danni started this place up? She only knew about Short Creek because I'd met Marisa in Boston, and Marisa talked about Short Creek.

Danni nosed around up here and saw this old farm for sale and got her Brilliant Idea about an arts center." She was playing with the ends of her hair again.

"No, I didn't know you did carpentry," Kate said. "So you and Andy have something in common. But who's Marisa?"

"We were friends. Marisa and me and Erik, we hung out, and then after Danni bought the farm—" She broke off and laughed, a shrill bark. "I didn't mean it that way."

Kim, on the other side of Harri from Kate, looked puzzled, so she said, "'Bought the farm' is slang for 'died."

His eyes widened.

Kate said quickly, "No, Danni's fine. She really did buy a farm, Kim. Can you believe it, with all the rocks around here? EMAC used to be a farm."

The surprise on Kim's face faded, but even though Kate had spoken slowly she wasn't sure he'd understood.

"Those were the good old days," Harri said. She pushed her plate away and folded her arms. "I can't stop thinking about Marisa."

"Such a pretty name," Kate said. "Are you still in touch with her?"

"No." Harri looked down too quickly. "She grew up in Short Creek and made it big in Boston and then New York as a singer. Everybody said she was the next Janis Joplin. That turned out to be a little too true."

"She got into drugs, then?"

"Yeah, heroin. What a funny word. Heroine, with an 'e'." She pulled her plate back and poked at a piece of squash with her fork. "I knew her in Boston, before she was such a star. She was good to me. I almost came back up here with her, what, two years ago? It was spring break, and she was planning a big concert up here to honor her hometown. And she had a wreck, on one of those switchbacks on Farm Road, you know?"

"Oh, no, that's awful."

"She—she was killed. That was the end of her. All those dreams. All that talent." Harri looked up, tears in her eyes. "She had such a beautiful voice. She was tough as nails, too, in the business end of things. I thought I'd know her for the rest of my life."

"Oh, honey, I'm so sorry."

"It's not fair." Her voice had risen, and she clutched at her hair. David and Farley stopped talking and looked at her. So did the others at the table.

"It's just not fair," she sobbed. "Marisa was the best." Stumbling from her chair, she ran out the back door.

David broke the silence. "What was that all about?"

"Beats me," Kate said.

"I know who she's talking about," Hallsy said sadly. "Marisa was my girlfriend in Boston. That's how I heard about EMAC. I didn't know Harri knew her, but I agree with her. Marisa was the best."

* * *

She and Farley often drank coffee or wine on his deck after dinner. On the way to Peacock that night they talked about Harri.

"The amount of pain in her life, already, as young as she is," he said, "is an enormous burden. I feel for her. Addiction is one of the toughest problems a person can face."

"Danni will stand by her, but a sister can only do so much."

"Good luck to them both," Farley said. "That sounds flippant, doesn't it? But I don't mean it that way."

At Peacock, he poured two glasses and switched on the outside light as they went out to the deck. A couple of vehicles rumbled along the road as Kate told him about the two attacks on Erik that afternoon. His face darkened. "I hate houligans. There's no excuse for gratuitous violence." He swirled his wine, thinking. "I wonder if Erik's houligans and yours are the same? Throwing beer cans by day and ravens by night?"

The night cooled and they went inside.

Kate didn't stay as long as she usually did. After her second yawn, she reassured Farley it wasn't the company or the hour. "That was a heck of a long ride I did with Erik—twice up the big hill—and I haven't been getting enough sleep. I'm done in." Her legs burned, and the wine had hit her harder than it usually did.

"You should sleep well tonight, then." He took her empty glass.

Just outside the back door, something big and soft made her stumble. She caught herself and turned. Farley was staring at the dark bundle that had tripped her.

"What," he said, as if he'd never seen real fur before, "is that?"

"It's a woodchuck," she said. "A dead woodchuck." She was suddenly sober.

"That's odd. I wonder why it died. And why here."

"Yes, it's weird," she said. "Sometimes people put out poison for animals they consider pests, raccoons and rabbits that get into gardens and eat up the veggies. Woodchucks can do that too, but there aren't any gardens near EMAC." She looked around in the bushes for a stick, found a sturdy one, and used it to push the woodchuck toward the back of the deck. The animal was big, close to ten pounds.

The head had an odd angle to the body, and was that a trail of blood? She bent over for a closer look and then she was not only sober, she was scared.

She stood up and used her flashlight to look at the woods around them. "Farley. It wasn't poisoned. Its throat is cut."

He peered at it. "You're right. How simply awful."

She shoved it off the porch.

"Well," he said. For a moment he seemed at a loss for words. "Not such a peaceful place after all. I'll tell Danni about this. How very odd." He looked around uneasily. "You be careful going home. Do you want my bear spray?"

"No, you should keep it handy, near the door," she said. "And please lock up." She flashed her light around again. "Somebody must have put the woodchuck out here after we went inside, Farley. A few minutes ago. It's still bleeding."

He swayed a little, caught himself on the door frame. "I didn't hear anything, or anyone. Did you?"

"No."

"Be careful, Kate."

"Yes. You, too. Lock up."

She waited until she heard him snap the lock into place before she moved down the trail. Wound tight, she jumped at a rustling sound in the bushes. Just some vole or mole or mouse. Owl food. Snake food. Chill, she told herself.

She got the key in the lock on Bobcat's door, took a good look over her shoulder then pushed through the door and hit the light switch.

Green bedspread, bright kettle, rug with moose and paddles. Her home. Her workspace. It looked the same, but it didn't feel like the secure refuge it had been.

She leaned against the inside of the door after she locked it. God, she was tired. Exercise and tension were taking a toll.

She was frightened for Farley. And angry.

Fear and anger don't make good bedfellows. Kate woke several times with a start. Had she heard a noise? She finally tried her trick of reciting the phonetic alphabet in her head.

Alpha, Bravo, Charlie, Delta. Her mind began to untangle itself from the strange happenings at the arts center.

Echo, Foxtrot. What was G? Start over.

Alpha, Bravo, Charlie. Her muscles eased. Delta, Echo. Foxtrot, Golf.

PAM FOX

Golf. H? Hotel.
Finally she slept.

SEVEN

Erik's comment about his relationship with Billy had startled Kate. She didn't make friends to keep an eye on them. Take Danni, her oldest friend—Kate trusted her completely. She'd made a big difference in Kate's life. Not only recently, but earlier, right after they met.

Their friendship was more complicated than most.

Kate had found Danni exotic: an Eastern urban girl, from Cambridge. "Which is almost Boston but better, yay, Hahvahd and MIT. My parents like to pretend we're Brahmin, but that's a lot of bull." Kate wasn't sure what a Brahmin was, but she laughed at her roommate's exuberance. Danni dressed like a model even though she got some of what she wore at the Goodwill store. She knew what to do with a beret, an odd, iridescent scarf, a polyester skirt that swirled like silk. And of course she had the figure. "I don't mind being called a clothes horse," she said happily, fluttering her mascara-laden lashes at Kate, flipping through the course catalog. She was looking for the easiest courses.

"Let's see. Oh, God, we have to take a science. Just one, fortunately. We need to stay away from physics, from chemistry. How about biology? Oh, no way. There's a lab. Ugh."

Kate loved it that her new friend was including her.

"Geology. That's our ticket," Danni said. "There's a lab for that, too, but you can bet we won't have to cut up cats in it. That work for you?"

Looking back, Kate was sure that Danni's breezy pragmatism had been an antidote to her own "depressive tendencies" (the language of the college counselor she saw a few times her freshman year).

But Kate took biology. Cutting up cats wasn't much different from skinning and gutting the rabbits her father shot in the desert outside Tucson. She remembered the first time she'd seen him do it. She was about six, and the tailgate of the pick-up truck where he put the rabbit was on a level with her eyes. He was disappointed he'd only gotten one. "Looks like potato stew tonight," he said as he chopped off the four paws and head in short order and pitched them to Ranger, the hanger-on dog they'd inherited when they moved to the trailer. Then he slit the fur down the middle and pulled the skin off like a jacket, sliced the belly open and tossed the guts to Ranger, too. It looked easy when he did it.

The cats in the biology class were in bags of formaldehyde and smelled awful. The lab certainly wasn't outdoors as she had hoped, and besides outdoors here wasn't the wild, clean desert. Western Massachusetts stifled her at first with its overwhelming green, its leafy clutter. Where was the sky? And sometimes the humidity staggered her. Even with Danni's friendship, she had to admit being homesick.

Homesick for what? She didn't miss her mother, exactly. And her father had been gone so long she'd gotten used to missing him. When she was a kid he used to take her to bars (root beer for her). When she was a little older, he'd let her join him camping and hunting. Sometimes when he got home from work they'd go to the dump for target practice. She'd gotten so good at picking off rats with a .22 rifle or a Glock pistol that her father bet a buddy she could outshoot him. But Kate got six rats and her father's friend nailed nine.

"She got 15 yesterday," her father said as he reluctantly parted with a ten-dollar bill. "Just froze up, is all."

It was true. She didn't like being watched. She'd hung her head.

Danni shivered when she heard that story. "Rats. Oh, God." Then she looked even more horrified. "You didn't eat them, did you?"

"No."

"That's good, Kate. Really good. I'm not sure I could live with someone if I knew they ate rats."

"No rats. Just rabbits."

"Bunnies. Only slightly better."

"But you can live with it?" Kate couldn't help smiling.

"Yeah. But let's not talk about it any more."

* * *

The complications started when they took an art course together. "A gut," Danni predicted. "Slam-dunk." But her drawings (or her clothes or her attitude) annoyed the art teacher, who gave her a C. Kate got an A, drawing "like an angel," according to Prof. Evans.

"She liked you," Danni shrugged. "But that's okay, in fact that's how you get through college. Or anything. Smile, schmooze, and go for it."

That wasn't Kate's style. She did the work, and was thrilled to see how fast her drawing skills improved. Even though it was a studio course, she did most of her work outside of class hours—she couldn't think with a dozen other art students working in the same room and Prof. Evans prowling around and peering over their shoulders.

She drew everything: Danni, the illegal third roommate FatCat, piles of books, plants, shoes. She drew from life and memory, and loved the look and feel of the materials, the paper and charcoal and pencils and colored chalks that could be rubbed into clouds or pressed into crisp lines.

Danni survived her C and majored in art. "I can do this stuff. I can't major in anything where I'd have to spend all my time reading. This is the ticket to my next piece of paper. What do you think the A in B.A. stands for?"

Meanwhile Kate collided with Dr. Baxter and the difficulties of oil paints.

"You have a certain facility," he said, "but you are not taking advantage of the properties of this medium." He was short, with a permanently displeased expression. His comments on Kate's work started at critical and went downhill from there. And he made them in front of the whole class.

She listened to his comments with an impassive face and then went to her room and cried.

"Oh, Kate, don't listen to the old buzzard," Danni said. "He's got a stick up his ass." That made Kate laugh—she'd never heard the expression—but it didn't help her deal with the buzzard. He discouraged her so much that her grades slipped, and not just in art.

After getting a kind lecture from her Aunt Sarah and a sterner version from Uncle Pete, Kate changed majors to biology. "I'd rather cut up cats," she said. "At least I know I can do that."

She found biology relatively easy. She memorized facts and then put them down on tests, and her answers were right or they weren't. She didn't miss the anxiety she'd felt in art class as she sweated under the critical eyes of the professor and sometimes those of fellow students.

Although she did miss the excitement of drawing, the way time disappeared when she worked on her charcoal or oil-crayon pieces, she was not going to stick her neck out in Dr. Baxter's direction. And he was the head of the art department. Prof. Evans, who had encouraged Kate, hadn't gotten along with Baxter and was no longer at the school.

And then Danni had one of her BIs. She was always having Brilliant Ideas. Like smuggling FatCat into their room. Like wearing items from Goodwill that merged with her own clothes so well that she got away with "forgetting" to pay for them. Like getting a job at the library reshelving books and then doing her homework instead, deep in the stacks. "Who's going to know? I can hear anybody coming a mile away." Why she stole clothes and took a job when her parents were so well off was a mystery. Maybe it was the thrill of deceiving people, being in control.

Kate loved FatCat even though pets were against the school's rules, but she didn't go shopping with her roommate anymore. She worried that Danni would get caught implementing one of her various schemes—there were probably more than the ones she told Kate about. Revising the BI acronym to Bad Idea, Kate tried not to think about Danni's stunts. But she couldn't resist the one that involved her.

She made art Danni presented as her own.

It was win-win, Danni said. Kate got to draw, and to sketch out ideas for larger compositions. She got to play with the beautiful materials Danni bought. And she got critiques from Dr. Baxter and others, "untainted by his personal reaction to the yahoo from the desert," as Danni put it.

They were careful: Danni messed up the work, drawing over things to imprint them with her own style. Soon their styles merged, and they became collaborators. Still, the comments Danni brought back were useful to Kate.

"You're auditing," Danni told her. "Think of it that way."

"I'd never be drawing this much without the structure of the course."

"So who gets hurt? Nobody. You're ahead, I'm ahead." And they high-fived.

* * *

Kate never told anyone, not even Mike, that she had, more or less, two degrees. Or a double major—a public biology major and a private, invisible art major. She didn't tell her brother Cam or her sister Vickie, either. Both of them would have told her she was an idiot to let herself be used like that. Both of them would have hated Danni, her best friend.

The invisible art major wasn't one she could put on a resume, of course.

* * *

She stayed with Danni's family the summer after graduation and took an emergency medical technician course at Northeastern, and in six weeks she was wearing a uniform with Metro EMT patches, riding in a van with a lightbar on the roof and AMBULANCE painted backwards above the grille.

She was scared for months.

The first time she picked up a scoop stretcher at a scene, a piece of equipment she'd handled like a pro in class, she couldn't get it to connect under the patient. When she encountered an unconscious man in a jail cell, she couldn't think, for too many seconds, of the first thing she should be doing. (Not that it mattered, in the end, since once strapped onto the gurney and loaded into the truck he opened his eyes and apologized. "I just had to get out of there," he said.)

She got better at it. Somewhat. It took years to get really good at the job. She had to give herself time.

Danni went to Boston University for a Master's in nonprofit management. "It's too hard to make it as an artist," she said, "but art is all I care about. Well, except clothes. But that's art, too, isn't it? I'm really not a painter, even though I wish I were."

90

Eventually it occurred to Kate that she might have cheated Danni out of discovering that she *was* an artist, and what kind. In that case, her crime was much worse than Danni's.

She'd brooded over this, and over her less-than-stellar performance as an EMT. And then, about a year into the job, a child died beside her.

* * *

She'd transported others who might have died later, men clutching their chests with terror in their eyes. The best thing she and her partner could do for them was get to the nearest hospital as fast as possible, flashing the red lights all the way but using the siren sparingly because it scared the patients even more. As a Basic EMT she couldn't give them anything—not nitroglycerin, not even aspirin. "If you're ever in a car accident, just pray that the truck that shows up says 'Paramedic' on the side," she told Danni. "They're in radio contact with the doctors, they can give IVs with drugs. If you get us Basics—well, we're just a bare-bones taxi."

The little girl had green eyes, and she was wheezing when they got to the fourth-floor apartment. Six years old. "She's got asthma. This is the third time this month we've had to call," the mother said, sounding annoyed. Kate's partner called the base on the woman's phone, and in minutes the paramedics were there, shoving chairs out of their way and laying the child on the floor. They put her on a stretcher and got her out in a hurry, down the wooden stairs on the outside of the building, in the rain. One of them looked around. "You," he nodded at Kate. "Come with us."

It was quarter to five on a Friday, and the Mystic River Bridge was choked solid with traffic. The medic driving did a great job, poking the siren and using the outside loudspeaker to get the green Toyota to the left, the white

91

Caddy to the right. Massachusetts General Hospital was just on the other end of the bridge. Their progress came in feet, sometimes inches.

In the back, the paramedic asked Kate to hold this tube or put tape on that one. He stuck some EKG buttons on the girl's chest and got a scribble on the scope. The girl's eyes looked up at Kate, and she felt a little shock of recognition, as if the child were her younger self. He set up an IV and injected something into the line. He and Kate looked at the scope, the needle. The girl's eyes changed in some way Kate found impossible to describe. The medic seemed completely calm as he leaned toward the driver and said, "Just so you know, she's agonal."

He got a nod in response. Kate didn't know the word, but it didn't sound good.

When they got to MGH the truck doors flew open and four men raced the gurney into the ER, past waiting patients and into an alcove. One of them yanked a curtain across the opening, but it only went halfway. A crowd of people in white coats ripped the girl's dress off. One of them pumped her chest with the heels of his hands while others rolled IV stands into place and worked on her arms.

The parents had arrived somehow. They were sitting with a priest, the woman sobbing.

And then it was over. The curtain was pulled open on the empty bed, and the enormous overhead lights dimmed out.

* * *

"Can you tell me where the parents are?" The voice was impatient. It came from a woman in heels and a dress, holding a clipboard. She tapped a pencil against her cheek and leaned a little closer. "The parents, please."

Somewhere inside herself, Kate turned and pointed to the crying mother, the stricken father, the priest. But the part of her the social worker could see did nothing, just stood and looked back.

The woman tossed her head and said, "Oh, for heaven's sake," and disappeared from view. The sound of her heels on the hard floor sounded disapproving: tsk-tsk-tsk.

Kate went out the emergency room doors and waited in the rain for her partner in the Basic truck to pick her up.

* * *

A few days later Cam called her. "Ma's in trouble. Can you go out there?" And she did. Quit the ambulance job and flew to Tucson.

Later she thought it might have been a mistake. "You think everything you do is a mistake, afterwards," Vickie said.

"Maybe because it's true," Kate said bitterly. She hadn't done her mother much good. The problem was a fallen uterus; the doctor recommended a hysterectomy, and Kate's mother was terrified of anesthesia. So she dealt with it in her own way, drinking hard and harder. Beer gave way to whiskey. "Ma, you're doing far more harm with alcohol than anything they'll give you in the operating room," Kate said too often. But Ma didn't stop, and when Kate started to pour Wild Turkey down the kitchen drain, her mother grabbed it, swearing. And drank straight from the bottle.

Kate went for long hikes in Sabino Canyon and wished she hadn't come. She sobbed to Cam and Vickie on the phone.

And then one December weekend they both showed up, cheerful with a kind of black humor.

"Here we are. We're the mother-nabbers, parent-pirates, coming to take her away, ha ha." Cam liked to clown.

Vickie gave Kate a long hug.

Thank heaven for Cam's health insurance. He'd put their mother on it, and it included drying out alcoholics who met certain criteria.

"'Unable to perform daily tasks of personal hygiene,'" he read, sitting on the bed where his mother was sleeping off six or seven shots in the middle of the day. He leaned in close and said in a loud voice, "When was the last time you brushed your teeth, Ma?" She mumbled and lifted a hand, swatting it in his direction. "Check. 'Unable to orient in time and/or space.' What day is it, Ma? What year? What's the address here?" She turned her face to the wall. "'Unresponsive.' That pretty much describes the situation, don't you agree?"

Kate and Vickie nodded glumly.

"Check, check, check," Cam said, and reached for the phone.

Kate visited her mother after a week, when they let her. Her mother railed against her. "Bitch! Traitor!"

She walked, sometimes all day. She liked Phone Line, a narrow trail along a rock wall high above the crowds of tourists and power walkers on the paved road of the canyon floor. Phone Line took her to Blackett's Ridge and stopped at a nest of rocks in the sky. Esperero. Sabino Lake. Seven Falls. She watched sunsets. She ate rice and seaweed. She lost weight. She visited her mother.

"Jesus Christ, Kate, you look like hell. Are you drinking?" her mother said.

Kate laughed so hard tears came. She cried until a nurse came and led her gently into a dark room and let her pretend to sleep for a while.

She stayed with her mother while the desert bloomed that spring. Brittle-bushes exploded into yellow globes; saguaro put on white caps; even the scrawny ocotillo plumped up its coach-whip stalks with red flowers. Her mother submitted to the hysterectomy and recovered nicely. She and Kate took short hikes, sometimes packing picnic lunches.

"Gotta get some weight on this daughter of mine."

As the temperature rose, Kate drove her mother's old car up Mount Lemmon to Summerhaven. They walked around the top of the ski lift and enjoyed the amazing air at 9,000 feet, or parked at the visitor center and hiked the Butterfly Trail. Once in a while they ate at the Iron Door or the Sawmill. A couple of times Vickie took the bus down to Tucson from Durango and the three of them went to the Desert Museum or a movie.

"Ma, you scared the heck out of us," Vickie said.

"Please don't do that again," Kate said.

"Course not," her mother sniffed.

* * *

That had been a low point in Kate's life. It had cost her a lot, emotionally, to take care of her mother, and she wasn't sure she even liked her mother. She couldn't stop blaming her for driving her father away. But duty drew her.

* * *

Duty had called her to Tucson, but it couldn't keep her: Massachusetts had become home. She went back and got the job as a reporter for a weekly newspaper. Then the weekly became a daily, which meant she was busier and got a major boost in pay. Kate stayed in better touch with her mother after that rescue operation, hoping future disasters could be averted. She wrote letters—her mother wasn't on the Internet—and called more often.

She spent a lot of time outdoors, just as she had in the desert. She found a guide who offered weekend courses in tracking. One of a group of ten or so, she followed him around Quabbin Reservoir, finding tracks of fox and otter pressed into mud, smelling the sweet-hay odor of the scent stations beavers left.

In the winter they found weasel trails that disappeared under the snow and re-emerged, the tunnel visible when the snow over it collapsed. They learned to tell the difference between cotton-tail rabbit tracks and those of the larger snowshoe hares. A cloud of fur on each foot kept the hares afloat on snow like their namesake gear, and the paw prints they left had the shape of ice-cream cones.

The guide showed them tracks that started in the middle of a clearing, as if an animal had materialized out of thin air. Impossible.

Commonplace, he told them. Made by flying squirrels that glided from trees fifty yards away.

The group spent a day following a coyote's track in a wide circle that brought them to a bushy rise overlooking the place they'd first gathered that morning.

"Coyotes are smart," the guide said. "He's probably watching us right now. I swear those guys can laugh."

She learned a lot, including the way black bears climb beech trees in the fall and sit up there eating nuts. Plenty of evidence pointed to the behavior, like the branches the bears ripped off, stripped of nuts, and discarded, which caught in the crowns of trees. The guide told them most people never noticed the "bear nests" because people in the woods almost always look down, not up.

* * *

On one of the tracking trips she met Mike. Tall, bearded, intense, she described him to her friends as Mr. Outdoors. Soon they were going on trips together, hiking or cross-country skiing in New Hampshire, finding tracks or sign and puzzling over them, backpacking and tent-camping on weekends.

After eight months of dating she'd moved in with him, and her life felt settled. He worked in a biology lab at Tufts University, a postdoctoral position that could last for one year or a dozen, and they lived in Danvers, north of Boston and much less expensive. The *News* office and the town hall were a ten-minute walk from home, so some days she didn't drive her truck an inch.

When she looked back on those three years, it felt like a peaceful era in which nothing changed, a time of pleasant work and fun-filled holidays and good friends and movies and wine. She met Mike's sister, his mother, his friends from the lab. He met Danni and Marjorie, and one Thanksgiving Cam and Vickie came to visit. Twice he and Kate flew to Tucson for Christmas. Once they went to Montreal for no reason at all.

Then he worked harder, longer.

And then, of course, the roof fell in.

And now? Now her efforts to rebuild her life were being sabotaged by someone who left dead birds and animals in his wake and was trying to scare her away from a precious opportunity. Who was it, and why was he doing it?

* * *

Taking the Loop back to Bobcat after an hour's walk, she breathed deeply. She'd been at EMAC almost two weeks, and she needed to let go of those memories, all of them: Mike, her mother, the guilty secret with Danni, the six-year-old girl in the ambulance. What were memories? Wisps of electricity in the brain. Ghosts.

Breathing was her anchor to the present. Breathing was an elevator of air that kept her alive, fueling her cells and firing nerves. She swam in air, she drank it. This cool, invisible stuff with its scent of pines and hay and faraway ocean brought her the news: she was free and safe. She had work to do.

In. Out.

She made each inhalation, each exhalation, last as long as she could. In. Stretch those lungs. Out. Collapse them. In again.

She was almost to the cabin. A small object on the porch gleamed, and a few steps later she stooped to pick it up.

The air went out of her in a rush and she sat down quickly on the bench. A bullet lay in her palm. Longer than the ammo she was familiar with. Fatter than the rifle rounds she'd used years ago in the desert.

Something was scratched into the brassy jacket. She turned it, reading the four letters as they came. T. E. K. A.

KATE. A bullet with her name on it.

EIGHT

The next morning, Kate closed the door firmly against the wind and a twinge of guilt, and locked it. She should be staying at Bobcat to display drawings and greet visitors to the Open Studios event.

But she didn't have any drawings. And Danni had kindly given her a job for the day. While most of the other EMAC artists displayed their work, demonstrated techniques and offered snacks and chatter to the visitors, Kate would move among them to gauge reactions, eavesdrop, and take mental notes about what worked and what didn't, all with an eye to improving the event next year.

"Be my undercover artist," Danni had said.

That was a role Kate knew only too well.

She was determined to set aside, temporarily, the crazy happenings—wooodchuck, bullet, and all—and focus on her friend's generous project. The Eastern Maine Arts Center deserved Kate's best effort.

Danni had chosen a mid-month Saturday for the event. "Watch Artists Work," the posters around Short Creek said, under the banner "Summer Fun Art Fling."

Kate snugged her Red Sox cap low on her head and walked toward the Big House. It was a few minutes before nine o'clock, but already a few people were leaving the parking lot, heading toward the studios scattered around the Loop. A fit-looking couple in their early sixties came toward her, wearing top-of-the-line hiking shorts and tees. The woman strode eagerly past, rings and earrings flashing. The man nodded to Kate, looking bemused, perhaps at his mate's single-mindedness. I bet they go to yard sales an hour early, Kate thought, and then changed her mind. They bought their Columbia and North Face outfits new—they didn't get that look at yard sales.

A woman pushing a stroller trailed the couple. Two boys orbited her, chasing and pushing each other, jumping on and off the low rock wall along the path. Held together with gravity and hope and the shape of the stones, it wasn't made for such sport. Kate stifled a warning and let herself be grateful it wasn't her job in life to deal with energetic children.

In the parking lot two men unfolded themselves from a small convertible, stretched, then laughed at nothing and joined hands. The car had Maine plates but these men didn't look like locals. Danni's publicity campaign must have done wonders. Other cars were pulling in, including one with Massachusetts plates.

Kate smiled at the men as she passed, and from the sound of their boots on the gravel she knew they were following her to the front steps of the Big House. A cardboard sign in the shape of a double-ended arrow was marked "Reception" in this direction and "Studios" at the end that pointed to the Loop.

The Big House looked great. The hanging baskets were bright with bloom, yellow and pink. Andy had re-gilded the letters in the sign and trimmed the yews under the front windows. Kate, on her way back from a walk the day before, had seen him working on the bushes. He'd smiled and waved. "Get ready for a crowd," he'd said. "My wife knows so many people she even knows the ones she doesn't."

And there Danni stood, ready with maps and smiles, on the porch under a Welcome banner bracketed by clouds of gold-colored helium balloons.

A few more cars were nudging in off Farm Road. Nice-looking cars. Good thing the residents had parked their vehicles near the barn the way Danni had asked. Kate's truck camper would look scruffy compared to these shiny sedans.

Danni smiled at the two men behind Kate, handed them maps.

"Gosh, Danni, that looks like a Mercedes pulling in." Kate grinned. "Who did you mail those flyers to?"

"I think the Portland paper ran something after all. I didn't hear back from them, but this is a lot more audience than a thousand flyers gets you. And a bunch of phone calls." Danni had on one of those little black dresses that fashion pundits said every woman should own. A gold scarf lay casually around her shoulders, held by a heavy bronze pin. "Maybe Deep Pockets sent some friends."

"You look great, Danni. As usual. If I tried to make a scarf do that, it'd end up tied in knots around my ears."

She laughed. "Yes, Andy says I'm the only dress in the county. But I have to be—I've got to counter the stereotype that we're a bunch of drop-outs or hippies in paint-smeared jeans." Then, in a different voice, "Hel*lo*, welcome to your Arts Center."

Kate stepped back to make room for a group of three women, one of them wearing a fur coat far too warm for the weather.

"Let me give you this map of the studios," Danni said. "On the back, you'll find a history of our support for nationally acclaimed and emerging painters and writers."

Since I'm not acclaimed, Kate thought, I'd better start emerging. She smiled at the women, aware that her best jeans and her newest fleece probably made her look like a homeless person to them.

The women moved through the double doors, and Danni's voice became her own again. "Kate, a lot of people came early. Maybe the paper got the time wrong—it was supposed to start at ten. Could you make sure all the food's getting out to the studios okay? And could you get Andy to open the gate so people can park near the barn?—Hel*lo*, welcome to your Arts Center. . ."

The building was cool. Someone had lit a fire in the last few minutes, and flames were nibbling on the kindling in the huge fireplace. Paintings had been hung on the walls; others were propped on a series of easels that led to the center of the room. Spotlights frosted the hair of the women clustered around the first canvas. "Oh, Farland *McQuay*," the fur coated one said.

Kate moved past them. The last canvas was unfinished, and on a table beside it lay a brush and a fan of fund-raising brochures. Nice display, Danni, Kate thought.

A tri-fold screen had been set up in front of the glass doors to the dining room, with a PRIVATE sign pinned to it. Inside, calmness changed to controlled chaos. Chairs had been pushed to the walls. Some of the high-schoolers Danni had hired were carrying trays of food from the kitchen to the tables—sandwiches and fruit, cookies and sodas, cheese and bottles of wine. At the tables other students were packing rectangular picnic baskets. Erik must be in the kitchen cutting up cheese and cantaloupe like a demon. Each basket had the name of a studio on it, and a couple of the residents, looking for their baskets, mingled with the students.

"Three to Muskrat and Kingfisher, two to everybody else," Erik shouted from the kitchen. He peered out from the pass-through, mopping his forehead with a towel. Kate could see other people behind him, so at least he had help. He looked alarmed when he saw her. "What's with Bobcat? I don't have an order."

"Relax, Erik. I'm a woman of leisure today."

"The hell you are," said a loud voice behind her. She turned: Reggie and his sidekick. "These baskets are too heavy for Sherri. You can take them out. Let's get this stupid circus over with."

"Reggie, you are so thoughtful." Sherri stretched up to give him a quick kiss.

"Isn't he, though?" Kate smiled innocently at the pair and moved toward the back door, one of the big baskets in each hand. Sherri was so well endowed she had enough to carry.

"Hey, what about me? I'm just a poor fragile womanchild myself." Joy was right behind her with another basket. Smaller than Sherri, she had the feisty spirit of a New Yorker. Kate grinned at her.

Andy and Ryan and a couple of other men were strapping baskets onto the racks of three-wheeled ATVs with bungee cords. Four on the first vehicle, a double stack high enough that Ryan, in his red bandana and blue and white checked shirt, had to swing his leg over the handlebars instead of over the seat.

"These're for the south side, Peacock, Chickadee, River Otter—" Andy shouted over the engine noise.

Ryan waved him off and shouted back. "Yeah, yeah, no problem. I've got it."

Kate held her breath as the ATV took off. The load jerked but stayed aboard.

Andy looked around and his eyes met Kate's. "Ryan doesn't take orders well," he said. "He's too used to giving them." He took the baskets from her and Joy.

"Danni said could you open the gate to the—"

"Yeah, yeah," Andy said, his impatience echoing Ryan's. "It's open."

Poor Andy. Kate thought of the coffee table in Danni's living room. A superb carpenter, an artist with wood, Andy was now Mr. Fix-It for EMAC. Light-Bulb Changer, Bush-Trimmer. Mr. Behind-the-Scenes Support Staff for his wife's brainchild.

103

Mr. Do-What-Danni-Says.

More people walked past the back of the Big House, heading for the studios. Who would get there first, hosts or guests?

"Gotta run," Joy said, and sprinted for her studio.

"Go, girl! Knock 'em dead," Kate called, and Joy waved in response without turning.

* * *

Kate had been in some of the studios before—Farley's, and Joy's several nights after dinner—but today was showtime. The no-visit rule meant most of the residents hadn't seen each other's work. At dinner most of them didn't mention their WIP, work in progress, because talking about it could dissipate the energy needed to accomplish it.

The only exception was Reggie, who regularly bragged, both about his own work and Sherri's. His praise for hers was so overblown that nobody but Sherri paid any attention. She glowed, a moon to his overheated sun.

* * *

Joy's studio was the perfect opening act. Had Danni already been planning the studio tour when she assigned cabins? Had she been able to scope out personalities as well as portfolios, half a year in advance? She would have had a few minutes on the phone with the artists, plus their portfolios and letters of recommendation. She'd waived that requirement in Kate's case, saying the letters were all packs of nice lies.

Kate had always been amazed by Danni's people skills, even at UMass. When she worked at the statehouse she used to joke that her abilities were being fertilized with bullshit, and the metaphor—as crude as it was—could be extended it to the present: what was EMAC but a flowering of her talents? The group of artists she'd gathered together at this remote place was impressive. Farley was the only one who'd already made it big, but Kate figured at least some of the others were on their way. Danni would pick winners. It took one to know one.

* * *

"So how does an installation artist give a studio tour?" Kate had asked Joy at dinner a few nights ago.

"I can feel that aura of yours, Kate. Curiosity, in spades." Joy smiled. "The answer to your question? Easy. I put a four-ton rock in the middle of my studio and let people look at it. And then, unlike you guys, I let them touch it. Poke it, pat it. Whatever they want to do." She looked around the table with an evil grin. "Why don't you all give up your intellectual frittering and make real art?"

Kate groaned. "I should never have asked."

"Please, what is fritter?" Kim asked. "To eat?"

"You're right, Kate," Hallsy said, helping himself to a second serving of mushroom risotto. "You set us up." He said it with a wink. The same words from Reggie would have made Kate flush with anger.

"Forget Reggie," Danni had said once when Kate had complained about him. "Think about *you.*" It was really useful advice. Reggie was, after all, merely the equivalent of a large, loud mosquito.

"'To fritter' means to waste time on meaningless activity," Joy said. "It's what most people think about all art."

"And what you think about most of it yourself, Joy," David said. A few of the maligned artists sitting at the table laughed. He looked around with an air of exaggerated innocence. "Hey, I'm a writer. What do I know?"

* * *

105

A large rock did indeed occupy Joy's studio, mounted on a simple pedestal. At first she talked about the characteristics of the rock, its colors and textures. People had gathered inside the door, so everyone was on one side of the room, as if they were a traditional audience at a lecture being given by a rock.

Then Joy invited them to walk around the rock. Murmurs and shuffling. It took some verbal encouragement, but after a minute or two the rock was surrounded.

Joy was clearly comfortable in front of an audience. "Can you feel your attitude change, now that the rock is no longer in a position of authority?" More murmurs in response. "What about this rock makes it art? Would you look at it the same way if it were on the floor? If you walked past it in the woods?" She invited them to touch the rock, and a few hands ran over its surface, smooth here, grainy there.

"If a rock rolled over in the woods, would anyone see it?" Some small laughs. "What are we looking at? At the rock or ourselves? At an object, or our attitude toward it?" Joy looked around. "What's art, what's you?"

"But it's *your* rock," a woman said. "You chose it from all the other rocks, you got it in here somehow. It means something to you."

Joy nodded. "I'm a little psychic, you know? This rock talked to me." She let some seconds go by. Then she said, "You know what? I've changed my mind. I don't like this rock anymore." Arms wide, she seized it, staggered to the window, and pitched it out.

A stunned silence. Joy broke it with a laugh.

"That rock was paper," she said. "Papier-maché. Many newspapers were harmed in the making of that rock." She got outright laughs at that. "I staggered for effect. The thing weighs maybe fifteen pounds, tops.

"So now you've seen proof that I'm a raving lunatic," Joy went on. "I admit it. I do what's called installation art, which means I mess around with objects in the real world. I don't put them in a frame or on a pedestal—or at least not for very long.

"But wait, don't leave," Joy went on, although no one had moved. "I'm the crazy one here, the one who lives in a tiny apartment in Manhattan and dreams of Space with a capital S—dunes and prairies and mountains and swamps and windy skies. Everyone else here at the Center does things on paper or canvas like a proper artist. So don't run away—all the other studios will have drawings and paintings and photos you can take home with you, like pets." She gave her listeners a wicked smile.

"I make things in big spaces to make up for how small everyday life is. That's just what I do. You'll find descriptions and photos of some of my installations in the notebooks you see around this room, and there's some of my work along the path to the next studio. Thank you for putting up with me. Please support this wonderful, crazy place called EMAC."

She got a smattering of applause and a lot of smiles, and groups gathered around her notebooks. Kate enjoyed the democracy of the scene: a boy wearing a baseball cap backwards standing next to the woman wearing the fur coat and a lot of makeup.

Kate made her way to Joy. "Hey, I'm disappointed. That wasn't a very big rock. At dinner the other night you said it was going to be a few tons."

"Are you kidding? Amazing how much time it took to make something that's mostly air. And paper maché is messy. That was as big a rock as I could stand to make."

Kate followed Joy outside, where she picked up the rock and dropped it back through the window.

"It went great. You were a hit."

"Thanks. I just hope my rock stands up to getting tossed out the window all day. I didn't make an understudy." She took a deep breath, arched her back and raised her arms. "Oh, I love this Maine air."

* * *

Kate had looked through the installation photos one night after dinner when Joy invited her to Muskrat. She liked the set of linked kites that, aloft, looked quite realistically like a flock of geese in a V. It was unremarkable to see them— except for the fact that they flew and flew and didn't move in the sky.

Another kite, much larger, was a great laughing dragon made of silver Mylar that reflected the sky and landscape it flew in and over. Joy had some great photos of it flying over a lake at sunset, its scales shining red and orange.

Joy had told her how scary it was to paint pictographs on a cliff in Utah, how she'd had to sit in something called a bosun's chair, dangling on a rope. She'd hired a mountaineer to handle the ropes and check them every three minutes. "Literally," she said. "He was at the top, making me go up and down when I asked, and he had to yell 'You're okay!' every three minutes or I'd freak out."

The pictographs were ochre and black, and stylized. Authentic-looking until you recognized their subjects: cars, cell phones, airplanes, books.

Kate's favorite installation was an enormous stone cat on a beach, with sandpipers perched along its back. According to Joy, some of the birds were real and some were artificial, but in the photos it was impossible to tell which was which.

* * *

More people were headed down the Loop toward them, toward Muskrat. "Gotta go," Joy said. "My public calls." She looked down the road and shrugged. "Okay, it's about to call."

Kate wondered how many times Joy would put on her show today.

Joy turned in the doorway. "I'm afraid nobody will notice my latest installation." She flashed one of her mischievous smiles, then disappeared.

Kate looked around as she walked toward Kingfisher, Nava's studio. No dragons, in fact nothing unusual at all. Mixed woods beside the road: lots of pines and a few maples. An occasional birch. What was different on the path? Last year's leaves lay in shallow drifts on either side. She leaned to scoop up a leaf that caught her eye, perhaps a bit bigger than most. It had some color, a little red and yellow, while the leaves around it were the color of paper bags.

It felt oddly heavy in her hands. She turned it over; it was signed on the back: "joy in the world / Joy Grimm / October 2018." Acrylic on what, parchment? Now that she was tuned in to the color, she saw more, scattered on the path and beside it. Joy had been busy.

Just before Kingfisher, a posterboard sign leaning against a tree read "Please leave me here / look for me everywhere. Joy!" with one of the faux leaves attached to it. Next to it was a bushel basket with a few more of Joy's leaves in it. Kate added the one she'd picked up.

She spent a few minutes with Nava. The work she'd put up was done in pen and ink, small drawings, mostly cityscapes, done in spindly lines, but she pointed out a couple of canvases tucked away in a corner. "I'm probably jumping the gun," she said. "I should wait until after I get my eyelid surgery. But I'm so excited about working on larger pieces and going nuts with color." The old artist wasn't ready to show the canvases yet. Kate left Kingfisher hoping she'd be as vital and willing to explore new things when she was Nava's age.

How well would Gabriel and Case do, dealing with the public? They often skipped the communal dinner, and even when they were there they didn't talk much. Except for their owl conversation after dinner her first night, Kate wasn't sure she'd heard either one of them say more than "Pass the salt." But they did a good job of demonstrating the great variety of textures that could be coaxed out of ordinary-looking lead pencils. The two of them said just enough for one person.

Even Reggie's pompousness went down better than she'd feared—the group at his studio listened to him attentively. Kate thought his canvases were garish and confused, but according to Joy he was doing well at a top gallery. His success hadn't lessened his appetite for an audience. "Note the way the massive orange shape is balanced by the greenish triangle," he said. "Do you see, do you feel, the tension between them? Think of irresistible forces. Think gravity. Think love at first sight. Romeo and Juliet. They knew. These shapes know, too." He sounded so affected to Kate that she almost laughed, but murmurs of appreciation rose up around her.

She took a quick look inside Sherri's cabin. The watercolors looked dull to her, their compositions askew. People weren't lingering. Sherri would have to make do with the loud encouragement from Reggie she ate up with dinner every night.

Kate smiled at Sherri and left, wondering if she'd ridden Reggie's coattails into EMAC.

And then she had a thought she didn't like one bit. She herself had ridden into EMAC on another person's coattails—Danni's. She'd submitted no letters of reference and no portfolio—she didn't have a portfolio. All she had was Danni's memories of work she'd done years ago.

And what were memories? Wisps. Ghosts. Gone.

* * *

The next two studios were a study in contrasts. Hallsy's paintings were bright abstracts, most with incorporated objects—a gear from a bicycle, a weathered board. Kim's palette, both artistic and personal, was black and white. The photographs were ambiguous: landscapes or body-scapes? While Hallsy's cabin was full of conversation, Kim's was quiet, the only voices coming from a small speaker. Buddhist monks chanting, Kate learned from the CD cover.

* * *

David's studio, Chickadee, was near the end of the tour.

"I'm very much enjoying my time here." David was explaining to a couple, probably for the twentieth time that day, what he did. "I love the quiet, and the fact that there's nothing else here but my work. I get up and I write. Then I eat lunch. Then I write. Life is simple. At home, nothing is simple."

"What do you write about?" a woman asked.

"I'm working on a novel. I'm the only writer here now, but our director is looking for more. So if you know any writers who could use some quiet time to work, please tell them to apply."

"What's your novel about?"

"It's about the dark side of love—jealousy, anger, betrayal, that kind of thing. A heavy topic, I know. But an important one." He smiled apologetically. "It'll be my third. Haven't come up with a good title yet. I'm taking suggestions. Anyone?"

The woman shrugged and turned away. Nobody had title ideas, nobody wanted to ask questions about jealousy. David didn't have lightweight rocks, or interesting images on the walls, just a computer on his table and a thick file folder next to it. People drifted back out into the late sunshine. Kate stayed at the back of the bunch, as she had all day. It was the best place to see everybody, to see what was going on. She was the Undercover Artist, after all.

At the door, she glanced back. David was looking up, toward the loft. A long pair of legs came into view on the ladder, followed by the rest of a tall young man.

David saw Kate watching. He hesitated, then motioned her back in.

"This is my son Larry," he said. Both of them looked uncomfortable. "Look, could I ask you a favor? Larry's kind of a, a stowaway. Just for a few days. I know you're friends with Danni, but could we please keep this among ourselves? He'll just be here a few days, and I'm buying his food. No cost to EMAC. When school starts, he'll go back to his mother."

"Oh, gosh," she said. The request made her uncomfortable, but she couldn't think of a good reason to object. "I guess it can't hurt for him to be here." She looked at Larry, who kept his eyes on his father.

"Thank you so very much, Kate. I really appreciate it," David said. He closed his eyes for a moment.

"Thanks a bunch, *Dad,*" Larry said. Kate was startled by the hostility in his voice. He looked at her, muttered "You, too," and bounded from the cabin.

The way he moved triggered something in Kate's memory. She went quickly to the door and watched him. Larry was running back toward Muskrat with the strong lope of a practiced runner. She knew that bounding gait. He was the person she'd seen running away from the Big House when she got back from having breakfast with Danni her second day at EMAC.

Her guess that day had been right, in a way. The mystery figure was a schoolkid. He just wasn't local.

She looked back at David, who shrugged and gave her a rueful "what can you do" look as she left.

Being a stowaway at the Center didn't mean Larry was guilty of anything else. But hadn't Nava said something about David's son getting into a lot of trouble? If there were any more pranks, if she thought Larry might be responsible, she wouldn't have a problem going back on her reluctant agreement to keep his presence a secret.

Danni had told Kate that none of the other artists had been visited by weird nocturnal sounds, dead birds or animals, or snakes in their beds. And Kate couldn't imagine why Larry would want to harass her.

Unless he was disturbed. He'd seemed unaccountable angry, but of course she knew nothing about the dynamics between father and son. Maybe Larry was out of control, capable of lashing out at anyone for no reason. A very few adolescents were like that, and they were all the more dangerous for their unpredictability.

Kate sighed. The day had just gotten a lot more complicated.

NINE

To think that two weeks ago she didn't know Farley, and now he was practically like a father to her. An encouraging, understanding presence, just the way she imagined her own father would've been if he hadn't gone missing. The difference was her real father never said much, while Farley was pleasantly talkative—a man of words as well as images. And somehow elegant, even though he wore jeans like everyone else. Must be the tweed jacket that gave him a professorial look.

A sign on Bobcat's porch pointed visitors up to Peacock. The trail looked more worn today—a lot of feet had come this way.

Both the front and back doors were open, so Kate took the front steps for a change. They were steep, and narrow. Danni's workers must have salvaged the stones, because the edges were rounded and they dipped in the middle from wear. Not quite as tricky as the trail to the Stone Throne that Erik had shown her, but she could see why Farley had said they were scary.

The cabin was crowded, with people clustered around canvases. Rather than hover near his pictures the way Sherri had, Farley sat beside the fireplace and answered questions as they came. Classical music featuring an oboe played in the background. A woman asked him where he'd studied. Another asked how long he'd been drawing.

"Since I can remember."

A girl who looked about ten asked him why he'd become an artist. A boy on the verge of being a teenager, wearing a skull and crossbones T-shirt, burst out, "Yeah, like how do you get famous so people will buy your stuff? I like to draw but my father says artists are always poor and live in attics." He got a few sympathetic chuckles from the group, either for his predicament or for his father's.

Farley leaned forward, elbows on knees. "You don't have to be famous to earn a living. You find your way. Perhaps you work as a technical illustrator, or you draw a comic strip, or you work in advertising. Or maybe you do something else, like be a lawyer or a forest ranger, and draw for yourself, for fun."

He paused, and when he began again his own face looked like a boy's. "Remember to follow the joy, not the money. For some people making art is like eating and breathing, it's that necessary. Do what's important to you, whatever it is, and fit the job in around that. If you do work only for money, you'll find you hate the work. Worse yet, you'll never use the deepest part of yourself, so in the end you'll hate yourself." His face was luminous as he sat back.

The boy looked startled and then embarrassed at Farley's intensity. He looked at his feet for a few seconds and then came up with a serious look. "Cool," he said. "Thanks." And he glanced over his shoulder at a woman who'd been carefully listening to Farley. Kate guessed she was the boy's mother.

A new drawing caught Kate's eye, a large cartoon done in black marker on white cardboard, showing an aerial view of the Center with outsized studios crowded around the Loop.

Kim lay on the roof of River Otter, looking as comfortable as a cat. Hallsy, in a captain's hat, had raised a sail on Grouse. The porch of Loon, Reggie's studio, sagged comically under his weight, and Sherri was perched on his

115

shoulder like a parrot. Gabriel and Case stood outside Black Bear and looked like the American Gothic couple in the famous Grant Wood painting, a huge pencil replacing the pitchfork. Muskrat was stretched tall and thin, like a tree, and Joy was leaning out a window holding a huge leaf in each hand. Nava sat in front of Kingfisher, apparently talking to an owl perched on the curved top of her cane. David poked at a typewriter, and the paper in it scrolled out Chickadee's window and across the field, where it stopped at the feet of a fox with spectacles who was reading it upside-down.

Kate looked for herself. She wasn't at Bobcat. Well, that was accurate. She found herself on her bike on Farm Road, zooming down the hill below Peacock, hands on the drops, helmet so aerodynamic it looked like the weird kind professionals wear at time trials. A bear was using an outhouse next to the old buildings on the river—answering, Kate thought, the old question of whether bears shit in the woods. Another bear was driving an old pick-up truck with a gang of bear cubs in the back. A puzzled-looking moose looked on from the edge of the woods around the buildings.

Danni, wearing a cheer-leader's outfit, was drawn mid-jump in the Big House parking lot, holding a megaphone pointed toward the studios. Andy dangled from the EMAC entrance sign by one hand, painting in the letters with the other; Erik leaned out the back of the Big House with a dinner bell in one hand and a clove of garlic in the other.

Farley himself was smoking a pipe on Peacock's back deck, his feet up on the rail. Kate didn't think he could actually get into that position, but hey, it was a cartoon.

What a great collection of caricatures. Kate looked up at Farley. He was watching her. They shared a laugh that neither one could hear through the chatter in the crowded cabin.

You could tell the artist was a city guy—bear cubs come singly most of the time. Occasionally a sow has twins, but cubs aren't born in litters like the half-dozen tussling in the back of the wacky-looking truck. Still, the cartoon was perfect for the end of the Open Studio tour, a recap for visitors of the artists they'd seen at work. Farley was a doggone genius.

People came in and out in small groups. The afternoon was waning. Visitors put on sweaters and coats and drifted down the path toward the parking lot. Car doors slammed. Kate was glad she'd seen a few local people in the crowd. She recognized a woman from the post office and Billy from the Gas N Go. The skull-and-crossbones boy was from Short Creek, too—she'd seen him in the library. He probably got little encouragement for his art, but maybe that would change based on Farley's advice.

"Hey, Farley, you were great with those kids." She wished she'd had such good advice when she was that young.

"I'm a total expert when it comes to children." He smiled. "It comes of not having any myself. Now come out on the deck and let me have a smoke."

She snagged herself a cup of coffee from the big Open Studio urn and followed him to the deck. The maples rustled their thick summer dresses. Crickets throbbed.

He packed the bowl. "I love to sit out here with my pipe. Especially at night. Well, you know. You've joined me often enough. Peaceful, isn't it?"

"I'm a little surprised by the traffic we hear across the road, some nights."

"Doesn't bother me. You want traffic, move to Manhattan. This place is serene compared with that island of madness. Nobody leans on the horn out here, at least. And no sirens."

He lit the pipe with a plastic lighter that looked tacky compared to the jacket he fished it from. "Maybe someone's going to fix up those old buildings and use them for something."

"Most of the them seem to be in pretty good shape. The site is great, right on the river like that. Nice place for houses."

"Or studios."

"Great idea," Kate said. "Or how about a gallery? Danni was talking about opening one in Short Creek, but the site by the river might be cheaper. If she could buy the land the mill's on, refurbish those buildings—"

Farley laughed. "Danni's entrepreneurial spirit is rubbing off on you. I think she'd love that idea. May have thought of it already." He leaned back. "Of course, she hasn't finished renovating all the cabins on this property yet."

"Right. EMAC's a work in progress."

"No dust on Danni. She makes things happen. Want something done? Give her a few minutes," he laughed. "Peacock is so new the nails are still vibrating."

Kate took a hit of the coffee. "Danni's doing a lot of good for this town."

"And for artists. When I first met her I knew she was more than a good organizer. She has heart, and she understands artists."

Kate heard a noise and looked into the cabin. Andy was carrying the coffee urn, and Ryan had a trash bag slung over his shoulder like a grotesque version of Santa Claus. They stopped in front of the big cartoon, and Ryan scowled. As the two of them turned toward the front door, he shoved a chair out of his way. *"Shit,"* he said.

What was his problem? Maybe he was angry that he wasn't included in the drawing. She turned back to the conversation with Farley.

"Manhattan is home to a lot of talented people, but it's also the most self-important place on the planet. Capital of

118

the Empire state. Spearhead of the imperial order. It's good to be out of there for a while."

"Yikes, you sound like you hate it."

"All New Yorkers know love and hate are not incompatible." It had been years since she'd been around a pipe—her grandfather used one—and the rich, cherry flavor of the smoke made her sad.

It was as if he read her thoughts. "Happiness and sadness, too. If you can't be happy when you're sad, when will you ever be happy?"

"Huh. You give good advice to adults, too."

"That isn't advice. Just how things are for me. And painting—when it's going well, anyway—it's beyond happiness or sadness."

"And if it's not going well? Or not going at all?"

"Then it's hell. But a hell with an escape hatch labeled 'Work.'"

She'd never be able to work the way he did, with someone else watching. When he was in that wicker rocker on the deck, he was never *not* working, even when she was there. She felt lucky. To be sitting here with this important artist, who also happened to be very kind, and wise—

Kate took a deep breath. She'd been getting up her nerve. She really wanted to talk to him about this.

"So Farley, um, when Danni and I were roommates at UMass, some of her work, you know she majored in art, and some of it, her work, some of it was—was really mine."

He was looking down at the road, not at her, which helped. "And you're feeling bad about that."

"Yes." She felt tears in her eyes. This conversation had been years in coming.

"Why?"

She was stunned. Why? Oh, God, how could he not understand?

He held up a hand, still not looking at her. "Could be many reasons. I'm wondering which of them is most important to you."

Many? Really? "I keep thinking about how Danni doesn't paint any more, doesn't call herself an artist, only an arts administrator. If I hadn't done all that work, all those drawings and paintings, she would have had to do them herself. And she would have learned to work, and would have discovered what a good artist she is. I saw what she did on her own, before we agreed to that, um, arrangement, and she was good, and I, I—" Her face was wet.

"Robbed her of the opportunity of self-discovery?"

She gulped, found her voice again. "Yes. Exactly. Because you only learn what you can do when you have to do it. You and the medium—it's a conversation. And most of the time you have no idea where it's going to go, or if it's going to go at all."

He looked at the sky, which had turned that pre-sunset electric blue. "Kate, you have to think of where you are in your life right now. You certainly know how to work. Now you have to get to it. Forgive yourself whatever mistakes you see in your past."

Then he looked at her, and the earth-tones of his face and jacket and the rocking chair ran together in her tears.

"Before you lose yourself in guilt, consider that Danni is at least as culpable as you. It was a deal. A deal is a two-way street." Then in a lower voice he said, "And did you never consider that you, too, were robbed?" When she didn't answer, he went on. "Robbed of direct appreciation of your talent, and of the fellowship of other artists? And the presence of the larger art community in your life? You've been alone, Kate."

Had she thought that? Not fully. Maybe an occasional glimmer of what-if, wondering how her life would have developed if she'd overcome one professor's scorn and officially majored in art. But she'd never thought about the effect her under-the-table deal with Danni had had on her personality, the solitary quality of her life. That was just how she was.

Danni had been her closest friend in college, and she'd been grateful. It had never occurred to her before that she'd lost part of herself, an important part, by giving someone else so much control.

They went inside Peacock and talked as Farley tidied up, cleaning brushes and making sure the caps on tubes of paint were tight. People didn't have to accept themselves as a set of givens, he said. "We all have parts of ourselves we'd like to change. So that's what we work on. Life's a conversation, the way you said making art is a conversation. Sometimes we're the medium as well as the artist."

He glanced at his watch. "It's almost six. Dinner? Give me a moment to put the cartoon in the closet. It's distracting."

"Really? But you've got other canvases around the room."

"Those are finished. I did the cartoon in a hurry, for fun, and I keep seeing things I'd like to change."

They went out the back, and Farley didn't lock the door. He sometimes forgot, even though Kate had told him she always locked hers after finding the snake on her bed. She opened her mouth to remind him but her thoughts veered off to what he'd said about guilt. She remembered Danni flipping through the UMass catalogue looking for easy courses. Maybe she couldn't have graduated as an art major without Kate's help. Not from lack of talent, but lack of drive. She had plenty of drive when it came to EMAC, but it was a different kind. She liked being at the helm of a project, highly visible, dealing with people. Not sitting alone with a piece of paper and a graphite pencil.

Art was hard. Danni wanted to do what came easily to her. She'd made her career choice. It wasn't Kate's fault.

Farley was quiet as they started down the path, perhaps sensing she was mulling over his comments. She asked, "Are you still working on changing parts of yourself?"

He looked at with surprise. "Of course." Then he laughed. "You think I'm perfect? That's a good one."

"Pretty darn close," she said, keeping her voice light. "That cartoon is terrific, Farley. Maybe it's not perfect in your eyes, but it's close enough for the rest of us. You should hang it in the lounge. Everybody deserves to see what sweet, funny elves you've made of us."

He smiled. "You're full of good ideas, Kate. Why don't you run that one by Danni, too? Might happen sooner than her buying the old mill. It's certainly a lot less expensive, especially since I wouldn't charge a nickel." He stopped to zip up his jacket.

She took another few steps, then half-turned to see if he was coming.

Something grabbed her ankle. She flailed, trying to catch her balance, and then fell, landing hard on the downslope.

What the heck? She scrambled to her feet. Farley was coming toward her, his face concerned.

"Stop!" Thank goodness he was slow, or he'd be on the ground too.

An ankle hurt, one palm stung. She'd put out a hand to keep from rolling. She brushed twigs and dirt off her clothes and examined the trail. It looked clear, harmless.

"Kate, what is it? What happened? Are you all right?"

"Just a sec." Light rang silver on something across the trail, low. Then it was gone.

On her knees, she waved her hand up and down near the ground. Crawled forward and repeated the motion. The third time, she felt resistance, and bushes on either side of the trail jerked.

The clear filament across her palm was nearly invisible. "Fishing line," she said. "Somebody booby-trapped the trail." She followed the line to the right and yanked it, but it was tangled up in the bush and didn't give. "They wanted to hurt you." She hated to think what a fall like the one she'd just taken would have done to Farley.

She looked up. "Do you have a pair of scissors? A paring knife from the kitchen would work, too. And Farley? On the way out, would you *please* lock your door?"

* * *

She cut the line and stuffed it in her pocket. They followed a few last visitors into the Big House. Inside the door, Erik had set up a table with coffee. The cups were ceramic, not styrofoam, and a young man in a white shirt poured.

Kate had been in the lounge that morning, but she'd been in a hurry. This time she noticed a sign on a stand: "Work by Current Residents," with an arrow to the left.

Danni was talking to a couple who looked like they'd walked out of a Chamber of Commerce ad. The woman's long skirt had glittering strands woven through it.

"Hi, Kate. Hi, Farley." Danni waved at them. She still looked chirpy after a day of schmoozing. Coming closer, she whispered, "Woman looks like a Christmas tree with tinsel. But that's her third glass of wine. Pretty soon the tree will have lights." She giggled.

"Hey, Danni. This is really first-class. Who's going to wash all the cups?" Kate asked.

"The caterers, hooray!"

Farley raised his cup. "To art. And caterers."

Kate clinked her cup against his, and they drank.

Danni said, "If I have any more caffeine I'll be bouncing off the ceiling." She looked exhilarated by the success of the day, but her face changed when Farley told her about the trip line and Kate showed her the filament. "Oh, my God," she said. "I'll call the police as soon as we close up here. That's no prank—that's criminal."

"Maybe Ryan and his guys could be security guards for a while?" Kate suggested. "They're around a lot anyway, and they could patrol the property on their ATVs. Even if they don't catch anybody, they might prevent another nasty stunt."

"Kate, that's a brilliant idea," Danni said. "Thanks. I'll tell Ryan."

* * *

The lounge looked great with the new art on the walls. Kate and Farley joined a few visitors in the slow-motion walk of gallery-goers everywhere. A small group had gathered in front of the largest canvas, one Kate recognized as Reggie's. Of course he would want to be Biggest in Show.

They came up behind another couple. The man was heavy and wore a pinky ring on each hand; his wife was bejeweled to the point of crustaceousness. Danni joined them, put a hand on the man's well-tailored sleeve.

"Do you suppose that's Deep Pockets?" Kate whispered to Farley.

"I don't know," Farley said. "But look around. Whoever he is, our benefactor knows people who own a lot of jewelry." His voice was low. "And now he and his friends want to own more interesting things. Art. And artists."

Kate was startled. "Farley, I didn't think you were a cynic."

"Not by nature, no. But experience? Well, this is not the place to talk."

They had edged along, looking at a series of prints by Kim. Monoprints, dark rectangles, almost identical. One was green-black, the next maroon-black.

"Like having your eyes closed in different places," Kate said, and Farley laughed.

"Let's see what they think of my number," he said, taking Kate's elbow and guiding her toward the corner.

It was quieter here—the murmured comments about Reggie's opus and Kim's understated studies stopped, and nothing replaced them. The little crowd was looking at another large canvas, a semi-abstract in which a white shape glowed above a riot of foliage. Or what might be foliage. The color and texture was right, though you couldn't make out individual leaves.

The white shape, floating on the dark background—what was it? It looked heavy, and yet it was suspended. It was more or less rectangular, smudged here and there with brown and gray. She heard the heavyset man ask his wife what it was. "I don't know, honey. A bar of soap?"

A kind of group intelligence had emerged: a soft snort of mild but general dismissal greeted the bar of soap theory. It was as if this collection of well-to-do art fans had discovered that they could accept the painting for what it was, a luminous white shape, a floating—something.

Hallsy came up, punched Farley in the arm. "Way to go, old man." To Kate he said, "So where's yours? Too shy to show?"

Kate winced. Hallsy meant no harm; he didn't know how much trouble she was having with her work.

Farley put a finger to his lips. "We, as others before us, prefer to remain anonymous." If Hallsy hadn't spoken, those around them would have taken them to be other visitors, not artists.

Turning to Kate, Farley murmured, "Here's a little something for you," and slipped a note into her hand. "Look at it later."

And then someone else came up—was it Joy? Kate, still looking at the painting, wasn't sure—and Farley moved away with her and Hallsy.

Kate looked at a couple of smaller paintings of Farley's, realistic natural scenes that she quite liked. If she were working, she might choose the subjects he had. The big barn. One of the buildings by the river with a van backed against it. A bicycle on its side in tall grass. The details were meticulous, done with a small brush. You could almost count the nails in the barn wall. The van looked clean and new, like some chitinous insect emerging from a brick chrysalis. The spokes of the bicycle—how had he done that?—shone in a way that rhymed with the blades of grass.

Someone came up beside her, and Kate gave him a glance. Dark suit, dark shirt. Nothing about him shone or gleamed—not a lapel pin or cufflink to connect him to the other, bejewelled art supporters.

He didn't seem to notice Kate. She didn't look at him squarely, but her peripheral vision told her he was tall, with a fringe of dark hair below a bald head shining in the spotlight that angled toward the paintings. Kate could have sworn she felt an intensity flowing from him. Had she absorbed Joy's ability to read auras?

No, she'd picked up on something else: the hand at his side was clenched into a fist.

He stood rigidly in front of the painting of the van, and then he turned and walked quickly away.

126

TEN

Sunday. She couldn't stay in bed and it was only six o'clock. She sat on the loveseat and drank coffee and looked at the birches. They must be growing; that's what trees do. But they didn't look any bigger than they did yesterday.

What a crazy thought.

She felt better in a jumpy kind of way.

What was different? The Open Studios event had been a total success for Danni and EMAC—was that the source of new energy? Did it come from seeing the other artists at work, feeling part of a community? Maybe Kate was growing stronger the way trees did, without showing much difference on the outside. Days of exercise, talks with Farley—maybe they were finally paying off.

She looked at the drawing he'd given her the previous night. A cartoon of her in bicycle gear riding a smiling fox and blowing a hunter's horn. *From your sketchbook to mine,* he'd written above his long-tailed signature.

She sighed, let her head fall on the back of the loveseat. The ceiling in Bobcat was bare wood, beams exposed. The anatomy of a cabin on display.

Windows open, breeze recruited, wild air astringent with the scent of pines.

She was air. And water, and the fire along her nerves.

Maybe she could learn to love herself in this cabin. To love the world, to capture what it said to her and claim it on paper. The world! Open it. Sketchbook like an open window, open door. What was it her father used to say? She wished she'd had more time with him, wished she could see him again.

One March day when she was in high school, Kate and her mother had just sat down with a pizza when the trailer's front door blew open. Her mother laughed and said "Close the doors they're coming in the windows, close the windows they're coming in the doors."

"What? Who's coming?" Kate asked, and her mother stopped laughing.

"Your father used to say that, before Cam was born. The bastard."

Kate knew her mother didn't mean Cam was a bastard. She took her mother's laugh as a glimpse of a time when her parents had been happy together.

Her mother sprang to the door, slammed it and lit a cigarette, drawing on it fiercely. That's how she did everything, fiercely. But she was living a life she didn't love.

Kate moved restlessly around the cabin, touching the things that were hers. Cracked leather jacket. Hummingbird earrings. Shiny sculpture of bicycle. So little, so much. Her life was a ride on spaceship Earth. She opened the door and the rush of wind in the trees became the soundtrack of her thoughts.

She wasn't her mother. But she was paralyzed with energy and the fear of using it.

Feverish, she dropped her sketchbook into the daypack with a set of pencils and the oil crayons. How could she have forgotten this feeling? So familiar, nearly lost. Something she had to make peace with. Anger and energy were almost the same. It was impossible to bear, the pleasure of looking, touching, being angry, alive. Being her hurting, human self.

Latch cool to her fingers, puff of air from the door closing, click of lock. Slight give of wooden steps, firmness of earth. The wide day.

She walked for an hour, or two. What was time? A trail through light and shadow under a sky generous with clouds. She stood by a pond deep in the woods and lost herself in the patterns the breeze made, soft triangles that gleamed and were gone and were everywhere again. Fields were like that too, so many grasses so much alike, green and tall and leaning, all agreeing with the wind, bending the same and overlapping. They rustled, a choir singing one note.

Ferns, green and bronze. Could she draw them? Sketchbook on her knees, her hands trembling over the page. The pencil warmed in her fingers, the drawing came to her. She flipped the page, started another.

A flock of gray birds, small, quick, flitted through dark branches, twittering, the scratches of high sound joining and overlapping, near and far. Round white bellies, slate wings. Sprinkling the air with small voices, the birds flickered, were gone. She wanted to move like that, high, wild. Imagine climbing air, swooping, braking. Landing as gently as light.

They were gone but she could hear them: they were in her, the birds. Just-audible calls, thrilling the space in her mind.

The road back to Bobcat, the porch. She sat on the bench and watched the clouds darken. Lightning arced, thunder shook her. Fat raindrops splatted against the worn wooden steps. She went inside and sat in the loveseat and looked at where she'd been, what she'd drawn. Ferns. They looked right and wrong, like words in a language she was learning.

She opened an old sketchbook: a houseplant she'd drawn years ago. She remembered the leaves' blend of red and green, the silvery undersides with fine hair, the square stems. It had lived on a bookcase near a sunny window, making leaf after leaf, all the same. It had flourished.

She could flourish.

Could she? Her hand hovered, too eager.

Coffee. It would comfort her.

Excited by the wind, the maples outside the kitchen window were doing what she was, thrashing, making space for themselves in the world.

She watched water run over the white of the sink that was modulated by the grays and greens of leaves at the window. Water on enamel, water over her hands.

Which were water.

Blue flame under the bright green kettle made her unaccountably happy.

Back at the table, she set the steaming cup beside her sketchbook. Rain against the window made a pattern and the cloudy light shone through, casting that pattern over her drawing. The texture lay across the whole page but became more open in the bottom third. A conversation of leaves and rain, pattern and pattern. At last she knew what to do.

* * *

Kate stood, her shoulders aching. She vaguely remembered turning on the light at some point—it seemed years ago. She'd heard the bell for dinner with a part of her mind that registered the sound like a mosquito's whine, a nuisance to be ignored. Somebody in the room was hungry and wanted her to do something about it.

She ate a piece of cheese. Somebody in the room was exhausted, was walking toward a bed, was lying down in her clothes.

* * *

The next day she worked for four hours. She'd awakened early, the sky barely light, and splashed cold water on her face. Made coffee and sat at the table, took a deep breath. Opened her sketchbook. She wanted to make sure she still had the momentum, that she was really onto something.

She was. She worked some of yesterday's sketches into drawings on larger paper. They were all about patterns, about small things accumulating. Soft triangles on the surface of the pond, the chorus of grasses, the slight variations ferns made on the same shape. She could still hear yesterday's birds in her mind. They rhymed with the lines she made, the shapes.

About ten o'clock she jumped off her front porch and made the U-turn up to Peacock. She couldn't wait to tell Farley the good news.

He was on the back deck with a new canvas on the easel—only a few lines on it—but when he saw her he wrapped his brush in tinfoil. He was thrilled for her, joy in his face and voice.

"Excellent, Kate, excellent. I knew you had it in you."

"You knew, maybe, but I didn't." Her laugh was shaky. "It's such a relief." She perched on one of the chairs. "I feel like I'm who I used to be years ago, in college. But I'm different, too. It's so strange."

He nodded. "You've recovered something important. Don't lose it again, okay?"

"Why was it so easy to forget I'm an artist?" she wondered. And answered herself. "I'm always falling for distractions. And putting myself down, even to myself. And to other people, for a joke."

"Bad habit." He was still beaming. "Not uncommon, though."

"There are reasons. Like how I feel about Danni. Ever since we were roommates at college it's been hard not to compare myself with her. She is so dynamic, she has such a huge effect on other people's lives. I just admire the heck out of her."

"Admiring her doesn't mean there's the slightest thing wrong with you."

"But look at what she's doing. The whole art community in Boston and New York is going to hear about this wonderful place she's made. The art that's done here will get spread all over the country. A few more years of the kind of effort she's been putting into EMAC, and she'll have artists coming from outside the U.S., and then she'll be affecting the art scene all over the world." She stopped to catch her breath. "And here I am barely able to take care of myself, one little person. Her life is so much bigger than mine."

"Kate, Kate." He looked stern. "You must know, after yesterday, after this morning, that your life is just as big as anyone's. As big as you can bear to make it. It's the doing of what you're good at that counts." He played with his pipe. "How did you feel when you were working?"

"Really working, instead of thinking about work the way I've been doing all this time?" She thought a minute. "I'm not really aware of myself at all. I mean I'm making things happen, with my hands, my brain, but it's like I'm not there."

"Kind of like being God, isn't it?"

"That's right. Exactly." Of course he knew. His work was different from hers, but they both went to the same mind-space to make art. Another of her giddy laughs came, quavering like the end of a female barred owl's call. "Whoever's holding the pencil, she's not the one who washes the dishes and answers the phone."

She glanced at the canvas in front of him, nearly blank. Come to think of it, she hadn't ever seen him start a painting. The ones he worked on when she sat with him on the deck were well underway. She'd surprised him, coming so early: usually she visited in the afternoon, or after dinner. So he had more than one work mode. That was a discovery to think about, to learn from.

"Now you've found it again, the way you can lose yourself," he said, "focus on that. Not who won what award or why you can't do what someone else is doing. Danni's great—she's done marvelous work here, for all of us—but it's a different kind of work than what you do. And nobody else could do it but you."

"So—'All comparisons are odious'?"

"No, just irrelevant." He scooped tobacco from a paper pouch and tamped it into the bowl. How could the stuff smell so nasty until you put fire to it, and then smell sweet? "Danni puts all her energy into what she's doing. What she's good at. So do I. So should you. So should everybody."

Kate felt like she was flying.

"Art," Farley said, pointing the pipe stem at her, "is the biggest thing going. It's bigger than you, me, and Danni all rolled up together. It's bigger than Peacock and Bobcat and the Big House. And," he added, a twinkle in his eye, "it's even bigger than Reggie Blair, though he may not think so."

* * *

Kate worked off and on the rest of the day, taking breaks that turned into short naps. She drew at the table by the window, and she drew on the porch. When Farley saw her on the bench with her sketchbook open on her lap, he waved and kept walking down the Loop to the Big House. For the first time Kate skipped the communal dinner, eating a protein bar almost without seeing it. She felt so energized the day seemed to last a minute. When dusk gathered around Bobcat she went inside and kept working, drawing from imagination. She drew a loaf of bread and a wineglass. A cat with its paws tucked under itself. A lizard like none she'd ever seen.

Finally she stood. Muscles stiff from so much sitting, she craved a walk. At the door she hesitated. She loved walking at night. But some hateful person had poisoned the atmosphere at EMAC. He could be outside Bobcat now, lurking and planning more nasty surprises.

Her anger flared. Not the deep anger that was a form of energy, that helped her work, but the reactive kind, the kind she felt when another driver cut her off in traffic. Whoever killed the woodchuck and wrote her name on a bullet was scum, and she wasn't going to let him deny her the pleasure of a walk. The way he was sneaking around showed him to be cowardly, and the chances of a direct confrontation were low.

She went out and took a deep breath of cool night air. Locked the door.

The night was crisp and sweet as a MacIntosh apple. The moon wasn't up yet, and the sky sparkled. Walking along the Loop, she thought of the nocturnal creatures who must be out here with her. You never knew when you'd see wildlife, even at night. She'd seen a porcupine nursing a pup once, at dusk, the mother upright on its hind feet. Another time a great-horned owl floated silently over her head, hunting in moonlight.

She turned off her flashlight to let her night vision come up. Less disruption for the animals that way. Foxes prowling for rabbits, grouse asleep with their feet locked onto hemlock branches, deer curled with their heads resting on folded front legs like dogs in front of campfires. The deer's only fire was in their cells, its fuel the twigs and forbs they ate all day, with maybe a few ears of the corn Erik sometimes tossed behind the barn for them.

To all those creatures she was incidental. Perhaps a fox found her scent on the breeze and turned away. Perhaps a deer heard her footsteps and raised its head and then laid it slowly down again, eyes open, wary.

Others were less concerned about her presence— raccoons and opossums, skunks and porcupines. The woods were alive with sleeping songbirds and hundreds of thousands of insects and billions of bacteria working the soil like slow farmers, laborers keeping geological time.

A truck engine in low gear growled up a nearby road. Insulated by his vehicle, the driver would be unaware of the stars, the bracing air, the vast collective creature that was the night. Most of her species wouldn't think of the others. People's lives can be cramped into almost exclusively human territory. Especially in a city, surrounded by thousands of other people with jobs and to-do lists, driving cars and selling things and throwing away great hunks of trash. Cities were machines that people ran.

Or was it the other way around?

She scuffed old leaves as she walked. They were all real, of course, signed only by the trees and the season, not by Joy Grimm. An earthy smell rose from where she'd disturbed them.

She came to the intersection of the Loop and the path that led out to the cabins that hadn't been renovated yet.

Deep in the woods, a light.

It was possible someone had broken in—teenagers looking for a place to hang out, or a homeless person. The cabins were livable: Danni had told her they needed few repairs but a lot of cosmetic work, and of course they needed to be connected to power. Kate had poked around them a few times on her walks and had never seen signs of amuone living there.

But a light was a light.

Feeling sneaky, Kate walked down the path and then around the cabin, hoping for a place to look inside. If it was some free-loader she wouldn't bother him, she'd just tell Danni in the morning. Unless he was damaging the place, in which case she'd call tonight. It was a good thing the Big House had a landline.

She found a window with a small gap between the curtains. She kept far enough away that the light didn't fall on her face, and looked in. A woman sat at a table with a Coleman lantern on it, counting a huge pile of bills. Her head snapped up and she stared straight toward the gap.

Harri.

Kate didn't think she could be seen out here in the dark, but held her breath until the other woman went back to counting. The bills looked like 100s. And so many of them.

Harri with that much cash was a red flag. She must be dealing, practically under Danni's nose.

Kate went to the front of the cabin and knocked.

She waited. Stealthy noises inside the cabin. "Harri," she called. "It's Kate."

The door opened a crack.

"I saw your light and just wanted to stop in and see how you were doing."

Harri didn't answer. She seemed to be holding onto the door for support.

"Please. Let me come in for just a minute. I want to be sure you're okay."

"I'm okay," Danni's sister said. After a moment she opened the door and stepped back.

She must have turned the lantern down; the room was dim. No piles of money in sight. A closed suitcase on the floor. Next to it a sleeping bag, some oranges, a box of crackers, a gallon of water.

On the table, a photo of a woman in front of a microphone, head thrown back, hair wild. Kate touched the corner of it. "Is this Marisa?"

"Yes. She was my best friend, you know? I was in a rehab group with her."

"I'm sorry."

"She was in such good shape." Harri paced, hugging herself, her ragged sweater two sizes too big. "She wanted to give a big concert for her hometown, and she came here to set it up. Then we heard she'd died in a car crash. We were devastated."

"Oh, Harri." Kate reached out to touch Harri's arm, but the younger woman spun away. "Look, you shouldn't be here alone," Kate said. "This kind of isolation is helpful for somebody with a project to focus on, but—"

Harri's eyes narrowed to slits. "Oh, it's okay for you and your wonderful artsy friends but not for homeless drug addicts like me?"

Kate was stunned. "No, no, that's not—"

"That's what you think. It just doesn't sound so nice out loud. But I'm not staying with Danni any more. I think Andy doesn't want me, and I'm not sure Danni does either. I want you to promise," she said, stepping closer, "I want you to promise you won't tell Danni where I am. She thinks I went back to Boston."

"She's worried about you."

"No, she isn't." She wiped her face with a floppy sleeve. "I came up here to be with Marisa's spirit for a while, okay? Not to hang out with Danni."

"She loves you, Harri. She'll always stand by you."

"Well, do me a favor and don't tell my loving sister where I am. I want to do a little snooping around. There's something going on here. I've talked to some people in town who know a few things."

"What are you talking about? What do you think's going on?"

"Things that are none of your business. For a while I thought you were okay, but it looks like you're just like Danni. All sympathy, no brains."

Ouch. Where had that come from? "I only want to help, Harri."

"I don't need help."

Strong-minded as her sister, but more vulnerable. If she was dealing it meant being around drugs, and she was going to slip sooner or later. If she hadn't already.

"Are you going to stick around here for a while, then?" She made an effort to keep her voice soft, casual. She was asking a lot of questions, and what Harri did was really none of Kate's business.

"I said I'm fine, okay? I think you should leave."

"Okay, Harri," Kate said. "I'm going. I was just passing by, saw your light." No need to get into a fight.

"Yeah, sure, whatever," Harri said. "I should have kept the lamp turned down." She opened the door.

The night didn't seem as peaceful anymore. Kate walked back to Bobcat with her flashlight on, letting go of her meditations about the Maine night to focus on a small sphere of human troubles. Should she tell Danni where her sister had gone? Kate hadn't promised not to tell, and Danni might be relieved to know Harri was okay. Well, sort of okay.

That was an old story, wasn't it?

ELEVEN

"Hey, Kate, c'mon in," Dannie called. She'd left the door to the hilltop house open, and Kate followed her voice to the kitchen. "Glad you're here. I'm going to call you Scout because 'undercover artist' is too long. It's a job description, not a name."

She looked tired, even though she'd given herself a day off before inviting Kate over for dinner and the Open Studios report. The event had called for a lot of work, and it had been a such a roaring success that she must be facing an emotional let-down. But she sounded her usual perky self, voice rising over the rush of water into a large pot she'd maneuvered into the sink. "Go say Hi to the boys."

Andy and Ryan were in the living room, intent on a TV baseball game, Tigers against Yankees. Ryan's red bandana didn't look like it had been through a day's worth of outdoor work. Maybe putting on a fresh one was his idea of changing for dinner.

Kate waved at the men and they waved back. She hung her leather jacket in the closet with her Red Sox cap tucked in its pocket. The day had been cloudy, and some rain had fallen as she'd walked up the Farm Road hill, but that old leather jacket had seen worse weather.

She and Danni sipped wine and worked on dinner. Kate chopped veggies—Romaine and yellow peppers and red onions—and tossed them in a huge blue bowl.

Danni was slicing meat from a cooked chicken. Dinner wouldn't take long.

"Is Harri joining us?" Kate asked carefully. She hadn't decided whether to tell Danni where Harri was or not. If she did, and Danni approached her sister, Harri would never trust Kate again.

"No, she's not here anymore. I guess she's gone back to Boston." Danni shrugged. "She left a note saying it was time to go." She sighed as she chopped the chicken into bite-sized pieces. "Unpredictable, as always. I just hope she's okay."

"Yes." Even telling Danni she'd seen Harri at a Big House dinner didn't make sense, because it might get Erik in trouble.

"It's funny how things work out," Danni said. "Harri's the one who got me interested in Short Creek. She was friends with Marisa Michaud—the singer, you've heard of her?—before her career took off. Marisa grew up here, raved about it to Harri, and Harri and I took a trip up here, just for fun. I'd been dreaming about starting an artists' colony for a few years, and I saw the farm for sale. Well, it wasn't a farm by then, the owner had built a bunch of cabins to rent out to hunters. That's how EMAC got real. That, and a hunk of money from my father. And more from Deep Pockets."

"You and Harri took a vacation? That must have been before Harri and Marisa got into drugs, right?"

"Yeah. Or before I knew they had. I liked Marisa a lot at first—she had more energy than me, can you believe it? But of course after what she did to my sister I hated her."

Hard to imagine anyone with more energy than Danni. "Hey, any word back from the police about all the weird things going on at the Center?"

Farley had told Danni about the woodchuck right away, of course, and she'd sent one of Ryan's crew to remove it and wash the deck. They'd all let it slide as some kind of practical joke, although a gruesome one. Likewise the dead raven and the snake. But the bullet with Kate's name on it was an outright threat, and like the fishing line incident it was criminal. As she'd promised, Danni had asked the Short Creek cops to investigate.

"A uniform came out and talked to me, and drove up the Loop to have a look," Danni said. "But there's just not any evidence to work with. I told him about the bullet and the woodchuck and raven and the snake. He said everybody should be alert and lock their cabins. Especially you and Farley."

"Duh," Kate said.

"Yeah. Helpful, right? I gave him the bullet and he asked me if you still had the snake." Danni snorted.

"I picked up the bedspread carefully the next morning," Kate said. "But I didn't really expect my scaly pal to be there. No self-respecting snake wants to hang around with humans."

"Glad it was in your bed and not mine. I would have freaked." She cranked a can-opener around a can of artichoke hearts. "But why you? Why anybody? Damn. I thought we were through with all the crazy stuff." She dumped pasta into the pot. "I asked Ryan to have his guys check around, especially at night. That was a great idea of yours."

"You should think about people in town who might not like EMAC," Kate said as she drained a jar of olives into the sink. "Thank goodness the noise that made Farley and me practically wet our pants turned out to be just an owl, like Erik figured," Kate said. "One of the librarians in town helped me find a book by some journalist who followed an ornithologist around. Said the barred owl call made his blood run cold."

"Did he wet his pants?"

Kate laughed. "Probably, but he didn't say so. Oh, and the snake was just a racer. Common, according to Erik, but mine was bigger than most. I took a picture of it with my cell phone to show him. No big deal."

"You've got to be kidding. Snakes? Any snake's a big deal in my book." Danni shuddered.

Rain streaked in the window. In half an hour fettuccini with chicken and artichoke hearts was ready for the table. "Dinner's on," Danni called, but the men didn't hear her over the TV. Wine bottle poised over the first glass, she looked at Kate. "Go round 'em up, Scout."

"Oops, sports police," Ryan said before Kate could open her mouth. He zapped the screen blank with the remote and then got up and slid the door of the cabinet across the TV. "All gone," he said with a mock-curtsy.

They celebrated the day they'd all worked hard to make a success. Kate thought her job had been the easiest, but she could see it was useful. The four of them clinked glasses, and then Danni turned to Kate. "Shoot, Scout."

She went down her list, making suggestions. Better lighting for Grouse, where Hallsy had improvised by borrowing photographer's lights from Kim next door, which were uncomfortably bright. Ramp access to the Big House and to the cabins that had porches, for wheelchairs and strollers. Attention to the road in places—gravel to fill in potholes and low spots. A couple of people had stumbled, and a little boy had fallen down. The roughest area was between Loon and Red Fox.

"Yes, we've been meaning to get that road re-gravelled," Danni said, looking at Andy ruefully. "You'd be amazed how much little bits of rock cost."

"You could put boards over the wet parts," Kate said. Danni made a face, so she added, "Okay, tacky suggestion." Danni liked things to look proper.

She went back to her list. A few benches between cabins. The south side, between River Otter and Chickadee, and between Chickadee and Bobcat, had the longest distances. Opening the barn and putting the Ping-Pong table out there, along with other games for children who needed activities that fit their ages. A slow walk around the Loop with adults looking at artwork would drive some children wild with boredom.

"Adult supervision," Danni said, nodding. "We'd need babysitters." She wasn't objecting; she was planning.

"But overall, it went really well," Kate said. "They loved Joy, and Farley was just the right person to end with."

"That's our Danni. She knows where to put people," Andy said.

"I wish I could say I planned the order," Danni said. She didn't seem bothered by Andy's comment, which could have sounded snarky. "But sometimes dumb luck helps me out. I knew Joy would be a hit, but it's good to hear Farley was too, in a different way. I put him in Peacock because it's got the best heat. He asked for that, mentioned his arthritis." She twirled her wineglass, took a sip. "He's such a sweetie. And I love his work."

"Yeah, he's a star," Kate said. "And he deserves to be."

Danni smiled. "Oh! I saw his crazy cartoon. We should put it up in the lounge, permanently. It's a hoot. The literary fox cracked me up."

"Not everybody loved it," Kate said. She looked at Ryan, who glanced at Andy.

"Hey, no, I thought it was great," Andy said.

Ryan stood up. "I gotta go. Danni, thanks for another great dinner."

"What about the game? Oh, sure, whatever," Andy said. He got up too, and the men left through the kitchen, the rumble of their low voices cut off when the door to Andy's workshop closed.

"What, you don't think he liked the cartoon?" Danni asked.

"I saw Ryan and Andy looking at it when they picked up the coffee urn at Peacock. Ryan said, 'Shit, man,' or something like that."

"Ryan's usually so upbeat. He should be—his trucking company is doing gangbuster business," Danni said. "And he gives the Center a lot of freebies, like those ATVs his guys ride to deliver lunch baskets and take their tools wherever something needs fixing. He leaves one of them in the barn, with the keys in it, which can help Andy get stuff done." She poured herself another glass of wine and held the bottle toward Kate.

"No, thanks."

"I'm really glad they're close. So Andy has someone to hang out with, when I'm not here." She stroked the stem of her glass. "You know, I get to travel a lot. I worry Andy is getting, I don't know, isolated. We had more friends—all different kinds—when we lived in Boston."

"So why not take Andy with you when you travel?"

"He hates flying." Danni yawned. "It's funny, he wasn't too happy about moving up here at first. Now he says it's great. These days I don't know what he's thinking half the time. We used to read each other's minds."

The night she'd gone to dinner at the Big House, Harri had said something about the couple not being as close, and now Danni thought Andy was shutting her out? Kate's concern for their marriage went up a notch.

"In fact, I worry a little that—oh, I don't know," Danni said.

"What?" When her friend didn't answer, Kate said, "Out with it. You wanted a woman friend to talk to, remember? Here I am."

Danni sighed. "You know how a rocket sits there on the launch pad and pours out billows of smoke, and barely moves at first? The past five years have been like that, even with all the support from Deep Pockets and my Dad. I've been working like a dog. Then Farley's name put us on the national arts map. A few more like him and we'll be on the way to lift-off."

"That's all good, right?"

"Yeah, but I wonder sometimes if Andy is maybe a little jealous. Some men have a hard time when their wives are successful. I never thought he'd be that way, but there was never a test. Until now."

"Ouch. Can you talk to him about it? Maybe get some counseling? It helped me."

"I've thought of it more than once, but I'm hesitating because he's seemed happier, recently. Bought himself that black pick-up in the driveway, which is great, because when he was a kid his father went bankrupt and the family always struggled. Maybe he's redefining himself. Maybe he's finally adjusted to a big change." Danni yawned again, and her jaw cracked. "Oh, gosh. I'm all in. Thanks for the support, Kate. I'm glad I put the problem into words: makes it more manageable, somehow. Let's talk some more, but not tonight. Let me run you home."

"Heck, no, the walk'll do me good." She glanced out the window. "And it's stopped raining."

"You sure?"

"Danni, you're asleep. Here, let me help you clean up." Kate moved fast, whisking dishes into the kitchen before Danni could get up.

"Hey, thanks, Kate, but don't worry. Andy can do these. His job, when I cook."

But they'd heard Andy's truck start up, and he hadn't come back in. Kate figured he and Ryan had gone off to watch the game at the sports bar in Short Creek. They probably thought she would stay longer, and she and Danni would want the living room to chat.

She loaded the dishwasher, and Danni wiped the table and counter. After a final yawn, Danni hugged her goodnight.

* * *

145

The sky had cleared, and the wet driveway answered the black sky's glitter. She swung her arms and walked fast, feeling the cool air rouse her body, burn off the sluggishness of dinner and wine. Breathe in, three steps, breathe out, three steps. It was dark, the moon busy somewhere else in the great round night: she paid attention to the sound and feel of her boots as they hit the ground, kept her left foot on pavement and her right on roadside gravel.

Farley had been right, she'd always thought of herself as a loner. But maybe it didn't have to be that way. Could she imagine herself as a member of a tribe now, her work connecting her not only to the small group at EMAC but to artists all over the country, all over the world? A society of people struggling to create small moments of beauty for themselves and others? Maybe she could make her time here more than a break from her old life, make it instead the passage to a different life she couldn't yet imagine.

The spotlight over the EMAC sign was a welcome sight. As she crossed the parking lot, she yawned. Not as wide a yawn as Danni's, but definitely a sign she was tired. A healthy night's sleep was at hand, not the depressed over-sleeping that had dulled her brain until the last two days. If Farley's deck light was on, she'd stop by, but not for long. And no more wine.

His light was on, outlining Peacock with a leaf-green halo. She was headed up the path above Bobcat when something caught her eye. Some large bundle at the bottom of the stone steps.

She should have brought a flashlight, but the decision to walk home in the dark had been spontaneous, as much a reaction to Danni's falling asleep and Andy's being gone as a wish for exercise. She fished her key out of her pocket—she'd put one of those little lights on the ring, the kind that are supposed to last forever. Lifetime guarantee, a phrase that always made her laugh.

146

Pressing the button on the tiny light, she made her way along the little-used path to the stairway. The light was so dim it showed her one flagstone at a time.

Then it showed her an almost-familiar face, so white it looked bright.

Farley lay face up, his fixed eyes looking past her into the starry sky.

TWELVE

She knelt beside him, stunned. His tweed jacket was soaked, and water pooled in the corners of his eyes. Why on earth would he have come down these steps, in the dark, the rain? She looked around for the flashlight he would have carried, didn't see one. But her keychain light didn't have much range.

Pain clutched her chest, her throat. "Farley." She touched his face. It was cold. Cradled his head in her hands, tears welling up.

A softness at the back of his head. She pulled her hand away, felt something damp on her fingers. Sticky, with a few hard white bits. Blood and—bone?

Fear cascaded from Kate's brain to her body. She found herself holding her breath to listen. Not a sound. She looked around, but the night was moonless, opaque. She was suddenly cold.

Reason came back to her in small steps. First, she could do nothing for Farley. Second, she needed to tell—whom? Danni, the police? Both, probably. That meant going back to the Big House with its land-line phone.

That was the next thing to do.

Go to the Big House. Call.

She hated to leave him.

This isn't Farley anymore, she told herself. Go.

She laid her leather jacket gently over his face, tried to remember that face alive, giving her one of his kind looks. Hold onto that picture, she told herself. Not this.

The reasoning part of her mind was telling her things she didn't want to hear. Farley wouldn't have been on the front stairs. He was afraid of them. The wound at the back of his head was too large to be from hitting a flat surface like a flagstone. Or the rounded edge of the old stone steps.

Shaking, she pushed the thoughts away. Stumbled down the path, face streaming.

* * *

The next morning a sign on the Big House door read URGENT MEETING 10:00. Not everybody came in for breakfast, though; Danni must have sent Ryan around to all the studios to let people know. Walking from Bobcat, Kate had seen him on an ATV.

The night had been beyond horrible. Kate called 911 and then Danni, who kept saying "What? What? Kate, what are you saying?" as if she couldn't, wouldn't, wake up. Not for this news.

She'd driven her SUV right up to Bobcat, the way she had on Kate's first day there, and rushed inside. They hugged. It was like a second take in a movie, a bad re-take. They weren't laughing this time, but crying. Because everything had changed.

Then Danni dropped into a chair, said she didn't want to see Farley, she'd take Kate's word that he—she didn't finish the sentence. Mostly they sat, waiting. Danni cried off and on, pulling her red cardigan close around herself. Kate had retreated to some cold place in her mind. She wanted to know what had happened. She didn't tell Danni how unlikely it was for Farley to be on those steps. Maybe there was some innocent explanation, which the police would provide.

It was twenty minutes before they heard the cruiser pull up outside. "Good thing it's not an emergency," Danni said. "Although it sort of is."

A uniformed cop, a young guy with a moustache, was joined by an older one wearing jeans and an Old Navy hooded sweatshirt. They left the engine running. Kate told them the story, and the three of them went up the trail to the point at which Kate had first noticed something at the bottom of the stairway. The uniform had a powerful flashlight, the kind that looks like a night-stick, and they could easily see Farley—no, the not-Farley—from there. She didn't need to see all that again, and went back down to Bobcat to be with Danni.

Another vehicle joined the SUV and the cruiser out front, one that looked like a squared-off stretch limo, black. Men went up the path, came back carrying something. What had been Farley was put inside the black vehicle like a package. The rear doors slammed and tires crunched. Silence.

Kate and Danni went outside. The detective, who'd introduced himself to Kate as Jim, joined them and handed Kate's jacket to her. The uniform tied yellow "Police Line—Do Not Cross" tape to the post of Bobcat's porch and unrolled it to a tree on the other side of the path, blocking off access to Peacock.

Danni gasped and turned to Jim. "Wait, this isn't a crime scene," she said. "Nobody did this. It was a horrible accident." Then something came out of her that was part hiccup, part sob. "Wasn't it?"

The cruiser's headlights lit Jim's face harshly from the side, but his voice was gentle. "That's what we think, Danni." Of course, everybody in this town must know her. "It's routine. We'll come out tomorrow and have a look around, just to be sure. But it looks like he fell." He put a hand on her shoulder. "Right now I think you need to go home, see if you can get some sleep."

Danni wobbled a little on her feet, and he put an arm around her waist.

150

"C'mon," Jim said. "You shouldn't be driving. I'll take you home. Andy can bring you back in the morning for your car. Right now you need his big shoulder to cry on."

"Oh, God, yes," Danni said. She whirled and gave Kate a fierce hug and turned to follow the detective to his car.

* * *

Kate barely slept. She tried to empty her mind but it was impossible not to think. It had been raining, slippery. Why would he have used the front stairs? Maybe he was having a heart attack, a stroke. Maybe he panicked because of that. Or was confused. Maybe he woke up from a dream and forgot he wasn't at home, thought he was stepping into the next room.

Sleep came, finally, but not for long. Her watch said three-thirty. Ugh. She got up for a drink of water and saw lights through the trees up by Peacock. She slid the kitchen window open. Voices.

Funny the cops couldn't wait until morning.

She slipped into her jeans and boots and jacket in the dark. What the heck was going on up there? She was on the trail before she realized this was not a good idea. What was she thinking? It might not be the police. She stood and listened for a minute. At least two men, maybe three, and some kind of truck. She couldn't see it well through the trees. But she shouldn't go up there.

It might be whoever killed a raven and a woodchuck. And a man.

* * *

They'd gathered on the patio behind the Big House. Reggie and Sherri sat together, and Hallsy and David. Gabriel and Case, of course. Erik sat alone. Both Joy and Kim got there at about the same time as Kate, and Kim

151

leaned against a post while the two women dragged chairs up at the edge the group. Nava came last, leaning on her cane, and David got up and gave her his seat, standing at the side near Kate and Joy.

"What's this all about?" Reggie asked, loudly. "This is serious work time for me." He looked around as if to say it wasn't for the rest of them.

Nobody answered.

"Kate, you know anything?" Joy asked quietly.

Kate looked down, shook her head. She couldn't. At the sound of tires on gravel they all looked up, and Danni's car stopped with its nose in the bushes.

"Oh, man," David said. "Look at her. It's bad news."

Danni got out of the SUV slowly. Her hair was all over the place and she was wearing a pink tee under her red sweater. No makeup. No earrings.

She faced them without, somehow, looking at them, and in the flattest voice Kate had ever heard come out of her mouth she told them Farley had slipped on the stairs, hit his head on the steps, was dead. That arrangements would be made. That they might see a police car around, just a formality.

"They've already been, I think," Kate said. "Real early this morning."

Danni didn't seem to hear her. "So I just wanted to let you know, and do it with you all in a group. Getting bad news alone is just the pits." She swayed a little, looked like she was going to cry, then took a big breath. "There might be— a reporter, too. Short Creek is a small town and everything is news."

For the first time Kate thought what bad publicity this would be for EMAC. She'd bet Danni had thought of that last night. Not immediately, but soon. Farley's death turned his eminence in the art world from a blessing to a burden.

Sherri looked shocked, hand in front of her mouth, and then she whispered something to Reggie. Every few seconds Erik punched a fist into his other palm. Hallsy sat with his head in his hands. Joy went over to him and crouched next to his chair, put a hand on his knee. David looked grim. Quiet conversations sprang up.

Reggie stood, banging his chair into the rail. Kim leapt away like a cat. "I don't know about the rest of you, but I've got work to do." He didn't look at all disturbed. He left without looking back, and Sherri followed him like a dog on a leash.

Kim faced the group. "Sorry," he said. "Sorry for all."

* * *

Kate found Danni staring out her office window.

"Could you check about whether the police were there? Somebody definitely was, last night. I woke up, and there were lights on at Peacock. I thought it was weird, but I didn't want to check it out by myself."

"No, of course not." Danni fished a card out of her pocket and dialed a number. Said "You wanted me to call you" in that flat new voice of hers. Said "Kate saw lights in Peacock last night." Said "okay" three times and hung up.

"Danni." Kate sat beside the desk and took her hands. They were cold. "Look, you know I worked as an EMT, right? I'm no medical expert, but I felt a wound at the back of Farley's head. A—bad wound." She didn't want to say "bone fragments," at least not now. "Not the sort of thing you get from hitting your head on a step."

Danni looked at her.

"It's a horrible thought, but it's been bothering me all night. I think it's possible somebody—killed him." There were no other words for that.

153

Danni burst into tears. Kate was surprised she didn't do the same. But she felt things she'd never felt so intensely, and together. Anger, a new kind she'd never felt before. Sorrow. And a need for revenge. Whoever did this to Farley had to be caught.

THIRTEEN

When she could speak again, Danni said Jim wanted to meet them at Bobcat.

He wore a dark blue windbreaker with "SCPD" across the chest instead of the hoodie he'd had on the night before. By day he seemed taller, more official. "Let's go out to Peacock, have a look," he said. He drove them in a plain blue Ford, Danni beside him and Kate in the back seat.

He lifted the yellow tape and followed them under it. Kate thought it odd. Shouldn't they stay away from the scene? Didn't the police need to look for clues, dust for fingerprints?

But Jim strode up the trail, then took the flagstone path to the front stairs. Danni stayed on the trail. "Let's go in the back," she said.

Standing where Kate had found Farley, Jim gave the area a casual glance. No sign of what had happened last night, at least not to Kate's eyes. But she hated looking at the place, and was glad Danni had taken the lead.

Jim came back to the trail and followed them. "Let's go inside," he said as they neared the steps to the deck. "You can tell me what you heard in the wee hours, Kate."

Danni sank onto the couch. About to join her, Kate stopped. "Wait," she said. "Where's his work? The last time I was here, he'd finished four or five paintings. He'd leaned them against the walls right over there. And there." She looked around the studio. The easel lay on the floor, as if knocked down by someone grabbing a canvas from it. Not a painting in sight.

Danni got up and looked around, too. "You're right. Oh my God, that's terrible." She looked like she was going to cry some more.

"What's the matter?" Jim asked. Wasn't he listening? He must have spaced out.

"All his work is gone," Kate said. "All his beautiful work."

Jim didn't look impressed. He must not have a clue how important Farley was.

"It was very valuable work," Kate said. She swallowed hard. "Especially now. It's a huge loss. To EMAC. To—all of us."

Danni sat down again. "Kate's right," she said. "A major loss."

Jim pulled a small notebook out of his shirt pocket. "So tell me what happened last night."

Kate told him in a few sentences, but he didn't write anything down. She tried not to mind that he'd chosen Farley's favorite chair. It wasn't Farley's anymore.

"You get a look at the vehicle? Think you'd recognize the voices if you heard them again?"

"Neither. I didn't go up there, just looked from outside Bobcat."

"That's not much to go on."

"No."

"Tell him the rest," Danni said. "What you told me in the office."

Kate told him about the wound at the back of Farley's head, about the gleam of bone on her hand.

Jim shook his head. "Death's been ruled accidental."

"It has? So fast? But how do you explain—"

"I don't, actually." He smiled, even though he'd interrupted her. "I go on what the ME—the medical examiner—tells me. He says foul play, I got work to do. He says accidental death, I go fishing. And this is a small county that doesn't have much crime. So we get things done pretty fast."

"Oh, Kate, it must have been an accident," Danni said. "Of course it was. He was one of the sweetest, smartest—" She couldn't go on.

Jim turned to Kate. "I'm sorry." He spread his hands. "Look, it might be a good idea for you to come down to the station and report your ideas to the chief. He's a by-the-book kind of guy, so I'd be surprised if he overruled the ME, but you were first on the scene and you're a very observant gal."

"Sounds like it's not going to make any difference," Kate said. But Farley's face looked at her from an empty wall, her mind playing pointed tricks. "But I'll do it, just in case." She was already doubting herself. Maybe it was just dirt on her hand, grit. Finding him already seemed like a bad dream, the worst one she'd ever had.

Jim turned to Danni. "So can you give me an inventory of what's missing here?"

She wiped her wet face with the back of a hand and looked around. "Not really. I only came up here once, a couple of weeks ago. He was working on something, but I couldn't describe it. Kate? You hung out with Farley, didn't you?"

"I spent a lot of time with him, but mostly we sat on the deck out back." She thought a moment. "You know, the most easily recognizable thing, on the finished pieces," Kate said, "would be his signature. Distinctive. More of a sign, really, just three letters. If you're going to look for his work on the black market or something."

"That's right," Danni said. "I don't know that I could remember exactly how it went, though."

"I can," Kate said.

Jim held his notebook out to her, and the pen.

Kate sat beside Danni, turned the page sideways and drew the "Mc" and the "Q."

Danni nodded. "Yeah, that's it. He really loved the tail on that Q. Sometimes it went halfway across the bottom of a piece."

"Thanks," Jim said, slipping the notebook into his pocket. "You've been a big help. Kate. If we find any paintings we think are his, I might need you to ID them."

"She'd do a great job," Danni said. "She's got a mind like a camera."

"No I don't," Kate said. "I just liked his work a lot."

"Where was that big cartoon thing?" Jim asked.

"Oh, that." Kate found herself smiling for a second. "He put it in the closet." She opened the door. "Hey, it's still here."

Jim was beside her. "Well, would you look at that," he said. "He must have missed it."

"He?" Kate asked.

Jim shrugged. "Or they."

Danni pushed in between them. "Missed it or didn't want it. I mean, it's just a joke. Too bad to have this, of all his pieces. I suppose it's something, though. I'll have Andy take it down to the Big House."

"Some of the work was unfinished, like the one that was on the easel," Kate said. "But maybe the thieves couldn't tell."

"How did they know the place was empty?" Danni asked.

"That's why I can't go fishing," Jim said. "Yet. The death was accidental"—he glanced at Kate—"unless proven otherwise. But theft? That's a crime, even if it's only art." He turned toward the door.

Behind his back, Kate and Danni looked at each other. Only art?

Jim was below them, on the path, as Danni locked the back door.

Kate asked quietly, "So how did Jim know about the cartoon?"

"I don't know. Maybe I said something about it. Maybe he came to Open Studio day."

They walked slowly down the path beside the cabins. Jim was already in the Ford.

"Maybe you were wrong, Kate. Maybe he fell really hard. Maybe his, his skull was, I don't know, frail or something."

"Yes. It was dark. I was pretty upset. Am pretty upset."

"Yeah. Ditto."

"And it doesn't make any sense that anyone would want to kill him."

"Yeah. The gentlest guy on earth."

"But Danni? Just be careful, okay? I mean, I'm not even sure what I saw anymore, but if it wasn't an accident—"

"—then we should both be careful. Because we don't know what's going on."

"Right."

Jim was watching them, his arm hanging out the window of the idling car. "Kate, want a ride down to the station? The sooner you talk to the chief the better."

"Sure." She wasn't holding out much hope that her impressions would change the ME's report, but she should follow through. And she was too sad and rattled to work.

A voice in her mind that was Farley's told her not to lose her momentum. *You found your way back to your work,* the voice said. *Don't lose that now. No matter what.*

Okay, Farley. Got it.

"Danni, you want a ride to the Big House?" Jim said.

She managed a weak smile. "No, Jim, I think I can manage to walk that far."

159

He turned the car around instead of driving all the way around the Loop, and Kate got in. The interior was warm, with a faint scent of aftershave. She liked the way Jim drove on Farm Road, accelerating a little on curves so the car hugged them.

"What kind of art do you do?" He glanced at her once, then back at the road.

"Oh, I'm a throwback to the days of realism. I draw things, mostly natural things, like landscapes, trees, ferns."

"What do you think of EMAC?"

"Oh, it's great. For me. For everyone." She lied a little. "We were all getting such a lot of work done before this happened."

"Yeah." His voice was soft. "I'm really sorry this had to happen to you, to all of you artists. But you especially." Another glance. "You don't need this."

"Nobody needs this." She hadn't expected a cop to be this sympathetic. "You're probably more used to this sort of thing than most people are, though. And of course you didn't know him."

"You two were pretty close, then?"

"I only knew him a few weeks, but yes. We'd become good friends." She put a little emphasis on the last word.

Without looking at her he touched her hand briefly. "Nobody needs to lose a friend."

She was startled. And then she remembered an incident she hadn't thought of in years.

She'd been sitting in the back of a friend's car, parked at the curb. It was a small car and Kate had been uncomfortable, her knees jammed against the front seat. A couple and a boy about ten years old had come out of a bank, and while the parents continued down the sidewalk the boy had come straight to Kate as if he had been called. He stared at her with a smug look on his face and then rapped on the window, which was an inch from her face. She flinched and

160

struggled to move, but she didn't know the car and couldn't find the door handle. And then the boy was gone, sauntering back to his parents.

The incident had stuck with her. It was a small act of bullying, but an effective one—she remembered the surge of fury and helplessness she'd felt. But the mystery was why the boy did it. What had been on her face to trigger his behavior, to make her his victim?

And why was she thinking of this now? Jim was being supportive; his gesture was acceptable under the circumstances.

She must be really screwed up if she couldn't accept a little sympathy.

"Hey, don't worry about seeing Chief Fallon. A bit of a grouchy bear, but he's all right."

"Oh. Good." She realized she'd been quiet for several minutes. She hadn't been thinking about the chief, but it wasn't a bad guess on Jim's part.

* * *

The chief's eyes weren't quite right. One of them wasn't looking at her squarely, but it was hard to tell which one. She found herself looking back and forth between them, which probably made her look shifty.

Jim had taken her to the door. "Chief, this is the woman from EMAC. She saw a couple of things last night she wanted to tell you about." Giving her shoulder a squeeze, he left.

Fallon wasn't any more receptive to her ideas than Jim had been. "I'll pass your observations along to Dr. Powers. But George, he's been in the business for three or four decades now, don't think he'd be likely to miss anything." He picked up a pen. "Where'd you say you were from?"

"Uh, from EMAC right now."

He waited, pen poised, looking at her.

"Massachusetts," she said, after a bit.

"Whereabouts in Massachusetts?"

Under his flawed gaze she felt her face heat up with a combination of embarrassment and annoyance.

"Danvers."

He sighed and looked out the window for a moment. "I'm asking you for your address, Miss Collins—"

"It's Corliss. Ms. Corliss."

"Miss Corliss, are you always this uncooperative?"

"I came in here with some information. I didn't expect to be grilled like a suspect."

He gave her a fake smile. "Let's start over. I'm a law enforcement officer and I'm asking you for some I.D."

She pulled her wallet out of her back pocket and tossed the license on his desk. The address was Mike's place now, of course, but she didn't have to tell him that.

"Is this the woman who saw something?" A tall man stood in the doorway, big and bald, wearing a black turtleneck and black pants. His shoulders were broad, and the wrinkle lines at the corners of his eyes suggested he smiled often.

He wasn't smiling now.

"Hey, doc," The chief's voice was friendly. "She didn't see nothing. Just thought something." He was writing slowly, copying the information from her license onto a notepad. Either he was trying to aggravate her or he hadn't made it through second grade. "This here's Doc Powers," he said to Kate.

"So what are we thinking?" Powers asked, looking at her.

"I felt a wound in the back of Farley's head—"

"Of course you did. The man fell down a flight of stone steps, didn't he?"

His tone was affable enough, but he clearly had his mind made up. Kate decided to keep her mouth shut.

162

The doctor took a few strides and looked at her license over the chief's shoulder.

Fallon looked up at him. "Told me she was an EMT."

"An EMT?" The tall man's gaze flicked at her. "Well, even an EMT is entitled to an opinion."

When the laughter flew out of her, Kate was as surprised as the two men. She'd heard about people who laughed at funerals, and now she understood. Nothing was funny, but she was all stirred up. Farley was dead, and she was caught between two male egos the size of Reggie Blair's.

"Jesus," Powers said. "She's hysterical." His footsteps faded down the hall.

"Thank you, Miss Corliss." The chief pushed her license toward her.

"Miss" again. Yes, he was trying to aggravate her.

"Thank you for being a good citizen and coming in with your, ah, ideas. All of this must have been a terrible shock to you. Since the gentleman who died was a boyfriend of yours, you may not be exactly at your best, your most alert. In the dark. In the rain."

"He was a friend, not a boyfriend." She picked up her license and was down the hall and almost out the front door before she remembered her truck wasn't outside.

"Whoa, whoa, whoa!" Jim came up behind her. "I'll drive you back. Hey," he said when she turned around, "you look like a woman who could use a drink."

* * *

The Helluva Sports Bar had two huge television screens, but it was early afternoon and quiet. A couple of men in bib overalls drank at the bar. Jim and Kate slid into a booth.

"We didn't see eye to eye," Kate said. Jim's laugh was uneasy, and she realized he might have taken it literally, might think she was making fun of the chief. "I mean he didn't trust me. I don't know how it started, but we were both practically snarling by the time I left."

"I could see that. So I figured a little damage control was called for. Let me guess. Merlot? Chips and salsa?"

"I'm glad your mind-reading isn't perfect. You're right on with the wine, but I'll pass on the chips."

"Be right back."

She could hear him bantering with the bartender. He was being nice, almost too nice. It made her realize she missed— something. Not Mike anymore. She'd worked on herself enough to put him in the past. But yes, it felt good to be having a drink with a guy.

Even a guy she didn't trust?

She realized she was shivering, and she crossed her arms to stop it.

Jim came back with a mug of dark beer foaming over a frosted mug in one hand and her wine in the other. She took a quick sip before he'd even sat down. It released all its complicated tastes on her tongue and went down well, warming her, calming her.

"Ah." She gave him a small smile. "Turns out the original comfort food isn't even food."

"But this is," he said, as the bartender brought a dish of jumbo shrimp to the table.

"They look yummy," Kate said, even though she wasn't sure she could eat anything. Was there such a thing as too sad to eat?

"Hey, what's the matter?"

Wasn't it obvious? She got a tissue out of her jacket. "Sorry. It just hit me again, all of a sudden. It's like everything's the matter."

"Just as long as it isn't anything I said."

Stupid comment. She ignored it. Maybe she liked the idea of having a drink with a guy more than she liked having a drink with Jim. She'd just met him, and under the worst possible circumstances. She didn't know him. Why had she even come here? But the next thing he said made her like him a little more.

"It's like that when someone's gone," he said. "It keeps hitting you all over again, even though you haven't forgotten it for a minute."

FOURTEEN

Remembering Farley every minute—even when she was asleep, she was sure, since she sometimes awakened with his dreamed face in her mind—meant two things to Kate as late August spilled its warmth across the hills and valleys around Short Creek.

First, her difficulty working had vanished. Farley's quiet encouragement lived in her own mind now, and his sudden loss punctuated everything he'd said with an exclamation point of pain. Looking back, it was easy to see the reasons she'd floundered: she'd lost the habit of working on her art, let it fade under the pressures of job and relationship.

Not to mention the recently discovered guilt that came from taking responsibility for Danni's choice not to be a working artist.

She remembered Archimedes from high school math: "Give me a place to stand and I will move the world." He was talking about the power of a mechanical lever, but there were other kinds of levers. Talking with Farley, she had found a place to stand, a place that made sense of her life: daily work. Her world had been moved.

The second thing about remembering Farley was Kate's resolve to find out what had really happened to him that night. She wasn't sure he'd been pushed down the stairs, but it was a strong possibility. She'd keep an open mind and stay alert. She didn't trust Chief Fallon or Dr. Powers, so she'd have to figure it out herself. Her instinct told her this wasn't the end of it, that things were still playing out.

In the meantime, work was her lifeboat.

* * *

She filled her largest sketchbook with rough drawings, then bought a four by eight piece of plywood at the hardware store. A stop at Bear Pause gave her the gesso to prime it, along with tubes of acrylic paint. She started roughing out a scene from her walks: a tangle of vegetation on a riverbank, seen from below. A frog's-eye view. And in fact a frog sat at the lower left of the drawing, half-hidden by leaves. She hoped the frog wouldn't be the first thing a viewer would notice.

Such a wealth of textures and colors to play with. The bottom of the brick wall of one of the old buildings across the road. One side of the frame of its cellar window, paint peeling. Dark shadows under the white flakes, and the rose and ochre and blood colors of the bricks. She worked hard on the coppery-green skin of the frog, its sheen.

After a few days' work on the plywood panel, she took a risk and asked Danni to her studio. "I know realism in art is about as 'in' as rhyming in poetry, but it's what I do," she said, opening the door and standing back.

Her friend brushed past her. "Okay, Kate, time to stop putting yourself down."

Danni stood in front of the piece for a full minute. When she turned around her eyes were full of tears and she gave Kate a wordless hug.

* * *

Later, at Danni's, they laughed about it over coffee and Danish. Andy, the coffee psychic, came in from his workshop and stood in the kitchen, pouring a cup. He waved at Kate, smiled a hello.

"You know me. I'm *never* out of words," Danni said. "But I couldn't believe it. It was like walking into your cabin and then I was outside again, looking at plants, and frogs, and that old building—"

"What building?" Andy leaned in the doorframe, cup halfway to his lips.

"Oh, those brick things on the river," Kate said.

"Be careful," he said. "That was a sawmill, back in the 1920s. Old places like that can be dangerous, full of rusting machinery that can fall apart if you look at it."

"True. But still, I think they're beautiful, in a way, how they're going back to nature, vines going up the walls, and trees growing up inside some of them—"

"You go inside?" Andy asked.

Kate shrugged. "I've looked through a couple of broken windows, the ones that aren't boarded up with plywood." She turned back to Danni. "I've got a sketchbook full of ideas from that place."

"I hope you don't get hurt," Andy said, shaking his head as he went back to his workshop.

Danni's eyes met hers. "Do what you need to do, Kate. If you can, now. You have to."

"I know, it's weird," Kate said. "With what's happened, you'd think I wouldn't be able to lift a pencil. But Farley said something once about being happy and sad, about how you can be both ways at the same time. That's how I feel."

Danni nodded, wiped a tear from the corner of one made-up eye. "The man knew things, didn't he?"

* * *

"I think you should get away from there," Cam said.

Kate had called him from the phone in the Big House. They weren't close, but she knew her brother worried if he didn't hear from her every few months. This time, it sounded as if he was worried despite her call. She'd told him only that one of the residents had died, nothing of her suspicions or her talk with the police chief.

"But I'm getting so much work done," she said. Cam wasn't exactly an art fan. "And it's not all work. There's a party tonight, a kind of good-bye party for one of the artists. Well, two of them." Reggie the giant planet and Sherri his moon.

"So it sounds like other people are bailing. It's just too isolated. People way back in the sticks can be kind of strange, you know. And a guy just falls off his porch and dies? There are probably bears and alligators. Can't you just pack up and leave? What does Mike think about you being up there?"

"Oh, he's okay with it." He probably would be, if he knew—the more distance between them the better. One of these days she'd have to tell Cam that she and Mike had broken up. She'd told him about losing her job because that was a whole lot easier to talk about. Cam had been married forever.

Good time to change the subject. "Heard anything from Ma? I got the usual postcard. I really should call her, but there's no cell coverage here. Would you tell her that, please? I'm calling you on a land line, but it's kind of pricey. You know how she can talk sometimes."

"Yeah, I know. She's okay. I don't think she likes it that you're off in that wild corner of the country, either."

"How's Karen? The kids?"

"Oh, she's, um, fine." Kate wondered at the hesitation. Could he have some hidden bad news too? He didn't talk easily about himself. For all she knew he was going to get divorced the next week. "The boys are both in school now—

Ben just started kindergarten. So it's going to be a little easier for her." A voice called in the background. "She says Hi."

"Hi to her. I've got to go, Cam, but I'll call again when I get a chance."

"Well, remember what I said. It's not like you don't have a life to go back to."

* * *

Alligators in Maine? Kate shook her head. People way back in the sticks? He was in rare form. Ever since he'd moved to Florida he worried about alligators everywhere. Probably saw them under his own bed. She hoped his kids wouldn't grow up afraid of the outdoors.

No, she didn't have a life to go back to. She had a life right here. In her sketchbook, on paper, in all the colors and lines that came to her through her hands. Just thinking about the table in Bobcat gave her a deep, slow satisfaction.

Farley was gone. It kept hitting her. Her mind was on fire with these two kinds of energy, the good and the dreadful. She had been planning to call Vickie, too, and her mother, but she felt too sad, too restless.

She walked along the Loop, kicking a pebble until it went off the road. Sat on the bench on Bobcat's porch, then went almost all the way around again. Stopped at Nava's cabin.

Why not? Nava might not see too well, but she was smart and friendly. If she had been in Army intelligence, maybe she could help figure out what was going on at EMAC.

A knock on her door brought the scrape of a chair inside. Good. Nava wasn't too deep into her work to be interrupted.

She'd been reading the local newspaper, which was spread out on the kitchen table under a strong reading lamp. Kate caught a photo of Farley under the headline FATAL

ACCIDENT AT ARTS CENTER before Nava folded the paper up.

"Farley was one of the finest men I've ever met," Nava said, waving Kate to the couch. Her voice was deeper, different from the dinner-conversation version with its grace notes of tinkling laughter.

"Yes."

Nava lowered herself into a rust-colored, stuffed chair. They were silent for a moment. Kate was looking at her folded hands when Nava said, "Was it an accident?"

Kate's head snapped up. Nava's chin was lifted so she could look under her drooping lids, and the table lamp put highlights in her dark eyes. "Why do you ask?"

The older woman shrugged. "Farley was a careful man. To be on those perilous front steps, on a rainy night, seems suspicious, that's all. I don't have any special information, only what Danni told us, and what little was in the newspaper." Nava leaned forward. "But you, Kate. You were right next door."

"I was at Danni's that night. I walked back here. I was going up to visit him when I—I found him." Tears welled up, blurring Nava's face.

"That must have been hard."

"I wish I'd been there. If I hadn't gone out, maybe things would've happened differently."

"Don't punish yourself, Kate. Guilt is wasted breath. And you haven't answered my question," Nava said. "Not that you have to." Her tone tilted, echoing the dinner-time voice like faint bells. She was someone who once had been able to pose questions people did have to answer.

"Nava, honestly, I don't know what to think." She told the older woman everything she thought could have any relevance: Farley's fear of the stairs, the wound at the back of his head, her conversation with Chief Fallon, the skeptical medical examiner. "After all the creepy things that have been happening—"

"Creepy things?"

Of course Nava didn't know. Kate and Farley had told Danni about the woodchuck, but she'd kept it quiet because she didn't want to scare everybody. Kate had done likewise with the shattered raven and the snake on her bed, talking about it only to Farley and Danni. The police had been called about the tripwire made of fishing line and the bullet on Kate's porch, and at that point Danni had filled them in on all the incidents. But the other artists? They apparently weren't targets. She wanted them to concentrate on their work.

Kate told Nava all of it, including David's son Larry running from the Big House on Kate's second day at EMAC. "I'm confused, Nava. And Joy mentioned you used to be in intelligence, so I thought maybe you'd be able to see how all this craziness fits together."

"Ah, Kate. You've been through a lot. I feel for you," Nava said. "Yes, I worked in surveillance, security, data analysis, but that was years ago." Her chin dropped a bit, and the lights of her eyes were eclipsed. "I can't see the whole picture, but I can tell you this: you are clearly at the center of whatever's going on."

It seemed obvious once Nava said it, but somehow Kate hadn't thought of it before. "But why? I'm no threat to anyone, and Farley wasn't a threat to anyone either. Except maybe Reggie's ego."

"You do know something, and so did he. You just don't know what it is." Nava's head came up and her eyes shone again. "You'll have to think hard about this, Kate. My advice? Old advice, but I hope it will be useful: follow the money."

* * *

Kate walked back to Bobcat, head down. Follow the money? What money? Deep Pockets was the major source of funding for EMAC. Should she try to find out who he was? Danni had said she didn't know, but maybe she was sitting on some clues.

Jim was on the porch at Bobcat, peering in the window.

"Hey," he said. "Glad you're back. Want to go for a walk?"

She was restless enough to agree, and they walked around the Loop twice, not talking much. Back at Bobcat, she sat on the bench, outside.

"Sorry, I don't have any beer," she said. "Want some tea? We could drink it out here." Her studio was private territory.

He sat down close to her. Aftershave, a hint of sweat.

"Whatever you've got," he said, "is perfect."

She didn't think he was talking about drinks any more, and she was right. Her leather jacket creaked as he put his arm around her.

They kissed for a minute. She had to admit being held felt good. But she hardly knew him. And she was in no shape to start a romance. She pulled out of his embrace. "Hey," she said softly. "I've got to get some work done today."

He kissed her a few more times, and she began to worry she'd have to break things up in a more hard-assed way. But he left off with a lick and a nuzzle. "How long are you sticking around?"

"Not sure," she said. "Few more weeks?"

"See you later, then," he said. "I hope."

"Later." She wasn't sure she meant it.

* * *

The next day she got up early and worked on a drawing of ferns against sun-washed rock. After a few hours she took a break and realized how much she wanted coffee—rats, she was out, a wisp of a memory telling her she'd used the last scoop the day before. Too late for the Big House breakfast, but maybe there'd be coffee left. She put some of her newfound energy into sprinting along the Loop.

Yes. Great. She grabbed a cup and filled it. Nobody here but Erik, who was clattering around in the kitchen. She sat at a table and heard him come out, pour himself a cup. He sat across from her and put his feet up on a chair.

"Hey, Erik."

"Hey."

"You coming to the party tonight?"

"At Reggie's studio?" He snorted. "Nope."

"Oh, come on. You don't have to talk to him. Or look at him, even. A few other people are leaving soon, so it's a last chance to hang out."

He looked at her over the rim.

"There are some new folks coming in next week, aren't there? Anybody interesting?" Since he read the files in Danni's office, he'd know the score.

"Yup."

Erik must not feel like talking. So why had he joined her? She went back to the party topic. "Reggie invited us to put up work. Isn't that amazing? Of course he gets three walls, and the rest of us get one—it's his studio. You can see what we do all day."

"I know what you do all day. Doodle."

He must be in that mood she'd seen the day they talked at the top of the rock formation—he wanted to be annoying. Why did she like him despite that? "C'mon, you need a party. We all need something to cheer us up."

"That we do."

She didn't know why she was pressing him, since she didn't like parties much herself. But sitting alone in Bobcat wouldn't feel right, either. "What's not to like about it? Friends and wine and cheese and crackers?"

"Crackers? He invited the locals?"

He could get away with saying that because he was a local himself. Her laugh came out almost like a shout, and the excitement of the half-finished drawing on her table at Bobcat surged through her like lightning. She jumped up, slid her cup along the metal counter of the pass-through. "All of them—the whole flock of turkeys, toting Big Squirts under their wings! You better be there."

"Yo, Kate." He lifted his cup to her as she went out the back door.

She decided to take it as an affirmative. It might have been the first time he'd used her name.

* * *

Reggie's cabin was bigger than Bobcat, and the party was well underway when Kate got there. She joined Joy, who was sitting in an overstuffed chair. She must be tired; for once, she wasn't making much sense. Half-finished sentences dangled in the air, and she was attending to a carrot stick with dreamy intensity. "This is *so* good."

Kate looked at her. "It's a carrot."

"Yeah, sure, but. . . .sweet." She leaned back in the big chair and smiled dreamily.

Oh, she got it. Her friend was stoned.

Now Joy was contemplating a walnut. A giggle started somewhere in her stomach and rose upward, like a silvery fish surfacing. "This looks just like a, like a—." She couldn't finish. She pulled her knees up, trying to control a fit of laughter. "It looks—"

The laughter was contagious. Kate found herself smiling, then giggling a little, too.

"Hey," Reggie boomed. "What's the joke? I like jokes." Looking down at Joy, he said, "Spill the beans, old girl." He was wearing a tie—in honor of what, himself?—and held a flute of champagne in a pudgy hand.

At "old girl" Joy's eyes met Kate's. Tears squeezed from the corners of Joy's eyes and she got even smaller in the chair, kicking her feet, shaking with laughter. Reggie frowned and looked at Kate.

"She's laughing at a—a walnut," Kate said, trying to keep her own voice under control. "I wouldn't take it personally. I think she's been into the wine, or the dope, or both."

"Oh. That's too bad. I wanted to hear what she thought of my latest piece." He drank the flute off in one go. "See you," he said to Kate.

Off to fish for compliments in another pond. Kate decided she didn't care that Reggie hadn't wanted her opinion of his work.

She spotted a cooler against the wall. "Be right back," she said to Joy, who might be asleep. Squatting, Kate looked for bottles—beer from cans tasted tinny to her—and pulled out a Sam Adams and a Guinness. Put the Sam Adams back.

"I'm glad he's dead."

The quiet voice slammed into Kate, took her breath away. She stood, turned.

Sherri's face was twisted with anger. Or hate. "Your stupid friend Farley. He thought he was so great, but he was a prick." Her face was so close spit hit Kate's cheek, and she took a step back. Sherri turned away, heading for Reggie like a homing pigeon.

That was the first time Kate had seen Sherri alone. May it be the last, she thought, and went to the bathroom to wash her face.

* * *

Joy was quiet, worn out with laughter, head back, thin arms resting on the massive arms of the chair. She looked tiny, and spent. Kate remembered laughing herself silly with Danni in college over one of her first joints.

Opening her eyes and sounding almost like herself, Joy said, "Cat brain." She looked at Kate with a serious expression. "The walnut looks like a cat brain. I can't eat it."

"That's okay, Joy. You don't have to." She hoped cats had brains bigger than walnuts.

Joy put the nut carefully on the arm of the chair. A pleasant wash of cool air came into the studio through the screen door.

Kate looked out at the party. Reggie was talking to a couple of strangers—that's right, Danni said he'd invited some regional hotshots. The way his face was lit up meant they must be important, artists or critics or collectors. Sherri was clinging to him. Danni was in the group, too, of course, wanting a part in any PR that went down.

In another part of the room, Hallsy and Nava were chatting together, and Kate wondered if Hallsy found it strange that he had to look up in a conversation for a change.

Just your average party. Reggie had bought the food, of course—he wouldn't ask Erik, and wouldn't want to do the work himself. And he had money. So the hors d'oeuvres were great, stuffed mushrooms and peanut chicken skewers and bacon-wrapped apricots. Substantial, like Reggie.

Near the door, Kim was examining a large painting of a woman sitting in a tree. Erik slipped into the cabin and looked around. He nodded at Kate, joined Kim.

Everybody had a drink in hand, and party chatter swirled through the big cabin.

Joy shivered and glanced around the room. "What was that?"

"What?"

"I don't know. It was like a shadow came along. Something cold."

"I didn't feel anything," Kate said. "People are just talking. Like you say, 'Schmooze or lose.'"

"Well, it feels creepy in here to me. Sometimes I get these feelings, you know? The last time it happened—"

"Bastard!" It was Erik. He'd crossed the cabin and pushed past Nava. He was in Hallsy's face. "What did you do to her?"

Heads turned, the room went silent.

Danni moved in. "Take it easy, Erik." She put a hand on his arm.

He shook it off and pointed back at the big canvas by the door. "What did you do to Marisa?

Hallsy looked stunned. "Marisa? How do you—"

"I *lived* with her, you piece of crap. That's how I know her name. I know a lot of other things, too. Like how the guy she was with after she left me treated her like a dog. *Killed* her." His voice shook.

"That's complete bullsh—"

"You're nothing but a—"

"Erik." Danni pulled his arm hard, turned him toward her. "Stop. I know what you're thinking. But you don't know what happened with her. None of us does."

His arm was rigid, his fist clenched.

"Stop it." As close to shouting as Kate had ever heard from Danni. "Get ahold of yourself. You really will hate yourself if you don't. I promise."

Was that a threat? That he would lose his job?

Letting out the breath he must have been holding, Erik turned and walked stiffly toward the door. Halfway there he stumbled slightly, as if he were drunk. "Watch your back, Hallsy. I'm not done with you." He glared around the room. "You're all going to stick together, aren't you? Bunch of friggin' art freaks."

After the screen door slapped shut, people who had been frozen in place moved. Danni said, "Oh, God," and sat down abruptly. Kim turned back to the painting, looking confused. Joy struggled out of her chair, and David moved toward her.

Reggie said, "What the hell was that all about?"

Hallsy staggered to one of the overstuffed chairs. He moved uncertainly, like Erik had. It wasn't alcohol in either case, Kate guessed, but emotion.

"That was a nasty fight that nearly happened," Kate said. "Danni, you were amazing. You really saved the day."

"That was scary," Sherri said. "He was about to explode. With jealousy about—" she glanced at the painting—"that woman."

Reggie's outsiders were edging toward the door.

"Ma-Marisa," Kim said. "Erik has known her name. Title is 'She Still Sings' only. How he knows name?"

Hallsy's big shoulders were shaking. "Marisa. God. I loved her, I did."

"Of course you did," Danni said. To the group she said, "She grew up around here, was a terrific singer, dated Erik for quite a while. But there was nothing for her as an artist here, she wanted to go to the Big Apple and see if she could make it there. That's when you knew her, Hallsy—"

"No, she lived with me in Boston," he said. He looked exhausted. "Couple years. Then left for New York."

"Erik's crazy, thinking he owned her or something," Sherri said. "So he dated her, so what? I'd rather be with Hallsy than with Erik, too. I mean—" she looked quickly at Reggie, "not me personally, I mean most women would go with Hallsy. So she left Erik, and then she left you, Hallsy. She's probably with somebody like this big guy now." She beamed at Reggie.

Nice save, Kate thought. Totally wacko thinking, of course.

The screen door bumped shut. The art critics and hotshots were gone.

"Marisa—she's not with anybody," Hallsy said.

179

Most of them knew the rest of the story from the time Harri had dinner at the Big House, but Sherri must not have been there that night.

"Oh, well," Sherri said. "Whatever."

"She—" Hallsy sighed. "Car wreck. She died. She got into drugs real bad after we broke up and she went to New York."

"Huh," Sherri said. "Too bad." She hovered over a plate of mushrooms, chose one and popped it into her mouth. "These are great. Have some, Reggie."

Another round of silence. Insect noises through the windows, leaves rustling.

"I didn't think anybody would recognize her from the painting," Hallsy said. "And if they did, so what? It would be a healing thing for them. It was to her, *for* her. Aw, shit." He took a deep breath and let it out slowly. "Yeah, okay," he said, as if someone had made a suggestion. "I'm going to bed."

General murmurs of agreement unfolded. "It has gotten kind of late," Danni said. "Want company for the walk, Hallsy?"

"No, I'm fine. Goodnight, all." But Joy and David followed him out.

Danni picked up plastic wine glasses and paper plates. Kate joined in, starting with Joy's walnut. Reggie's contribution to cleaning up was eating the last of the salmon pate and going to work on a platter of strawberries. Of course he hadn't hired a full-service caterer with a clean-up crew.

"What a night," Danni said. "Things were crazy enough. Now they're even crazier."

"That cook of yours is off his rocker," Reggie said.

Danni ignored him. "It must have been a shock to see Marisa in that painting," she said to Kate. "She died, let's see, around two years ago. It was the summer after we moved up here." She shook her head. "Erik was a mess, poor guy."

180

"Poor Hallsy," Kate said.

"Poor all of us."

"This place was supposed to be peaceful, a quiet place to work, and now people are dropping dead and screaming at each other about it," Sherri said. "I'm glad we're leaving."

Kate was glad Sherri and her self-involved boyfriend were leaving, too. She now disliked Sherri more than Reggie.

What a night, indeed. So much for a party to cheer them all up. Kate wished she hadn't encouraged Erik to come to the party, but she couldn't blame herself for his altercation with Hallsy. Currents of passion she knew nothing about had flared into view. Powerful, but not relevant to her mission to find out who was behind what had happened to Farley.

FIFTEEN

Salute to the sun. Three times. She came to the standing position, eyes closed. She was in the birch grove, facing south. The sun touched her face. Yoga might help relax her, calm her, save her from the terrible picture of Farley that kept her awake sometimes. And from last night's difficult moments—Erik's torment and Hallsy's grief.

Don't think about last night. Don't think about anything.

Tree position. Her balance holding her. Gravity collaborating with her spine. She was vertical like a building. No, more active. Like a fountain, with water rising and falling at the same time. A tree was a slow fountain, drawing water from the earth and letting it go. Transpiration: how trees breathe.

She was a tree.

She opened her eyes. A fox stood at the edge of the road, looking at her. It was young, its fur a bright orange, and she could see light shine along the separate hairs. Because she believed she was a tree, the fox believed it too. After a few minutes it ambled away. She was not important to the fox the way a person would have been.

* * *

When she got back to Bobcat, she sat cross-legged on the rug. She wrote in her sketchbook. *Fox. Tree.* She sat for a long time and watched the light change on the floor, on the plant she'd bought at the crazy general store that carried some of everything, hardware and housewares and art supplies. Leaves like a clover but much bigger, and red. She'd never seen a plant like it. *Oxalis triangularis,* false shamrock: she'd looked it up online at the library. Its leaflets closed down in dim light, the three leaves collapsing together like an umbrella.

She sketched it. Flipped a page, moved to the table and drew the birches across the road, their slender uprightness broken by black dashes. The paper's vellum finish felt good under her pencil tip.

The trees she drew were real. She was a fox, moving among them in her gray fur, slipping into the graphite depths. Light slanted through the trunks in front of her fox eyes.

A new page: she drew a birch leaf caught in a tuft of grass, from fox-eye height. Closed her eyes.

Farley had been a gift. Farley was gone. The fox was alive. She was alive. She had to focus on what was here, now.

Farley had loved her like a father. He loved a lot of people. He knew people were connected, a web. He knew things she could learn from him, even now. He would be part of her balance for the rest of her life, helping her stand like a tree. Helping her see through different kinds of eyes.

* * *

The day had slipped away. In the dim studio she rose and stretched, tuned her radio to a jazz station and moved around the room to the music. Not with restlessness but calm, calm. Scooped up her jeans and put them on, tossed a shirt on over her tank top. Dressing felt like dancing. Slipped on sneakers. Sneakers! Footpads, paws. She walked along the road, noticing every tree, all of them her sisters.

Oh, Farley.

It was not easy, this business of being alive. But she would find her way. She would work.

* * *

Dinner was quiet. Erik had called in sick and Danni was in the kitchen. Hallsy hadn't shown up either, and Sherri and Reggie had loaded up their Lexus and driven away that afternoon. Nava, David and Joy, and Kim sat at the table, looking glum. And Gabriel and Case.

All the artists were mourning Farley in their own ways, but Kate's grief and Danni's were complicated by what they knew. They'd talked about it and agreed to let the official story stand: he fell. Kate wasn't totally sure Farley had been murdered, she only suspected it; and of course she had no evidence. She'd need strong evidence, solid proof in fact, to approach either Danni or the police. EMAC's director had to think about the place's reputation; she wouldn't go out on a limb.

By quarter past, Danni brought linguini in huge bowls to the table and went back for salad. She sat nearest the kitchen. "Erik hasn't missed a day in three years," she said. "I hope he's okay."

"Have you heard from Harri?" Kate asked.

Danni considered her pasta. "No. Not a word. Usually she at least texts."

"She's missing?" David asked. "Have you called the police?"

"I talked to my friend Jim, who's a cop. She's an adult. There's nothing officially wrong," Danni said.

Nobody talked for a while.

Then Joy said, "That was some party. I guess I drank too much. I remember the last bit, though. Poor Erik. Poor Hallsy. I hope they're okay."

Everybody was wondering if everybody else was okay. It was comforting.

Danni played with her noodles. "Marisa. She was beautiful, and talented, and funny. Harri loved her. Her career was all over the newspaper up here, the *Washington County Watch*." She fiddled with the ends of her scarf, like Harri with her hair. Must be in the LaMaze genes. The scarf was iridescent, like a grackle in the sun.

A tear fell into Danni's pasta.

"Hey," Kate said. "You're taking the rest of the night off, okay? Forget about the dishes, the kitchen. I'll take care of it."

"*We'll* take care of it," Joy said quickly.

Bless Joy. Bless women. You could count on them.

"Right. We will," David said.

Kate blinked. Okay, bless men too.

"You guys," Danni said, and stopped. Closed her eyes. Opened them and pushed her chair back. "You're just great," she managed. "Thank you."

Nobody said anything as she left.

We're great all right, Kate thought. Unless somebody around here killed Farley. She remembered how she'd felt, meeting him. How quickly she recognized his goodness. Why would anybody want to harm such a man? She pulled her mind gently away from pain. Toward that round, smooth feeling at her center, like a heart-sized rock warm from the sun. Farley would want her to fill her mind with that. Her new life.

"Let's get to it, crew," Joy said. They all trooped out the kitchen, plates and bowls in their hands.

Except Gabriel and Case, who slipped away like cats.

"Where was the cat when the lights went out?" Kate asked.

Nobody answered. David dropped a handful of forks and stooped to pick them up. Joy turned on the tap in the big steel sink and a few seconds later she wore scarves of steam.

"In the dark," Kate answered herself.

Yes. In the past week she'd answered herself. Energy ran in her like an underground river.

* * *

When the kitchen was ship-shape, they gathered on the back patio. The sky was furry with stars, and the artists paused as one. Nava turned on a flashlight. Then David startled them by vaulting over the rail.

"Way to go, David!" Joy said.

"Didn't think I was an athlete? I'm full of surprises." He looked at Joy. "Coming?"

Joy smiled at him. "I won't miss Reggie or Sherri, but it's sad our little arts village has to break up," she said, lighting her way down the steps with her cell phone. "Let's see each other a lot before we go."

"Yes," Nava said. "We've shared some important things, haven't we?" After a couple of steps right, toward Kingfisher, she paused, perhaps waiting for Joy to join her. Then she smiled and said, "Goodnight, you-all."

"Goodnight." A chorus.

David and Joy went left, toward his studio. Ah, they were holding hands. No wonder Joy hadn't gone in the same direction as her neighbor Nava. Kim joined Kate and the four of them headed along the left side of the Loop. She turned on a flashlight and pointed it at the ground.

They were about halfway to Bobcat when they heard footsteps. Someone came toward them in the dark, moving quickly.

"Hello?" David called. The figure switched on a flashlight and shone it at their faces. Kate put a hand in front of her eyes.

"Please turn that off," David said sharply.

The light dropped and a man's voice said, "Oh, sorry."

"Andy?" Kate said.

"Just checking on some things," Andy said, and went on past them.

She turned. "Is everything okay?"

He kept walking, didn't answer.

"Funny," Kate said, more to herself than to Kim. She had trouble making conversation with the Korean. She should stop thinking how hard English must be for him. And stop being unnerved by how polite he was.

"Who is, please?"

"Andy, Danni's husband. Haven't you met him?"

"No. I see him here." Kim waved his hand to take in all of EMAC. "Not meeting."

"Ah."

"Wow, he was in a hurry," Joy said over her shoulder. "Funny, at home I'm always in a hurry, but here? Up until Farley died, this place was such an amazing release from all the bad vibes, hurry, pressure, the things I have to fight when I'm in the City." Her voice caught. "Farley was so calm. He knew a lot about peace, the personal kind. And I was looking forward to knowing him for a long time. I mean, we lived ten minutes apart in Manhattan."

"He helped me a lot with my book," David said. "The guy had an emotional IQ through the roof. Said we should stay in touch."

They were outside Bobcat, and Kim went ahead of them toward River Otter.

"Yes," Kate said. "He was somebody I wanted to be friends with forever, too."

"Stay in touch with me, okay, Kate?" Joy slipped one arm around David's waist and the other around Kate's.

"Of course, Joy. You're not leaving for a few more days, right?"

"A week. But I just wanted to get that straight."

"Okay, you've got it."

"I'm working on a piece for Farley," Joy said. "I want to finish it before I head home."

"Only two more chapters to my novel," David said. "I've been so productive here it's unreal." He looked around. Kim was out of earshot. "And Larry's gone back to his mother, which is good for everyone." He winked at Joy.

"Goodnight, Kate," Joy said. "Give me a hug. I don't know why, I just want you to give me a hug."

Joy was so small. She always seemed bigger because of her energy.

"Goodnight, Joy. Goodnight, David."

* * *

Kate had left her cell phone at the Big House. She went back, scooped it off the table, and headed for Bobcat again. For a second she thought a light glowed in the blue cabin. Of course not. A case of wishful thinking, wanting Farley to still be living up there, making art, ready with a glass of wine and words of encouragement.

She read a little and went to bed. Sleeping restlessly, waking often, she finally tossed off the covers and paced around the room, remembering the cascade of frightening experiences that had happened near Bobcat and Peacock. It had all started with that blood-curdling sound Erik said was an owl. If it really was an owl, why hadn't it called again? Owls have territories, and habits.

Barred owl. Good name. If a creature could make a noise like that, it ought to be in jail.

She settled back in bed and just about to turn on the reading lamp when she heard something. Not an owl; a person. An ATV went past Bobcat, down the trail from Peacock.

At this time of night? She looked at her watch. Almost two.

With somebody out there, she didn't want to turn on her light and attract attention. Forget about reading. She hoped she wasn't going to find a dead animal on her doorstep in the morning.

Wait, it was probably one of Ryan's men, cruising the property to make sure everything was in order. She'd suggested that herself. The rider was trying to be quiet, not giving the machine much throttle on the Loop. The engine wouldn't have awakened her if she'd been fortunate enough to be asleep.

Relieved, she turned on the light by her bed and opened the Kingsolver novel.

A few minutes later, she knew the passing ATV wasn't about security. Her cabin brightened with a rosy light that had nothing to do with dawn.

It reddened. And flickered.

She jumped into her clothes and took a quick look out her kitchen window. Yes, Peacock was in flames.

For the second time she was running for the Big House to dial 911. She burst through the doors, into the little booth and grabbed the phone off its cradle.

No dial tone. The receiver felt strange in her hand. The cable connecting it to the phone had been cut, metal housing and all.

Her brother was right. Alligators lived around here. Human ones.

SIXTEEN

Biking up the hill on Farm Road, Kate could feel new strength in her legs. Maybe she hadn't needed her daypack, since she was only going to Danni's, but she'd grabbed it out of habit, and even with it on her back she felt lighter. Her daily exercise had made a difference.

She pushed the pace, wanting to burn off the anger she felt about the destruction of Peacock. She'd thrown down the landline's useless handset and run back to Bobcat to grab her bike and helmet. No need to hit the light switch, with firelight pouring in the windows. The noise startled her, the fire's constant roar like a waterfall, overlaid with pops and cracks like gunshots.

She'd seen Joy and David dash out of his cabin to stare, but she'd jumped on her bike and shot down the Loop and onto the road. She needed to move, and she needed to tell Danni more than the news about Peacock. The two of them had to put their heads together right now and figure out who was sabotaging EMAC. Andy, too, if he was there. Three heads were better than two.

Her truck would have been faster, but not by much, and Peacock was already lost—no fire truck could get there in time to save it. And there wasn't room for a third vehicle in Danni's driveway.

Kate stood on the pedals and drove the cranks with her weight, her mind racing. Peacock in flames. What was the point? Why destroy an empty cabin?

The handlebar light was dim, needed fresh batteries. When a vehicle's headlights threw her shadow in front of her, she was glad her way was better lit. Then she recognized the whine of the small truck's engine, and she knew it was trouble. Those stupid punks in the red truck. How did these guys know when she went for a ride?

Okay, so she was going to get wet. Big deal. Like Erik, she was waterproof. She was almost at the top of the hill, almost to Danni's.

The headlights in her mirror were blinding. Damn, the driver was cutting it close. Only a couple of inches between her left handlebar and—

She was down and sliding over pavement, her mind still processing it: the door had opened right in front of her. Her left knee hurt, and her shoulder.

Hands were all over her, grabbing her arms and legs. She was face-down in the dirt, and something heavy in the middle of her back kept her there. Fear rushed through her. She heard the ripping noise of duct tape being pulled off a roll.

"Get that helmet off her," a man's voice said. "Here's the bag."

The strap under her chin went slack. Someone grabbed her hair and yanked her head up, and cloth slid across her face. The weight on her back shifted as her wrists were taped together at the same time as her ankles.

"That'll do her." A younger voice.

She couldn't move. She was helpless, and blind.

"Wait." The first voice again.

She was rolled onto her back and something circled her knees.

"That's enough." A third, deeper voice. Older. "Time's important here, boys."

"Keep your shorts on, d—"

The dull sound of a body blow, and a grunt.

"Jeez, what the—"

"Shut *up,* you idiot." The older voice. It sounded familiar, but she couldn't place it.

A throat gathered phlegm, spat. It hit the pavement like an expletive.

Hands again, picking her up, carrying her. Something slammed her head to one side so hard she saw a burst of stars, and tears sprang to her eyes.

"Oops," a voice said, but it had laughter in it.

Sound of a tailgate dropping, then metal under her back, cold. Someone pushed her in by her feet like a piece of lumber until the older voice said "Hold it."

Something stung her thigh. Darkness took her.

* * *

She woke shivering, soaked in dew. The sky was light but the sun hid behind a break of conifers that edged the field where she lay on her back. She rolled onto her knees and a wave of dizziness almost took her down again. Putting her hands on the wet grass, she waited for the trees to stop spinning.

She had a headache so bad she could hear it.

What was wrong with her? Where was she?

A swelling above her right ear: touching it set off fireworks in front of her eyes. That brought it back: the truck, the ditch. The men's hands. Her helplessness.

Her wrists were sore and gummy with the white residue of duct tape. A couple of bloody nicks said whoever had cut the tape off had used a knife, and hadn't been careful with it.

She felt the back pocket of her jeans for her cell phone. Not there. She hoped she'd forgotten it, left it sitting in Bobcat. If she'd taken it with her, it was gone for good, fallen out or stolen by the creeps who'd grabbed her.

Her daypack was next to her, bulging, full. As she reached for it she thought it might be a bomb, and paused. Then realized the idea was absurd. She wasn't thinking straight. Whoever had kidnapped her could have easily killed her, had every chance to do so. But hadn't. Which would be comforting, maybe, if she understood why.

She didn't understand anything.

She popped the pack's plastic buckles and looked inside. Her fleece top, the water bottle from her bike, her Red Sox cap. She pulled them out. Underneath, her rain jacket, three apples, some Clif bars, then the usual pack-clutter of compass, flashlight, first-aid kit, tissues, hand sanitizer.

The shivering was worse. Her jeans were sopping. She got her arms into the fleece and zipped it up, grateful. How strange to be kidnapped and wake up with a pack full of supplies. She pulled out one of the Clif bars and stared at it. Her favorite kind, mint chocolate.

Her favorite, and hard to find. The hair on her neck stood up.

Whoever had put them in her pack knew her.

Something to think about, when she could think.

The fleece warmed her and the shivering eased, but she ached all over. Her eyes were dry and sore. The usual routine after a long ride was not to be concussed and drugged and thrown into the bed of a pick-up truck. The usual routine was a hot shower, then a protein shake and a good veggie stir-fry over brown rice.

Getting up would break contact with the cold, wet ground. She lurched to her feet, lost her balance, staggered a few steps. Held onto a sapling, steadied herself.

The headache like a drumbeat.

Drank some water. Too queasy for food. She wanted desperately to be back in her camper, in the bed over the cab, warm and safe in her sleeping bag. Her mind flickered there, then to Bobcat. The bright table at the front window, her sketchbook. Her work. She had to get back.

Then she remembered the fire at Peacock.

Her mind wasn't right, the memories coming back to her fragmented, out of order.

Who were the men who'd grabbed her off her bike? Who on earth was she a threat to? She couldn't figure it out. These must be the same people who'd—face it—killed Farley.

Or had they? The fact that they hadn't killed her, given all the trouble they'd gone to, suggested that maybe Farley's death *was* accidental. Had he fallen during a kidnap attempt? Maybe they didn't realize how fragile he was. Or maybe she'd been wrong about the size of the wound at the back of his head.

If he fell, it didn't make them any less responsible for his death, of course. And it didn't let her off the hook of figuring out who they were.

Nothing to do now but face the day and hope it didn't turn out as crazy as last night. She dug through the pack to the first aid kit, unzipped it and took out the emergency twenty-dollar bills, put them in her pocket. Shook two tabs of Ibuprofen out of the plastic bottle and swallowed them. Picked a few burrs from her socks and combed her hair with her fingers. She wanted to look as normal as possible, not like someone who'd been ambushed and drugged.

Her one driving thought: get back to EMAC.

The sun had cleared the trees and its light warmed her jeans. She slipped the pack on and started toward the smaller of the two roads she could see, the one with less traffic. The other must be a major route; it had big overhead signs, but she was at the wrong angle to read them.

Walking helped her feel stronger.

She had to find out where she was, and then maybe she could figure out why she had been left here. She'd avoid the low tan building to her right, with the tall radio or cell tower next to it. A radio station? She didn't want to trespass, especially onto an official-looking site. Avoiding attention was best, for now. She had to get home.

Should she contact her sister? Or Marjorie? No, she didn't want to get anybody else mixed up in whatever was going on. It was dangerous. And nobody could do anything to help. Kate had to go back to Short Creek to get her sketchbook, where she had poured out such a surge of ideas, and to get her truck. The camper was her home now.

She'd have to watch herself, think twice about everything. People with concussions shouldn't make plans. It wouldn't be smart to stay at EMAC, but she could camp nearby. She wouldn't leave the area entirely until she sorted this mess out. She owed Farley that.

And she needed to warn Danni. Something dangerous was stirring in Short Creek, at EMAC itself. Dangerous and possibly deadly.

* * *

The pack felt awkward, lopsided, so she stopped to repack it, kneeling, pulling everything out. A couple of dark T-shirts at the bottom looked lumpy, like something was wrapped up in them. Something heavy.

A pistol gleamed in the sunlight. A Glock.

She glanced around. Not a soul in sight. Dropped the magazine out to check it. Full. Seventeen nasty-looking rounds. She checked the chamber. Empty. Good.

Should she dump the empty gun in the grass? Or keep it?

It could have been stolen, or used in a crime. This pistol could get her in more trouble than she was already in.

She had no idea how long she'd been unconscious, how far she'd been driven. If she was still in Maine, it would be okay to carry. And New Hampshire? Vermont? She thought they were okay too. But Massachusetts—didn't it have a mandatory sentence for people with unlicensed guns? For all she knew she was in Canada. Big trouble for an armed American.

The Glock was hard to turn down, though. With its weight in her hand she closed her eyes and she was ten again, shooting rats at the dump with her Dad. She smiled. Didn't sound like fun to most people, but she'd loved being with him.

She'd given up guns when she moved East, but now she was up against something—somebody—dangerous and unpredictable. The pistol wouldn't be a bad sidekick to have at hand if the guys who bagged her yesterday came for her again. Could be a real asset.

Could be a set-up.

She sighed. She wrapped the gun in one T-shirt and the magazine in the other, and stowed them in the pack close to her back. She'd keep the weapon for now, find out where she was, and make a plan.

The low building she'd noticed earlier, with the radio or cell tower, was flying the Stars and Stripes on a flagpole out front. Closer, she saw the cars parked out front were blue and white, with light bars on top. Police cars.

Should she ditch the gun, go to the cops right now? She'd been assaulted, kidnapped. Think, Kate, think.

No. The chief in Short Creek—she couldn't remember his name—had been hostile, probably a criminal himself. Whoever left her in this field wanted her to go to this police station, but she wasn't going to fall for that trick twice.

Okay. She'd keep her cool, walk past the place. She had to look like she knew where she was going. If she wasn't thinking straight, if she was being paranoid, she'd just have to live with it.

She was sweating, only partly from the exercise.

As she neared the parking lot exit, an engine started. One of the cars backed out of its slot and came toward the road.

Sure enough, POLICE stretched in big blue letters across both doors. The driver gave her a once-over and then made his turn past her and sped off.

She let out her breath and kept going. Her bike shoes weren't great for walking, but at least they were mountain-bike style, so their soles weren't rigid. She'd slammed her feet into them the night before, urgently: ordinary shoes didn't work with the clipless pedals on her Trek. Even though the cleats were recessed they grated on the roadside gravel; they'd probably get wrecked.

She hoped it wasn't too far to a town, or a gas station. Any business would do. She just needed someone to tell her where the nearest bus station was so she could buy a ticket to Bangor. She had to go back, get her sketchbooks and pack up her camper. Then she'd go to the cops, but not the ones in Short Creek.

So the criminals knew what kind of Clif bars she liked but didn't know she was familiar with guns? And wasn't afraid of snakes? It was too confusing.

No, it meant the perps had met her recently. Didn't know her background.

Had to be somebody at EMAC.

* * *

How far could she walk? The Ibuprofen had lessened her headache, but the day was too bright. She pulled her Red Sox cap lower to cut the glare. Glanced in the roadside ditch: a broken wooden sawhorse lay on its side, MASS DOT stenciled in black on the yellow paint.

Massachusetts Department of Transportation. Yes, that must have been the plan. Whoever planted the gun in her pack figured she would be traumatized and hysterical, would rush straight to the police with her wild stories and then be discovered to be carrying.

At which point she'd end up in jail. Or a mental hospital.

She'd made the right call. Once she was in her truck camper, she'd go to the state police in Bangor. She could trust them.

And she'd have to trust this road would go somewhere useful.

Half an hour later, hot and tired, she was at a crossroads. Four corners: three stubbly fields and a cut-over patch of woods. A metal sign pointed back the way she'd come, to Interstate 95; a hand-made wooden sign with a sudsy stein pointed to the right: Frank's.

Okay, Frank's it was.

The pack got heavier as she walked. Frank's finally came into view, a shack with a Schlitz sign in one window and Budweiser in the other. The neon signs were dulled by daylight, but they were lit. A few cars and trucks were parked in the unpaved lot. Her watch said it was just after nine o'clock. Beer for breakfast?

The place was a dump, but it cheered her up. She ached all over, and nausea had given way to hunger. She wanted something hot. Even a two-bit bar had food. She hadn't had a hot dog in years, but the thought of one made her mouth water.

Vehicles out front—that was a good sign for any eatery, however humble. She passed an old gray Toyota with a Massachusetts plate, the familiar slogan "The Spirit of America" underneath the numbers. The big Chevy next to it had the same red-on-white plates. The next in line was a pick-up.

She bolted to the side of the shack and crouched, slipping her pack off, rubbing her shoulders. The darn thing was heavy.

The old red pick-up had Maine plates.

Of course they'd be here.

They knew that if she didn't run to the police as they'd hoped, they'd have more work to do. And they figured she'd come here, the only place for miles.

So what was she going to do? She couldn't walk away, because one of them might see her out a window. Damn. She was lucky nobody had already seen her, but if they had they would have rushed out here and been all over her. So she'd been lucky.

Now she'd just have to wait them out.

She settled in. Guys who have beer for breakfast aren't in a hurry. Occasional bursts of male laughter and the mumbling of a TV reached her from an open window.

Gravel crunched under tires. She pulled herself into the wall as far as she could. It wasn't far enough: a young face peered around the corner and looked at her, then disappeared. The screen door squeaked open and slapped shut. A man said, "Who's the hobo dude out front?"

Her heart jumped like a cat that's been barked at. Behind the building a rock wall edged the property; she threw her pack over it and then herself. The land dropped away steeply, but that's where she'd go if anyone came looking for her. She'd run down to the woods. Trees were good cover.

The windows on the back of the shack were high and small, for ventilation rather than the view. Through them came scraping of chairs, footsteps. Then a frail old voice said, "Way to go, Charlie, you done it again." Howls of drunken laughter.

Someone else said, "Shame on us, Charlie. How many times you fool us?"

"Last time it was a loose horse."

"Time before that it was a rabid raccoon."

"You sure know how to yank our bobbers."

"You keepin score, Frank?"

"Sure am," the frail voice said. "And don't forget he's beat you twice at darts. And the big bet on the Patriots last year."

"Yeah, yeah, okay, don't rub it in. Just get us another round—make that a pitcher—and a glass for Charlie here. So's he won't be drinking out of mine while I'm running off looking for hobos."

"Comin right up."

Thank goodness for her short hair and baseball cap. Drunk or sober, Charlie thought she was a guy. But she couldn't be seen again. She lay as close to the wall as she could get, edged her pack under her head as a pillow.

The kind of pillow that keeps you awake all night, she decided after a few minutes. But that was a good thing, given the circumstances. She needed to stay alert. That was a close call, and Charlie might still let slip the hobo was real. Good thing he was so interested in beer.

It was cooler next to the stone wall, under the branches of the hemlocks that grew on the slope, than it had been on the road. She wriggled her hips to make herself as comfortable as she could. Beer for breakfast was bad, but pitchers were worse. They sounded like lunch. A long lunch.

She ate an apple and thought about events at EMAC. Maybe more than one person was behind them. They fell into two categories, the first being being malicious pranks, like the raven and woodchuck. The second was more serious. Farley's murder, intentional or not, and her kidnapping topped the list. And the trip-wire, which could have caused Farley serious injury.

If there were two evil-doers, David's son Larry was high on her list for the lesser crimes. Young and troubled, he was hiding out at EMAC from who knew what kind of problems at home. But she didn't think he had organized her kidnapping. He was unlikely to know anyone local, and two or maybe three guys had grabbed her.

Gabriel had done such a good job with that sweet barred owl call the first night. Could he do as well with the owl's less delightful calls, if he wanted to frighten her and Farley? Aloof, the least social in the group, Gabriel and Case seemed pleasant enough, but she couldn't dismiss them.

On Open Studio day, Ryan had worn a blue and white checked shirt like the one on the guy she'd glimpsed riding away after the dead raven incident. But come on, how many shirts like that could she find in Maine, or in Short Creek itself? Clothes weren't good clues. Might as well say everybody wearing jeans was a hippie. And she wasn't even sure the ATV rider had anything to do with the raven.

Jim had been too friendly, too fast. She trusted him about as far as she could throw a police cruiser. But she found it hard to believe he could be so convincingly romantic with her and then conspire to have her kidnapped.

She still had no idea why she was a target. Nava had said she, Kate, was at the center of the mess, but Kate couldn't figure out how. Nava had also said to follow the money. Where did those two things converge? Kate didn't have any connection to big money, or know anyone who did.

Except for Harri, who was into something up to her neck. Her suitcase full of cash didn't lead Kate anywhere useful, though: Harri wasn't a likely candidate for violence, especially against other women. She was in trouble, but she had a good heart. Kate was sure of that despite Harri's unfriendly attitude at their last meeting.

Reggie had money, and he was arrogant and full of resentment. He blamed Farley for not getting that big award. Could he have lost his considerable temper and pushed Farley down the stairs? Kate could easily imagine that—an accidental murder. Manslaughter, wasn't that the word? "Slaughter" sounded worse than murder. But surely Farley wouldn't have gone near the top of the stairs during an argument with Reggie.

Sherri had said that awful thing about Farley. Kate didn't know her well, but it was possible she'd do anything for Reggie. Parasites like to please their hosts. Would "anything" include murder?

Her thoughts moved to others at EMAC. Erik was hard to read, with his mood swings. Most of the time he was friendly, and he'd shown her that special place high in the rocks, but he liked to needle her sometimes. Was he trustworthy? He'd snooped in Danni's files, reading applications—totally sneaky. He didn't make friends among the resident artists—as far as she knew Kate was the only one he'd spent time with—but it wasn't until he'd called them "art freaks" at Reggie's disaster of a party that she realized he had hard feelings toward them all. Was that enough of a motive to kill the most successful in the group? Living in the Big House, he had plenty of opportunity. And he was a local, who'd have friends in the area to help nab her.

No, the red truck linked his attackers and hers. She crossed him off her mental list.

Andy was worth thinking about. He'd had that strange reaction to Peacock that Danni had mentioned. If Andy didn't like Peacock for some reason, he could easily have set fire to it. And he probably knew enough local guys to kidnap all the artists at EMAC at once.

Sherri and Reggie. Andy. Case and Gabriel.

Then she thought of David. He'd said his novel was based on the dark side of love. Someone focused on the shadows in human nature might be good at coming up with ways to frighten people.

But none of the artists had connections with local thugs.

Right. Two kinds of ugly surprises, two evil-doers. With a common effect: disrupting EMAC.

Kate's mind was going in circles. She knew she wasn't thinking straight, but she couldn't stop. She was reaching, trying to consider all possibilities. Who wasn't on her list? Nava, of course. Joy. Hallsy.

Kim? She knew so little about him. Could his immigration application have been thrown off track by criminal behavior? She had a hard time imagining him doing anything nasty, let alone violent. She crossed him off.

With a jolt she realized she should think about Danni: ambitious, powerful, and willing to cut corners. That's what she'd done as an undergraduate at UMass. Ironic, wasn't it? Before her breakthrough, Kate had been thinking of leaving EMAC because she didn't want to pretend she was an artist if she couldn't produce, but Danni had begun her career in the arts with a degree she hadn't fully earned.

If Kate looked at it coldly, she could say Danni had been a petty criminal in college despite her family's wealth. Had she changed her ways? She was the whole show at EMAC, the only administrator, giving her plenty of opportunities for dishonesty.

No. Danni might maneuver people, or even cheat a little, but kidnapping, murder—out of the question. Besides, Farley was a top artist, his presence an asset to her pet project.

Could Danni have lured him to Maine and put him at the top of Peacock's scary stairs in order to kill him and steal his paintings? Was she putting a glamorous mask over some twisted quality, her failure as an artist herself causing her to covet others' work?

That, Kate told herself, was sheer lunacy.

SEVENTEEN

It was dusty behind the shack, and a breeze had kicked up. Kate suppressed a couple of sneezes. Not that she needed to—inside, a jukebox had joined the party, playing country and western songs. They made her think of her mother, in the trailer out there in Arizona.

She ate a Clif bar, drank some water. She may have dozed a little. Noises woke her. Boot scuffs, guffaws.

"Either she's invisible or the cops got her. Ha."

"Hope the little girl likes jailbird food."

"I'm going back over there, make sure she ain't sitting on her butt, crying."

"Okay. See you boys later."

Slammed doors, revved engines. Horns. Rattle-trap peel-outs on gravel. Engine noise receding.

Time to go. But it was too quiet. She'd have to be careful getting away from the shack. Could she do that without the bartender seeing her? Maybe not. Maybe she should wait until he closed up.

"You still out there?"

She flinched at the voice, which came from the windows above her.

"It's okay. I'm not the big bad wolf." What was supposed to be a chuckle turned into a wheezy cough.

Emphysema. Occupational hazard for bartenders back in the bad old days when drinking and smoking were inseparable.

"Come on in and have a sandwich."

She sat up. If he didn't know her pack was full of food, he probably wasn't in on the plot. "Okay, thanks," she said to the window.

The parking lot was empty. The owner of the voice, a small unshaven man with holes in his khaki pants from dropped cigarettes, stood at the door. "Huh. You don't look like the she-bear they was makin you out to be. You look kinda normal. Dirty, but normal." He smiled a little. "I'm Frank."

"Thanks. I'm Kate." She followed him into the dimness of the bar. "There's something dirty going on but I don't think it's me."

The bar was generic red-neck style, with a twelve-point buck rack mounted on one wall and a moth-eaten stuffed raccoon next to the register. "If you hear a car pull up, grab your pack and git in here." Frank held open a door behind the bar: a single bed and a wooden table like the ones in the bar, with a lamp and a few books. A reading bartender. Best kind. And live-in. Good thing she hadn't waited for him to close up and go home.

"Okay, thanks," she said. "The amount they drank, though, they won't be coming back real soon."

"You don't know 'em, then."

"No, I don't, as a matter of fact. Who are they, and why did they grab me?"

He shook his head. "Less you know, less you'd be responsible for. If I was you I'd git outta here as fast as you can git." He tapped a Pall Mall halfway out of its red pack, looked at it, then tossed the pack onto the bar.

"That's what I'm going to do. Just pick up my stuff back in Short Creek and—"

"My advice? Forget about your stuff, if it means going anywhere near the fellas in here the morning." He went behind the bar and put out a plate and two slices of dark bread. Kate felt her stomach sit up and take notice. It had been a while since she'd had a square meal. A Clif bar wasn't real food.

"The stuff's kind of important." She needed her sketchbook. She needed to work again, and soon; she'd promised Farley she'd keep her momentum.

Frank was looking into the half-fridge, which seemed to be full of olives and lemon twists. He fished a plastic container from behind some pickle jars, turned back toward her and slapped a thick slice of ham and another of cheese onto the bread. "As important as staying alive?"

She couldn't be standing here with a friend of five minutes giving her life-and-death advice. But she was.

The sandwich was thick, hearty, and came with a glass of cold orange juice. She forced herself to eat slowly: it was better for her stomach, which was just as jittery as the rest of her. Eating made her feel less scared and alone. She felt a little sheepish about the question, but she had to ask. "Don't suppose you'd have any coffee, would you?" She'd already looked around and hadn't seen any sort of coffee machine.

The old man went into the back room and came out with a steaming cup. A miracle for breakfast.

"I got me a coffee maker back there," he said. " Don't tell those yahoos. It's just for me. Me and my friends." He gave her a long-toothed smile.

She smiled back. Tension ran off her like water after a shower.

The only downside was the smell of cigarettes. Frank wasn't smoking at the moment, but the pack on the bar was nearly empty. And plenty of people had smoked here for plenty of years.

Frank leaned against the bar on the customer side, watching her eat at one of the little tables. He looked tough as an alligator, and he wasn't telling her a thing.

"Where am I, anyway?"

He nodded. "That one I can answer. Shad Point. Little town in northeastern Massachusetts. Got a high-security prison and a police station. The combo kinda makes sense, don't it?"

"I got a ways to go, then, to get back up there."

"Will you forget going back? I'm telling you, these guys are—" He took a deep breath. "They don't fool around." Then his face hardened. "Okay. Look, do what you want. Just watch yourself." He picked up her plate, tapped the crumbs onto the floor. "You'd better go. Two miles north of here's the center of town, such as it is. Drugstore, hardware, beauty shop, bus station. Take your choice."

"Hey, Frank, thanks. You've been—"

"Beat it, girl." He didn't smile, but his eyes were kind.

He didn't need to help her; he was sticking his neck out. What if one of those guys found out?

He must have had the same thought. "Stay out of sight, okay? Hear a car, hit the ditch."

When she was almost out the door, he said it again. "Just watch yourself."

She leaned back in. "Thanks, Frank."

He took a couple of steps toward her. "I'm supposed to be a bartender, but I'm no tender anything. I'm tough as the Plymouth rock." His small laugh turned into a big cough. "I have enough sense, like the rock, to keep my mouth shut. You do that too."

He turned his back. In a lower voice he said, "I just don't want to read about you in the paper, okay?"

* * *

This was her third ride, and she was glad to be back in Maine. In Shad Point she'd used her twenties to buy a bus ticket to Boston and then Bangor. She didn't wait in the station but in a nearby park, looking for anyone who took notice of her. But nobody did, the passers-by just a normal assortment of people, some in jeans, some dressed for offices, some in uniforms—a UPS guy, a nurse. Small-town people having a more ordinary day than she was having.

After that, with most of the money spent and no ID, hitchhiking was her only choice. She didn't want to do it after dark, so she spent the night on a wooden bench in the Bangor bus station. She would have stretched out on it, but it had a third armrest in the middle of the seat to foil wannabe sleepers.

In the morning light, by the side of the road, she pulled her baseball cap down and stood tall. Only about seventy miles to Short Creek. Hitchhiking wasn't safe for anybody, and like many things it was worse for women. The kid at Frank's had thought she was a man, and she hoped the drivers who picked her up would think so, too.

Her standard of safety had changed in the last few days.

* * *

On her first ride, in a Honda, she'd had to listen to a fundamentalist preacher on the radio. A sequined cross hung from the rear-view mirror. The driver didn't say anything except "Praise the Lord" when she got in and "Praise the Lord" when she got out.

Her second ride was in a semi. Rocky listened to hard-rock music and talked to her over it. Either that or he talked to his CB buddies. His handle was Motor Mouth. When he couldn't raise a buddy on the radio, he said, he talked to himself. "But that's no fun. Glad I got you to entertain."

He tugged at his John Deere cap. Everything he wore had writing on it, including his bright yellow jacket with patches all over it, NASCAR and MOPAR and PENNZOIL. Even one with the NASA symbol. He pointed that one out. "I'm a space shot," he said. "Ask my wife." Stickers on his dashboard, too. I Make Shit Happen. Student Driver. To Avoid Injury Do Not Tell Me How to Do My Job.

He fished a couple of pills out of his shirt pocket and swallowed them with coffee. Glanced at her, said "Aspirin." She figured they were more likely amphetamines, some kind of upper, especially given the amount of talking he was doing.

"Pure aspirin." He was short, and bounced in his seat when he shifted. "So much personality and it's all 100 per cent natural, just like they say on the cereal boxes." He told her his life story, which started in Tennessee and included three wives, four kids, so many dogs Kate lost count, and a parrot that a six-year-old threw out a window to see if it could fly. He'd worked on a ranch in Montana and on an oil rig in Louisiana, and as a kid he'd been a pearl-diver in Florida.

"Wow," Kate said. "That sounds like fun. But I thought pearls were mostly farmed these days." She couldn't remember where she'd read that.

Rocky enjoyed his laugh, took his time with it, finally told her "pearl-diving" was restaurant slang for washing dishes.

He drove fast and well, like an athlete, a road jockey, the shifts smooth. Kate tried to think of another sport that would tolerate the amount of talking he was doing, couldn't come up with one. Rocky had found his niche.

He was going north past the turn-off to Short Creek, so he dropped her at the intersection.

Ten miles to go. She walked along the road until she found a straight section where she could see a good distance. She'd need to scope out potential rides carefully. If she saw a beater of a red pick-up coming, she'd duck behind a tree.

Not much traffic. A few cars passed her by, and she found a grassy place away from the road to take a nap since she hadn't slept much the night before. It was mid-afternoon when she put her thumb out again.

* * *

Her third ride was in a flatbed Ford. The driver wasn't a wall of chatter like Rocky, and he didn't have a message about Jesus. He said his name was Sean. Somebody she could talk to, or might have if she weren't an outlaw from outlaws, like the star in an off-off-Broadway show about art and murder.

And he was the only one of the three she had to make up a story for. With the others it was just a matter of where she was going. With Sean, her answer to "where're you headed?" got a reaction.

"Short Creek." He snorted. "What's there for a gal like you?" He looked over his left shoulder, checking for traffic before merging onto the road.

What did "a gal like you" mean? What had he picked up on?

"Got some friends up there," she said. "Hey, you got a few horses under the hood." He'd cranked on some speed to pass a sway-backed white Cadillac beating along with no back shocks, one side of its bumper tied on with rope.

"Done some adjusting here and there. Don't judge a book by its cover. " He smiled briefly. "Okay. So who do you know in Short Creek? I got a few friends up there myself."

Oh, shit. But she had to come up with something.

"You know Don? Don Brown." The lie sprang out of nowhere. She couldn't tell the truth, because what if he was one of *them*?

"No. He your boyfriend?"

She laughed, though she could feel sweat prickling in her armpits. If you can't keep your mouth shut like a Plymouth rock, improvise. "Dawn. D-A-W-N."

"She work at the Crazy Cat?"

He knew Short Creek, all right. "I don't know where she works." A pause. "She's only been there a few weeks." Kate tried to keep her voice casual.

The pause lengthened. Past the old Caddy, Sean eased into the right lane, and his speed dropped a bit. She felt like a rabbit frozen in place, waiting to see if its camouflage worked. A change of subject might help. "So what kind of adjustments did you make to the engine?"

He glanced in the mirror outside her window, then at her. "I don't know what you're hiding, but you need a better story."

Oh, crap. What could she say to get this guy off her back? Could she trust him? Even if she could, the truth might make her sound like a nut case. But she had to say something innocuous or she might lose this ride, and it was late. She'd have to sleep in the woods.

"Look, Dawn's an old friend. I'm just—"

"Save it." He flicked off the radio, which was too low to hear anyway, rested his forearms on top of the wheel, and stared down the road. He didn't trust her, would probably drop her off at the next exit. Maybe she didn't need a better story, just a different driver.

"Okay. I've got two questions. Answer me straight and you stay in the truck."

She was getting a military vibe. The direct manner was part of it. Something else, too: his voice was used to giving orders.

"Okay. You a user? Got any dope on you? In your pack, in you? Cocaine, heroine, anything?"

That was a bunch of questions rolled up into one. "No."

They were coming up on a blue pick-up. A dog sat in the bed, tongue out and ears flying.

"You carrying? Got a weapon on you?" He glanced at her for the answer, not just the words of it.

211

She paused. She had to take a chance, because somehow she didn't want to lie to him. Besides, they were in Maine. No mandatory jail. "Yes. A pistol. In the pack."

"Okay." Must be his favorite word. He passed the blue truck. He drove fast, but he was careful.

He looked fit, without the bulging belly that was not only the trucker stereotype but often the reality. Sitting in a big rig, sleeping on the road, eating what Flying J or Irving dished out—that wasn't a lifestyle that kept drivers healthy. This guy looked lean and tough. And he'd asked about drugs.

Maybe he was a cop.

And maybe she was suffering from paranoia.

Drugs. Heck, she'd smoked marijuana in college, even taken LSD a couple of times. The acid trips were burned into her brain with an immediacy that hadn't faded over the years. But out of college, on her own, it wasn't any fun to smoke pot, and she didn't dare try a solo acid flight. Her only contact with drugs in the past decade had been reading about them in newspaper stories.

If illegal drugs were what had infected Short Creek, and Sean was part of the business, he would know who she was. Unless it was a big enough operation that he didn't know, and he was right now trying to figure out if she was part of it too.

All she knew about him was how he'd looked and acted in the past few minutes. Not a lot to go on. But she didn't think he was a good fit with the crowd she'd overheard living it up at Frank's bar. That was the good news and the bad news, because if he was on the wrong side of this he wasn't one of the soldiers. He was a general.

The other possibility was that he was with law enforcement. In which case he would still be trying to figure out whether she was an innocent bystander or part of the problem.

Her job was to figure out which side *he* was on, ASAP.

He did a driver's stretch, elbows straightening, shoulders pressed against the seatback.

"So. I'm a cop. In case you hadn't guessed."

Oh, great. "No."

"At least"—he swallowed—"I was one. Still am, except for minor details. Like I don't have the badge in the wallet, the marked cruiser. The pay." He spit the word out. "But I keep my eyes open, and you—you're a walking question mark. You're either about to make trouble, or you're in trouble yourself."

"Me?"

"At least you were honest about the weapon." He glanced at her again, the look less appraising this time, with a trace of approval. "So I'm giving you a break."

"You already knew about the gun." She threw it out as a test. In case he was with the guys who planted it.

"No I didn't." He threw her a puzzled look. "How could I? Not until you told me."

Good.

"So, okay. I got busted out for nothing. It was all made up—late on shift, insubordination, bad attitude, insubordination, skipping practice shoots, insubordination, you name it."

"Insubordination."

"Yeah. Bullshit. We got the heads-up from this kid, there was a deal going down, we would have nailed the whole gang, but the chief said no, the kid was way off, stay away from it."

"And you believed the kid? You busted the gang?"

"No. How could I, just one guy? But I had a look, that's all, just checked to see if they met like the kid said. And they did. And the next thing I knew I'm fired."

"Bummer."

"Then the kid was gone. Disappeared. Open case. Still." He drummed his fingers on the wheel. "That was six months ago. But I still drive these roads. Keep my head down, but I see what's going on."

He could be spinning a story. Or he could be somebody in pretty much the same situation as she was, trying to figure out what was going on in Short Creek.

"So now what? Think you can break up the drug ring yourself?" Kate asked.

"Hey, I'm not Superman. I don't know what's going to happen. I'm just hanging out, observing. For now."

He must have some kind of plan. But he wasn't going to tell her about it. Should she tell him about Farley? He'd been killed, she was sure now. Maybe by the same people who'd "disappeared" the kid who saw the drug deal coming.

No. Sean was a wild card. She had to get her work and her camper, and then get herself to a safe place. Then she'd go to the state cops. She'd get to the bottom of what happened to Farley, but she needed help doing it. Professional law enforcement. Messing about on her own would just get her dead, too.

"Short Creek isn't a very safe place to be," Sean said. "You got a friend somewhere else to visit?"

"I have to go, but I won't stay long. In fact, I'm just picking up some stuff I really want, and my truck, and I'm outta there."

"You really don't want to do that."

Here we go again.

EIGHTEEN

"Look, I know a thing or two about what's happening around Short Creek," Sean said. "I'm telling you, it's a place to stay away from, not a place to go to."

Harri with her suitcase of money. Tire tracks near the river. The old buildings. Things were connecting, finally making some sense.

"I need ten minutes, that's it."

"Let it wait. Come back in a couple of weeks. Or get somebody to ship the stuff to you."

Those were sensible suggestions. She thought about not having the sketchbook, though, and how that would affect her momentum. She needed it in her hands again, soon. Those rough images were powerful—they were her lifeline to the person she'd been when she was working hard. Just days ago! She didn't trust herself to start over from scratch after the physical and mental disruptions since then.

The agony of getting reconnected to her art when she'd first gotten to EMAC made her shudder. She'd been away from her work too long already. Wait a couple of weeks? Even a couple more days was impossible.

She could call Danni, ask her to send the sketchbook. But what about her truck? And Danni might want to go to the cops, who were her friends, and then the wrong people might find out Kate wasn't locked up in Massachusetts. And if something big was going on, the way Sean seemed to think, Danni might be in danger herself.

No, slip in and out. Then call Danni when she was clear of the whole mess. Warn her. She and Andy should get away from there.

"I have to get back. I need my stuff to work, I need my truck. I can't put myself on hold—I just got working again and it's exciting like you wouldn't believe. It's my life now." She realized she hadn't told him what kind of work. He could be thinking she was a carpenter or a bike mechanic or a masseuse. "I'm an artist," she said.

It felt good to say it.

He drummed his fingers on the wheel. The truck drummed down the road. She couldn't explain. Not in a way that anyone who didn't do art would understand.

"I don't suppose you can handle a motorcycle."

She laughed. "You suppose wrong."

"Okay. I'm thinking." His hands got tight on the wheel again. "It's not the bike so much as the helmet. They're not required in Maine, but some people wear 'em. And a full-face helmet's a pretty good disguise."

"What are you talking about?"

"About getting you in. And out. Fast." He looked at her with a controlled kind of warmth. "You said ten minutes."

"Wow. For real?"

"I'm one of those people you don't have to ask that question." He was all business again. "Just promise me you'll be fast."

* * *

Sean took back roads just before Jonesboro, the town next to Short Creek. The last turn took them onto a dirt road with soybean fields on both sides, just a two-track with grass in the center. Two miles later Sean pulled into a half-circle driveway outside a small, boxy house. The attached garage was ugly but efficient: room for three cars, with a roof high enough for a Greyhound.

The place was surrounded by cut hayfields—nobody was going to get near the place unseen. Sean was a careful man, careful in ways Kate had never had to be.

He pressed a remote on the truck's visor and the garage doors rose. A dark gray van and a white pick-up were parked inside, both facing out. Next to them were three motorcycles, a big touring bike with a fairing, a jacked-up dirt job, and a Kawasaki sport model.

"Yikes," Kate said. "A fleet. Do I get to choose?"

He almost smiled, but his eyes were on the rear-view mirrors. He scanned out the windshield before he got out.

The Kawasaki looked new, a lime-green 750. His helmet was too big, so he gave her a watch cap to wear under it. She couldn't figure out why he was doing all this for her, but it was too good a deal to pass up.

Sean looked sheepish when he asked her to take a short test drive. "I like the bike," he said. "Just want to make sure you know how to ride. Sorry."

"That's okay," she said. "I'll try not to pop a wheelie."

This time he did smile.

She rode the Kawi around the driveway, went left to the first corner and made a U-turn in the intersection, then came back. She'd been out of his sight for most of the drill, but the engine sound told him she knew when to shift.

"Almost done for tonight," he said. "But one more thing. I want you to follow me on the bike to a motel. It's not too far. I'll fix you up with a room and you can catch up on your sleep."

She started to object, but the thought of a bed pulled at her like quicksand. "I'll pay you back when I get my stuff from the cabin."

"That's fine." He gave her a knowing look. "You've had a tough few days."

217

She didn't respond. He'd earned her trust, but she still didn't know where he fit into the picture—what he knew, and how he knew it.

* * *

She'd slept for maybe an hour, then woke up with a jerk.

The night was quiet. But her mind was in turmoil, and after a few minutes she knew she wouldn't be able to sleep again.

She splashed cold water on her face and looked in the mirror. Bad news there. Eyes bloodshot, bags under them.

All the more reason to extract herself from EMAC and get someplace safe.

* * *

And here she was, waiting behind a pick-up at the stoplight in Short Creek. Nobody in town would recognize her on this bike. Nobody at EMAC would know her, either, which was a gift: her ten-minute plan didn't include fielding questions about her disappearance or her cool new motorcycle. It was a little after nine. Dinner would be over, the artists should be back in their studios.

The light went green and the pick-up peeled out. She gave the throttle a little torque, nice and sedate, not wanting to attract attention. Besides, she'd prefer to stay away from the smoke the truck was laying down like a crop-duster. Its rings must be shot.

Every second vehicle here was a pick-up, common as blue jeans.

But the one outside the civic center was distinctive. Hanging rear plate, red body lacy with rust, cracked windshield. The sight chilled her. But she'd be out of here soon. Ten minutes, one truck camper and one sketchbook to go.

She'd noticed the fuel gauge was close to empty, but she hadn't passed any gas stations since leaving the motel. She wanted Sean to have a full tank as a thank-you from her, and it looked like the Gas N Go was going to get her business.

She kept her helmet on while she tanked up. No paying at the pump here. She hoped Buster wouldn't come over to her, wagging his tail; she hoped Billy wouldn't recognize what he could see of her face.

A lucky break: he was on the phone and barely glanced her way. "Like I say, a lot of traffic," he said. "How many you figure are coming?" She slapped some bills down on the greasy counter and headed back to the bike.

While she'd been inside, a dark car had squealed up alongside the pumps. The muscly-looking dude filling it up nodded at her, so she nodded back.

She mounted up. The car screeched out of the station. It had a big antenna on the roof that had a bad case of whiplash from the maneuver. Didn't see too many of those around here.

Hey, he hadn't paid.

Well, it wasn't her problem. Billy was still on the phone.

* * *

She liked the bike even more now that she'd had a little time to get used to the low bars. She worked it, kicking down a gear into the curves, cocking her wrist for more gas on the way out of them. She kept her speed moderate as she went up through the switchbacks, thinking of Marisa's fate. As she turned into the EMAC parking lot, Danni's SUV was coming out, turning toward town. First test of Kate's disguise.

But it wasn't Danni at the wheel. The driver was a guy with a beard, wearing a black headband. Danni must have loaned her car to a workman. Kate hoped she wouldn't run into any more of Ryan's guys.

219

The Big House looked sweet and familiar, like home. When all this was over maybe she'd get to work here again. Maybe she'd come back for a residency next summer. Some of the others might come back, too, and next year this time she'd be talking to Joy and Hallsy over dinner.

But not Farley, that sweet man. Never again.

Kate steered her mind away from the pain. She had work to do.

NINETEEN

She rode the Kawi gently across the gravel parking lot and up the dirt road to Bobcat. She circled, parked facing back toward the Big House and popped the bike onto its stand. The charcoal smell of Peacock came to her on the breeze. The moon was full but low, its light lost behind the pines.

She took the flashlight out of her pack, slung it over her shoulder, and moved onto the porch. She had the key ready, but the door was unlocked.

Someone had been here, then. She'd left it locked. Tense, she opened the door, flashed her light into the dark interior.

Nobody.

Inside, she took off the helmet and watch cap. Cabin lights might attract attention, so she picked her way around with her flashlight. She wouldn't pack everything; she wanted out of here fast. She jammed a pair of jeans and a couple of turtlenecks into the pack. Forget about the free weights, books, the poor wilting shamrock. Relieved to see her cell phone, she grabbed it and the charger off the kitchen counter. Her wallet and truck keys.

Where was her sketchbook? Under ordinary circumstances she'd be worrying about the big Masonite piece that had made Danni cry, but things were far from ordinary. All she needed was that sketchbook—so hard-won, and the wellspring of future work. Where the heck was it? She felt close to panic. What if she couldn't find it?

Ah. On the table, exactly where she'd expected it to be; she'd just missed it in her first wild swoop. She wasn't at her best, for sure, with a head injury and too little sleep. Okay, breathe slow, she told herself. Calm down.

She froze. Was that a board creaking near the back door? She flicked her flashlight off.

The man in the doorway was nearly invisible. A faint silhouette, darker gray against gray.

She caught a whiff of garlic.

"Erik?"

He flipped on the overhead. "Kate! What the hell. Where you been, girl?"

Blinking in the brightness, she laughed with relief. "Waiting to be conked on the head with a rolling pin, obviously."

"It was handy."

"Kitchens are full of knives."

"My good knives? Nobody screws around with them. Not even me." The rolling pin looked dangerous enough in his hands. "So what's the deal? First you disappear, then Danni stops coming to the office, then some dude on a motorcycle shows up. Curiosity can get the better of a man. I thought maybe I'd ask the dude some questions."

"Okay, but let's do it with the lights out. You might not have been the only curious soul who saw me ride in."

He hit the switch. "Tell me."

"It's just so weird. I was kidnapped—got grabbed off my bike on Farm Road."

"Bicycle thieves?"

"Don't think so. I woke up in Massachusetts. Something's going on around here."

"What the hell? Somebody nabbed you and just took you for a ride?"

"The nabbers must think I'm onto something, but I don't know what. I've started thinking the same thing could have happened to Farley. They thought he knew something."

"Maybe they didn't knock you off because two artists dying would look fishy." Erik moved deeper into the cabin. "You think EMAC is behind it all?"

"What? No, of course not."

"It's just this place is lousy with money. I know Danni's family is rich as blazes—Andy's told me some stories about her father. Quite the wheeler-dealer on the Boston real estate scene." He shook his head. "But think about what it costs to run this whole place. The fancy food? Keeping the Big House from falling apart? Renovating all the cabins?"

She didn't like what he was suggesting, even though she'd considered it herself. "Danni writes tons of grant applications, she has lists of rich people she cultivates. And then there's Deep Pockets."

"Every wonder how Deep Pockets got so deep? In northern Maine?"

"He doesn't necessarily make his money here. Or even live here."

"Maybe he does both. And needs a good cover."

"Jesus, Erik. What a thought." EMAC as a front? To launder drug money? "Danni wouldn't do that."

"You sure?" He let the question hang, then said, "Danni might not know."

"Deep Pockets could be using her?"

"Using us all."

They sat in the dark as the thought unfolded.

"We put on a mean party, though," Erik said. "All kinds of excitement."

She didn't know what to say to the sarcasm. But the party made her think of Marisa. She'd died in Short Creek. Was she murdered? It was all too much. Everybody was in danger and everybody was guilty. "We've got to get out of here."

"Not me, girl. I'm going home to bed."

"Erik. You know too much now."

"What, you think the bad guys are mind readers? My lips are zipped." He stood up. "Look, I been worried since you disappeared. Now I know you're okay, I'm going back to all my bad habits. Like eating. And sleeping."

"Maybe you're right," Kate said. "If you didn't see me, if you don't know what happened to me, you're no threat. As long as nobody saw you come here."

"Maybe there's nothing going on. Deep Pockets is legit, and Farley fell down. You just watch too many cop shows on TV."

He was kidding, right? He was so hard to read. "I don't even own a TV. I was grabbed and taped up and thrown in a truck and driven to Massachusetts. Somebody must have had a reason, Erik."

"I don't know a thing, and that's the safest way to be around here. But you, you poke around old buildings, you walk all over the place any time of day or night, you talk to the cops and—ah, never mind. I gotta go."

The dimness in the doorway darkened for a moment as he went out.

"Erik—" She took a step, stopped.

Wait. Her top priority was getting away. Erik wasn't in danger, but she was. All she had to do was get on the Kawi, leave it where Sean had told her to, jump into her camper and be clear of all this.

She eased onto the front porch and waited a couple minutes, watching. Erik's footsteps faded down the Loop. The night was quiet.

Astride the big motorcycle, she didn't turn on the engine, just rolled it down the slope from Bobcat. The way they wired headlights these days, they came on automatically with the engine and you couldn't turn them off. She didn't want the lights and didn't need the engine. She had gravity on her side.

She parked the Kawi at the end of the bicycle rack behind the Big House and hung the helmet on the handlebars. She'd taken a few steps when a car pulled into the parking lot out front.

Footsteps, voices. Oh, hell. It was Joy. And David. Coming back from dinner in Machias, maybe, or a movie, or dancing. They came past the end of the Big House, headed for the Loop.

Joy was chattering. David said something, and she laughed. And then they stopped and kissed. Damn.

While they were busy with each other's faces, she dared to move, crouching behind the Kawi. She didn't want to explain her absence, especially since it might make others fearful. Or possibly endanger them. And what would she say? "Hi, Joy, I was kidnapped and let go, like a catch-and-release fish, so I'm back for my notebook and I'm really in a hurry"?

* * *

Kate looked away, looked back. She was burning with impatience. She didn't want to watch but she wanted to know what was happening. Joy had mentioned a boyfriend in New York, and Kate felt sad for him.

Things could be worse. If she'd talked longer with Erik, or if the happy couple had come back a few minutes earlier, she would have run right into them.

Her quads were burning from the stretch, so she sat. This had to be the longest kiss in human history. Longer than any she'd ever had, or seen at the movies. Longer than the longest hot shower she'd ever taken after a hard work-out. Come *on,* guys, she wanted to say. Go do it on your own time.

225

But she sat like a rock. What would she really say if they saw her? She'd be firm. "It's a long story," she would say. "I've got to go. Right now. Sorry about the accidental voyeurism. I'll explain later."

The two shapes finally pulled apart, reluctantly. Went along the Loop, toward David's cabin. Right past Bobcat. Yes, her timing had been lucky.

What a relief. Their footsteps faded.

Safe to move. She stood, took two steps.

TWENTY

A car door closed. Footsteps came across Farm Road. Double damn.

The quarter moon was higher now, in and out of clouds. A breeze ruffled the maple leaves, and the parked cars twinkled in the changing light.

She held her breath. A figure slipped under the roadside trees and was at the door of her truck. He opened it and the dome light lit his face for a moment before he reached up and switched it off.

Sean.

A muffled flashlight lit the cab as he had a quick look around. And then he dropped to the ground. She couldn't see him. What was he was doing?

A minute later he stood, gave a quick glance around and melted into the shadows. His steps crunched gravel and then went silent as he reached the pavement. Beyond the trees, a vehicle started up and pulled away. Its lights didn't come on until it was nearly out of sight.

So he wasn't the friend she'd thought he was. How confusing, after all his help.

And she couldn't use her truck.

Whatever Sean had done to it wasn't good news. Bleak possibilities crowded her mind. He'd messed with her steering? Planted drugs? Poked a hole in a brake line? She thought of Marisa again, her car plunging off a switchback.

The camper was her home, and it was compromised. She felt a wave of despair, which she squashed. She had to carry on, without Sean's help. *She* was the only person she could trust.

Sean thought she was snoozing at the motel and wouldn't show up to claim her camper until morning.

Now she had to wait some more. Sean would recognize his own bike and helmet. So wherever he was going, let him be good and gone.

She could use these minutes to warn Danni. She went in the back of the Big House and checked out the landline. Yes, it had been repaired, quickly. Danni must know somebody at the phone company. She punched her friend's number into the pad.

A man's voice said "Yeah?" It didn't really sound like Andy, but who else would it be?

"Hi, Andy, is Danni around?"

Silence, then a scuffling sound. "Hello?" Danni's voice sounded funny, too. Must be the phone. Maybe the repair had been faulty.

"Hey, are you okay?" I need you to be well enough to hear some bad news, she thought.

"Sure, I'm fine."

"Danni, I was right about Farley, okay? I just wanted to tell you that, and warn you. Be careful. Some dangerous people are behind all the weird things going on around here. Drug dealers, I think."

A pause. Of course this was a shock. "Oh, thanks, Kate, but we couldn't possibly make it to the midnight movie. Thanks for thinking of us, though."

"What?"

"So I think you should go yourself. Yes, you'll just have time if you leave now. Yes, go yourself, honey, okay? Go right now."

Rustling. The man's voice said, "Where you at now?"

Andy would have said "Where are you?" not "where you at?"

"I'm, uh, at the mall in Machias. Hey, the movie's about to start. Gotta run. Sorry you can't make it, Andy." Her hands were shaking as she hung up.

Okay, okay. Stay calm. Her warning was too late. Now the best thing she could do for herself and Danni was get the heck out of here, get some help.

She'd been clever, inventing a question Kate hadn't asked. If Danni had just said she couldn't talk right then, as she'd probably been told to do, Kate might not have picked up a clear distress signal. Along with the message: Leave now.

Too bad that guy on the phone would know Kate wasn't in a Massachusetts jail cell or mental hospital.

She started up the bike and rode through the parking lot, turned right onto Farm Road.

Sean must be one of the gang after all. He'd been trying to help her on the side, but something had gone wrong. Was his help a set-up, or had he changed his mind?

It didn't matter. She had her sketchbook. And the bike. She'd ride to Massachusetts tonight, dump the gun just before the border, ditch the motorcycle somewhere not too close to Marjorie's and ask to sleep on her porch again while she got things sorted out.

She came around the curve to the river. Box trucks and vans clustered near the old buildings, the headlights showing men rolling loaded dollies out of the wide-open doors.

For a second she thought the bike had backfired, then the steering went soft and she knew she was going down.

Everything happened fast yet seemed to be in slow motion. The woods tilted. Her helmet hit the pavement with a grinding noise.

She jumped to her feet. The front wheel was still spinning, the tire shredded. It looked like that raven she'd found outside Bobcat. She ran for the woods, glad she'd just bought gas. The less vapor in the tank, the less likely it was to explode in a crash.

Shouts and lights behind her, and this was much, much more trouble than she'd ever been in.

* * *

The pounding of her feet on the road came through her helmet like someone was beating on it. She jumped the roadside ditch and tore through some small evergreen trees. Branches slapped the visor and scraped past her arms. On the other side of the trees, she ripped off the helmet and jammed it onto a stump, then ran from it at an angle. The woods were denser here and she had to slow down some. But she kept running, her pack thumping on her back.

She stopped behind a big tree and looked back. Was anyone following her?

She couldn't see all the way back to the road, but the white helmet was bright in the blackness of the woods, catching a trickle of moonlight. Her breath came fast, partly from running, partly from fear.

Night noises came to her ears, small sounds, rustlings of leaves and twigs and small creatures, all of which was the forest's version of silence. If anyone was following her, she'd be able to hear footsteps.

Then a tremendous crash ripped through the night. The helmet flew off its perch and rolled over on the ground. Her whole body jerked in reflex to the noise, and a fear took her that went beyond being afraid. She entered survival mode.

She ran recklessly, noisily. Whoever fired the gun wouldn't be able to hear for a minute or two. The trees thinned, and she stumbled onto a path. Good. Following it meant she wouldn't leave a trail of broken branches and crushed ferns. Even though she was breathing hard, she upped her speed. She ran until her throat was raw, then stopped and gulped air.

In patches of moonlight here and there, she recognized the woods—evergreens mixed with beech and maple, the kind of ecosystem where she'd seen the brown creeper. Yes, this was the same trail. If she kept going she'd come to the rocks that led up to the overlook where she and Erik had talked, where he'd sat on his Stone Throne.

She loped down the path, part of her beyond thought. Faces drifted through her mind, Erik's, Danni's, Mike's, that guide they'd had in Vermont, in the snow, tracking coyotes, he'd said to think like an animal, a deer being stalked—

No wonder she was thinking about Vermont. She felt like a hunted animal herself, one that wasn't in her home territory. She was panting again. She needed to rest. Where could she hide?

She remembered the guide saying that people never look up. She chose the biggest tree she could find, an old beech, and climbed like a bear, barging upward, forcing small green branches aside and breaking dead ones with her head and shoulders or hands. She got to a high branch on the far side of the tree from the path and straddled it, then looked up. This was as far as she could go, though the bulk of the foliage was still above her. The odor of her own sweat came to her, and a green sappiness that must be the tree.

As quietly as she could, she slid the pack off her back and jammed it against the trunk, then pulled out the pistol. She'd never needed a gun so much. She worked the slide to put a round in the chamber. "Up the spout," her father used to call it. Dear God, she thought, may I not have to use this.

A light. Somebody—no, two people—coming this way, running.

Would their flashlight penetrate the leaves below her? Her boots and jeans and leather jacket were good dark camouflage, but her face would give her away. She pulled off the watch cap Sean had given her. Put her left hand inside it and held it to her face, looked over the top. Wool, with a hint of mothballs. The Glock ready in her right hand.

The men stopped next to the beech.

"You really think," one said. He leaned over, hands on his knees, his breaths raspy. "You think he's going this way? It'll take him—"

She recognized the voice. Ryan.

"Yeah, I know. It dead ends at the rocks." That was Jim!

"He's gone off the trail, I bet." Ryan stood up, his breathing still harsh.

"He was churning up the woods pretty bad, from the road. We'd have spotted it."

They looked around, the woods blotchy from the quarter moon.

"Lousy luck," Ryan said. "Some poor bastard with a nice bike rides right into the biggest drug deal in the Northeast."

"Bad luck for him. Bad luck for us if we don't nail him."

"I'm telling you, he'll go off-trail somewhere. We need lights. Something better than this stupid thing." Ryan pointed the weak beam of his flashlight at the trunk of Kate's tree. She held her breath.

"You went thundering off," Jim said. "I knew we should have taken a second to grab some gear, make at least half a plan."

"Oh, quit griping. Let's get a couple of those tactical lights. Turn this guy into a deer in the headlights."

The two men moved quickly back the way they'd come.

When they returned with good lights, they'd probably spot the litter of fallen twigs she'd broken on the way up, and the scrape marks her boots left on the light gray trunk. A big drug deal meant going back toward the road wasn't a good idea. Neither was crashing around in the woods, leaving a trail and making noise.

There was one place nobody would expect her to go. They'd spend their time looking for signs of where she'd left the trail, but if she went up into the rocks she wouldn't leave any trace. And the men might not even know there was a way to the top.

She stashed the pistol in her pack and slid down the tree. More twigs broke. It sounded horribly loud to her, and she held her breath for a moment.

The woods were quiet.

She'd have to chance it. Right now they should be moving away from her; in a few minutes she couldn't be sure where they were. She got the Glock out and put the pack on. With her index finger wrapped around the outside of the trigger guard, she crouched and ran down the path to the rocks.

She'd forgotten how high the formation was. The climb to the top went through a tight space, a chimney, just before a sharp turn. She had to take the pack off and push it ahead of her, the pistol tucked in the waistband of her jeans. She got to the flat place protected by shoulder-high rocks she remembered from the time Erik had brought her here: a fortress overlooking the grassy clearing where the trail ended. Back then she'd thought of it as a place a child might play. Now it could save her life.

Second thoughts crowded in. If Ryan and Jim came here, they would have found the scatter of twigs on the path, and seen where she had climbed the pine. They'd have looked along the trail from that point on. Maybe they'd be convinced that she hadn't struck away from it, bushwhacking.

Leaving the tree was a good decision. Hiding there had bought her time, but it was indefensible: branches didn't stop flashlight beams, or bullets. Now she wasn't sure how safe she was, because she didn't know if the men were aware that there was a passage up through the rocks.

233

Suppose they did know, even if they'd never gone to the top themselves. They'd know it was a dead end, that they had their quarry trapped.

Dead end, a frightening phrase. But it might not be true. The paw prints she'd seen with Erik told her a coyote had found a second way up.

She took a quick inventory. She had the gun with a full magazine, seventeen rounds. Her sketchbook, flashlight, fleece jacket, oil pastels, a first aid kit, four food bars and water bottle.

Jim. She swallowed hard. He hadn't fooled her, exactly. She'd ducked his advances, but she had to admit he was a good enough actor that she hadn't taken him for a killer.

Now she knew. Okay, Ryan and Jim. She was glad, in a way, because she didn't like either of them. She could relax about others she'd suspected, Erik and Andy and the two quiet Canadians.

A ragged breath almost turned into a sob. She couldn't bear it any more, the confusion, the pain of being close to someone and having them ripped away from her. Farley. Mike. And yes, in a much smaller way, Sean. She'd liked him, and he'd turned out to be one of the drug dealers.

The sound of a helicopter rattled the night. That was bad news. When she'd come across the clearing below, the sprinkling of noise the night insects made had stopped. Despite the turmoil in her mind, she'd been listening for that silence as a warning the two men were coming. A natural security system. But now she couldn't hear anything but the copter.

It was going to pass almost overhead. The roar seemed to come from everywhere, bouncing off the rocks around her. Rotor wash blew grit and dust into the air and left her gasping, and then in a rush it was past, tilting sharply as it crossed the clearing and grazed the trees. Damn, it was low.

God, she was tired. If she fell asleep she'd be a sitting duck. She had to hold out, get through this night. It would be easier to stay alert in when the sun was up.

But wait, her chances of escaping in daylight were insanely low. Two of them, at least, and one of her. And climbing to the top of the rocks, up where she and Erik had gone, would mean exposing herself, with her back turned.

Should she go up higher now? Leave the protection of this little nest of rocks?

The coyote track at the top of the rock pile promised another way out of there. A coyote couldn't manage this rock scramble. But could she find the other trail in time? It hadn't been obvious when she'd been there with Erik.

As she weighed the choice in her mind—stay here, ready to ambush her pursuers, or go higher and look for another way out—she heard something that made her scalp prickle. A sneeze, followed by a low voice. Jim's. "You idiot."

"Couldn't help it. Goddam dust from the heli—"

"Shut *up.*"

How had she not seen their lights? Had she dozed, briefly?

The voices came from the edge of the trees. They were hiding, which meant they knew she was here. And suspected she was still armed with the Glock planted in her pack.

The clearing below her was a great advantage, but the moon had gone so low she couldn't see much. They could be sneaking across that space even now.

Her fingers trembled as she opened the first aid kit and took out the lighter. She had a more urgent use for it than sterilizing needles for splinter removal. Shielding the light with her body, she held the flame against one of the oil pastel crayons until it smoked and, reluctantly, burned. She lobbed it over the rock and into the grass without looking—she didn't want it to light her face. She threw three more of the little sticks as fast as she could get them lit, then moved behind a different rock.

If she could start the grass burning, her visibility problems would be over.

Of course, theirs would be too. But she had a crack of rock to hide in, while they had an open area to get across.

She moved to the chimney and waited, careful not to look at the small fires even though she wanted to assess how long they would last. She didn't want to screw up her night vision. The vertical cleft gave her a deep shadow to hide in plus a good window to shoot from. She'd have to change positions often, of course.

What would they be thinking? Surely they would split up, to make it harder for her. Secure at the top of the chimney, she calmed herself as best she could and opened herself to the night.

She almost felt it more than saw it: movement at the left edge of the clearing. She looked to the side of it, the way you look at a faint star. A flash erupted ten feet to the right and a bullet thudded into rock somewhere below her. She aimed at where the flash had been and squeezed off a round, then dropped down. Two shots chipped rock over her head.

One of them was firing to cover the other moving across the field. She scrambled to the fort and looked over the lowest rock. Sure enough, someone was running, doubled over to stay low. She hesitated. Shooting a person you could see was harder than shooting at a flash. Who was it, Ryan or Jim?

It didn't matter. It was that guy's life or hers. She followed the figure in the sights, led him and fired. Hearing the shot, he zig-zagged. She fired a spread of three and he fell and rolled and held his leg and yelled, "Son of a bitch!"

Ryan.

She had twelve rounds left.

Then the helicopter again, its lights rising behind the trees. The men on board would have rifles and floodlights; they would not be bothered by a small grass fire; they could maneuver at will for visibility. Hiding in rocks didn't work if her hunters were overhead.

Jim hadn't come to Ryan's side. She fired twice toward dark edge of the clearing and stuck the pistol in the back of her jeans, ignoring the burn of the hot barrel. Ten rounds left. She worked her way up the the rockpile, feeling for handholds, footholds. She'd have to find the other way out. She'd have to become a coyote.

At the top she got the Glock in her right hand and used her flashlight sparingly with her left. She ran past the Stone Throne but couldn't find anything that looked like a trail. Just rocks and air. She turned back.

Gunshots from the clearing. When she didn't return fire, Jim would know she'd left. Sooner or later he'd follow, though he'd take his time, not liking the exposure.

Or he wouldn't follow her. Why not leave it to the guys in the helicopter? It was headed this way, low and slow.

She peered over the edge of the cliff, used her flashlight briefly. A few ledges, none very wide. Some scrub trees. It was possible the ledges would lead somewhere, that she could follow them horizontally and then climb up again or down, get someplace unexpected.

Get to solid ground. Run for her life.

It was possible, and it was her only chance.

* * *

She climbed down carefully. The first ledge led to a corner of nothingness, black air. She moved back, saw another, farther down. Could she get to it without momentum taking her right past it? She wasn't sure.

She took the chance; she had to. Big step down. Her right foot caught a scrap of rock and she got her left foot onto the ledge, narrow as a window sill. She held onto a small tree growing out of a crack, using it for balance. Didn't put weight on it—its roots were already sucking air.

The helicopter was close, kicking up grit. She squeezed her eyes shut and searched out sturdier handholds, a crack on her left and a nubbin of rock above her right shoulder. She held on with both hands. She couldn't see, didn't trust herself to move again with the noise hammering away, her whole body vibrating with it. The roar seemed to hang right over her for minutes.

Then it subsided. Shouts and gunshots in the distance. She hoped the operation at the abandoned mill was getting busted, but it wouldn't help her much. Anyone who could get to the helicopter would get away.

A long silence. Sooner or later Jim was going to move through the rock pile, looking for her. He would climb carefully because she was armed, but eventually he would be on the path at the top. This ledge was under a shallow overhang, so he might not see her right away. But he would figure it out.

She'd done her best, and had run out of options. She'd played for time and gotten some, but not enough. Agonizing, how close she'd come. She took a look over her shoulder. Yes, across the valley the horizon was beginning to define itself, a seam of hills against a dark gray sky.

It was strange to be minutes from the end of her life. She'd just figured it out—discovered what she was supposed to do, what gave her joy and, she hoped, gave others joy. She was leaving so much work undone. What a fool she'd been to waste those years not drawing. She bowed her head, her forehead touching cool stone.

A small noise above her, like a shoe scuffing. She didn't move. It would be over soon. In her peripheral vision, light washed the wall of rock. Then it flooded over her, and she saw how precarious her perch was. Part of her boot-soles stood on rock, the rest on air.

Someone said, "We've got her!" She braced herself, but the light went away.

She closed her eyes. She promised herself she wouldn't open them, because the shot might not kill her immediately. If she was alive when she fell, she didn't want to see the ground coming up at her. She hoped the first shot was fatal. A head shot would do it.

More scuffing, a thump; she flinched as something brushed her shoulder. She opened her eyes when a pair of arms went around her, held her hard.

"Kate! Kate, are you all right?"

TWENTY-ONE

Not much to pack. If you live in a truck camper, you live light.

And you don't work on large paintings. Danni had bought Kate's four-by-eight piece, the frog's-eye view of the riverbank, for the Big House, and the paintings stolen from Peacock had been recovered undamaged from one of the mill buildings. So future EMAC residents would see see her work and Farley's hung together in the lounge. Kate found that heartening.

She'd given statements, three times, to three different FBI agents. She'd replaced her oil sticks and worked four days in this beautiful place where her life and her peace of mind were no longer threatened. Waking early, walking, working: the three W's were her new joys, she'd told her old friend.

"Your stay here didn't turn out to be the quiet retreat I promised you," Danni answered.

Yes, the month had been frightening, but Kate didn't regret a second of it. It had launched her both as an artist and as a full-time RVer: instead of going back to Boston she'd decided to live in her camper and travel a while, maybe a year. She'd lived in Arizona and Massachusetts, but that left plenty of country she hadn't seen, and now she could. Why not? She didn't have a job or kids, the things that usually tie people down. She had enough money saved to last a while—the truck wasn't too bad on gas, and she'd always been frugal. Selling the large work to EMAC had helped; maybe she could make other sales or trades elsewhere as she traveled.

She'd recovered her Trek from the ditch where she'd been attacked. A thorough cleaning and lube were called for, and some clear nail polish to seal scratches on the front fork. The bike was already on board the camper, bungee cords holding it securely against the table legs. She'd parked outside Bobcat to save time, itching to be on the road.

Nearly everything was loaded, and she tossed the last few items into her daypack knowing she'd have to sort them out later: the little radio wrapped in a flannel shirt, her rain jacket, the Kingsolver novel and the copy of *Travels with Charlie* Danni had given her. She turned toward the door and Sean was there.

"Thought I might catch you in," he said.

"In the nick of time."

He glanced past her, took in the empty cabin. "Hey, you're not just going for a run."

"Going to visit my mother."

"Whereabouts?"

"Tucson."

He whistled, then grinned. "Long drive."

"I'm planning on taking it slow. Really slow. Maybe a year. Back roads, and hiking and drawing all the way. Lots of nice places to see between here and there."

"Huh." He seemed at a loss for a moment, then took a big breath. "Well. So. Um, need a hand with anything?"

"Great. Thanks. Want to take the groceries?" She hadn't had much in the cupboards, but no sense leaving even a little to tempt mice.

He peered into one of the bags before he picked it up. "Coffee and coffee. Oh, and coffee. You must live on the stuff." He looked in the other bag. "Whole-grain bread. Good. You're not going to float away."

The air had a fall crispness, and their footsteps sounded loud on the hard ground. "I want to thank you for your help," he said.

She laughed. "Thank me for blundering around in the middle of your drug bust?"

He grinned again. "Yep. You were the canary in the coal mine. When I heard your story, I knew a big shipment was coming down. The cartel needed you out of the way, but only temporarily. Knocking off another artist would have been suspicious."

"They came pretty close, though." She gave him a sad look. "Sorry about your Kawasaki."

"Hey, that's what insurance is for. Not your fault, anyway—Ryan shot out the front tire."

"Well, it was a good thing you showed up—so if there's any thanks, it goes in your direction. I was sure I was a goner. And then you rappel down a rope, grab me, give me a big grin and flash an FBI badge in my face."

"Yep. You did look kind of surprised."

"Dumbfounded."

"Too bad you saw me put that tracker on your truck," he said. "I just wanted to be sure you weren't around when the action started. And then the action started, and you turned up in the middle of it."

They'd reached the camper, and she opened the door and slid the duffle in, then the two paper bags. Done. Ready.

But Kate was no longer in a hurry. She took the few steps back to Bobcat and sat on the bench. "Want to sit for a while? I've answered so many questions, I wouldn't mind hearing a few answers myself. Tell me everything."

Sean sat beside her, cocked one knee up on the bench. "Actually, our first tip came from Harri," he said.

"That's such a surprise. I was sure she was back on drugs, seeing her with all that cash. I was worried about her."

"She'd been struggling, trying to decide whether to tell what she knew or not. She finally decided to come see us—she knew enough not to go to the police."

"Why didn't she talk sooner?"

"She was protecting Marisa's reputation." He paused, then laughed. "And protecting the stash of money Marisa had told her about. It was hidden in the floor of that cabin. She gets to keep it, since we have no way of proving it came from drug deals."

"Marisa, the mystery woman." Kate shook her head. "I don't really understand her role in all this."

"Marisa was Erik's high-school sweetheart. She made it big with her band, first in Boston, then went on to New York. She was selling CDs like crazy, going on tours, but the bad news was she got into cocaine and heroin. Tons of talent, and she had good business sense, too." He shook his head. "Not a healthy combination, for her or anybody else. She told her dealer about the mill site, a good place to warehouse the product—lots of big buildings nobody paid much attention to."

"She sold out her hometown? Told the drug runners what a good place Short Creek would be for a distribution center? Wow," Kate said. "I suppose she was right. It's hidden away, and not far from the Canadian border."

"Yep," Sean said. "But then she started having second thoughts. Erik might be able to tell you something about that. She came up here to plan a concert, which would have been the biggest thing this town had ever seen. She saw him, of course—"

"And he found out what she was up to?"

"Right-o. By that point she couldn't hide the drug use, but he must have found out more, that she was friends with some pretty tough characters. Those attacks on him were to make him leave town, but Erik can be stubborn."

"What about Hallsy? He said he was her boyfriend in Boston."

"Yep. We talked to him, of course, in case he had some leads to Marisa's nasty friends. But he didn't even know she was using back then. Either she was able to hide it, or she wasn't hooked yet. It was New York that did her in."

"Wait a minute. It wasn't New York that did Marisa in, it was Marisa." Kate was surprised at her defense of the City. She'd always disliked New York, but now that she knew a few people who called the Big Apple home, her attitude had changed. Joy, and Nava. And Farley. "She could have gone to rehab."

"Right-o." Sean gave her an appreciative look.

Engine noise. A familiar, silver SUV pulled up next to the camper, and Danni got out slowly. It would be a while before she got her usual high spirits back, Kate thought.

The two of them had talked late a few nights before. Andy was being held in Bangor without bail, along with George Powers, Billy from the Gas N Go, and some other Short Creekers Kate didn't know. Danni said the FBI had grilled her for days and had been all over her files and computers in her EMAC office and at her house. But they'd finally let her go without charges.

"Hey, Kate. Hi, Sean. Finished all the interviews?"

"Yep. Just filling in the blanks for your tree-climbing, sharp-shooting artist friend here."

"Good thing I wasn't really all that sharp a shooter," Kate said, "or Ryan would be at a funeral home instead of the hospital."

The door to Bobcat was still open, and Danni wandered past them and went inside, looking a bit dazed.

"The rest of the story?" Kate asked Sean.

"So Marisa was up here, having second thoughts, Erik was pushing her to get clean and get out of the drug business altogether. He told her EMAC was making a huge difference

244

for Short Creek, and all nice and legal. So she went to Chief Fallon. He wasn't in on the scheme, but anything he knew George Powers knew, too."

"And Powers was the biggest bad guy?"

"Yep, right-o. Except for the suppliers in South America," he said, glancing over his shoulder. He probably didn't like having anybody behind him, even a totally vetted Danni.

"Billy at the Gas N Go was in Powers' pocket. When Marisa's car needed an oil change Billy made sure the brake lines developed a slow leak." He shook his head. "She was leaving town that day, going back to New York. Billy knew she'd never make it. Erik was following in his car, so he saw her go over the Farm Road switchback. Lucky for him they weren't traveling together."

"So Erik suspected it was murder, but he couldn't prove it."

"Yep. He figured out enough not to go to the cops the way Marisa had."

Danni came out of Bobcat, closed the door. One arm was wrapped around the shamrock Kate had bought at Bear Pause. "Harri was here then," she said, "she'd come up with Marisa for a visit, and she and Erik and Marisa hung out together. Marisa got Harri started on heroin, damn her." She dropped down beside Kate. "Thanks for the shamrock."

"Glad it's got a home," Kate said. "Slide-in truck campers aren't great places for houseplants."

"You know, it was kind of an ethical litmus test," Sean said. "I suppose all crime is. Erik and Harri passed. Harri was using, but she stayed out of the organization. Erik didn't touch any of it. He and Harri were suspicious about Farley's death, of course, after Marisa's. Two accidents too many." He put air quotes around the word "accidents."

"Thank God Harri had sense enough not to deal," Danni said. "I talked to her last night, and she's glad the Feds got involved. She was trying to figure things out by herself, gather evidence. She might have outed the dealers eventually. Or she might have gotten herself killed."

"When you went missing, Kate, she and Erik figured you were a goner," Sean said.

"Billy flunked the litmus test. And Ryan." Kate said. She didn't mention Andy. "But Powers kept the chief in the dark?"

"Yep. Fallon's not the sharpest pencil. As medical examiner, Powers had a lot of control. But too many accidents might make even Fallon suspicious. It wasn't a bad idea to export you to Massachusetts." He gave Kate a grin. "Except you didn't follow the script."

"The script wasn't written for me." She smiled back. "They must have thought I was some kind of Easterner. Never seen a Glock before. Eeeek!"

"Right-o."

Danni put an arm around Kate. "I'll have to go pretty soon. The Feds finally cleared me for my trip to D.C. But I wanted to tell you something important. I found out who Deep Pockets is. Was." She looked at Kate with a sad smile. "Farley."

It took a few seconds to sink in. "Farley. Wow."

"Wow is right. I had no idea." She pushed her hair back, and her face changed. "Bad publicity, this mess. But Farley believed in EMAC, and we'll pull through. He left the place quite a bit of money, which will help, and he left other things, too. A legacy of art and"—she groped for the word—"of spirit."

"He believed in EMAC, but mostly he believed in you," Kate said. "He told me you had heart."

"Thank you for that." A hint of a younger Danni showed in her smile.

"Thank you. For—all this." Kate waved her hand toward the Loop, the field, the woods, the Big House. Across the road the birches trembled in a breeze, their leaves showing a touch of yellow. Kate would never forget them.

"I want to spend time in beautiful places like this, and draw," she said. "Get things into my sketchbook and into my mind. I'll take my time across the country, make my route up as I go along. Follow the weather. Maybe it'll take me a year, and then maybe I'll be ready for something else."

"Do you think you'll come back here?" Sean asked.

"Oh, for sure, I really want to come back to EMAC. It's where I learned how to work again. I'm so grateful to have met Farley here. I can't thank you enough, Danni."

"You're welcome here any time, Kate," Danni said. She looked at her watch. "Hey, I've really got to go."

Kate followed her to the car, and Danni put the potted shamrock in the passenger seat. The two women had a good hug before Danni drove off.

Sean was standing near the camper door, and she joined him. Mist rose from the field, and a faraway crow called.

"You're lucky EMAC is going to survive for you to come back to. We're not charging Danni with anything, but personally? I find it hard to believe she didn't know what was going on."

"Love is blind, Sean. EMAC is her baby. And remember, she was away a lot. She thought Andy was holding something back, but I'm sure she had no idea he'd gone completely off the rails."

"Yep, Andy was in it up to his neck. So was Ryan. That trucking company of his was a perfect cover for moving product. And laundering profits."

His voice softened. "Those two, Kate. They're the ones who killed Farley." He stepped back, as if to make room for her grief. "Danni doesn't know yet, but Andy told us everything. Says Ryan set him up. "

Kate shivered. The rainy night came back to her, Farley's white face—

"I'm sorry, Kate." Sean reached out, touched her shoulder. "The order came from Powers. He thought Farley had figured out what was going on—he'd been seen on Peacock's back porch so often, at night, and a painting of his had one of the drug vans in it. Powers wanted Farley taken out before he blew the whistle.

"He didn't know," Kate said. "His mind was on his work." She stared at the ground, felt tears rise.

"Well, Powers had a plan. And he wanted to use somebody Farley would recognize, feel safe with, so he wouldn't be alarmed when they showed up at his door, wouldn't struggle and leave evidence." Sean said. "It was probably also a test."

Kate looked up. This couldn't be the first murder Sean had dealt with, but his face was full of sympathy. "I get it," she said. "A test of their loyalty. And something Powers could hold over their heads so they couldn't quit."

"They told Farley there was a short in the electrical box at the back of Peacock, it was arcing, shooting sparks, the fire danger was extreme and he needed to go out the front. He was worried about the stairs. So Andy led him, holding his hand—"

"The bastard!"

"—and Ryan pulled a crowbar from under his shirt and hit him from behind. It was fast, Kate. He didn't suffer."

She felt sick, leaned against the truck.

"Andy says Ryan didn't tell him the plan," Sean said. "Says he was horrified."

Kate couldn't look at him. "Do you believe him?"

"I'm not sure. Shouldn't even be telling you this. But—I want to, Kate." His eyes held hers. "And there's one more thing I want you to know about that night. When they told him about the danger, that Peacock might catch fire, he said they should be sure to get you out, too. You were in his last thoughts."

Kate sat on the ground and cried like a child.

When she'd finished, Sean helped her up. She blotted her eyes against her flannel sleeve and gave him a wavery smile.

"Good thing I don't wear mascara."

"Your eyes look fine just the way they are."

"Thanks for telling me the whole story. I hate what happened, but knowing how it all fits together might help. In the long run."

"If you hadn't showed up like a red flag on a windy day, I wouldn't have known about the shipment. I bet on you big-time."

"Bet on me?"

"I called the Bureau, put my reputation on the line. They listened, then mustered the helicopter with the infrared gear. If they hadn't found anything, I'd have looked like a fool." He laughed. "Remember that story I gave you about being a busted local cop? If a major drug deal hadn't gone down that night, my cover story would almost have come true. Instead we collected ourselves a whole nest of snakes. "

"And now you've got admiring friends in high places."

"And one new friend who'd better come back if she knows what's good for her." He gave her a mock-menacing look, but couldn't hold it. They both laughed.

"Right. And I've got a new friend in the FBI, which is a miracle since I wrecked his bike and got his helmet shot up. A friend who is way different from the man who picked me up hitchhiking. That guy barely said three words, and two of them were 'Okay.'"

"Remember, I was playing a role. And I was preoccupied with the operation." His smile faded. "But I have been accused of being moody."

Kate wondered briefly whether the accusation had come from someone he worked with or someone—closer, in his private life.

"Well." His face got serious. "You'll keep in touch? Here's my contact info." He handed her a card with an embossed shield on it. "I wrote my cell number on the back. Call anytime."

"You bet I'll keep in touch, Sean. You saved my life." She tore a piece from one of the paper bags and took the pen he offered. "Here's my cell, and a friend's address and phone in Massachusetts. Marjorie will know where I am, most of the time."

He tucked it in his shirt pocket and looked at her. And then gave her a kiss. His lips were cool at first, and then warmed with hers.

* * *

She looked at the map. West past Bangor, then where? New Hampshire, Vermont, northern New York—all of them had plenty of state parks and campgrounds. She'd work in the morning, drive as long as she felt like in the afternoon. Life had just gotten a lot simpler.

Simpler for her. Danni was swimming in complications. She'd told Kate her top priority was to rebuild Peacock, but that labor of love could be only a small part of the work facing her. Expanding EMAC and ministering to its reputation would engage Danni for years to come. Kate wondered how many of those years her friend's marriage would survive.

Farley had been Deep Pockets. Kate smiled every time she thought of that. His bequest, plus the sale of some of the work he'd done here, would leave EMAC in excellent fiscal health. Yes, she'd be back. She'd found and then lost a dear friend here, a man who'd left her a legacy of freedom and optimism.

And hard, consistent work.

Farm Road unrolled in her rear-view mirror. She would find her way.

Thank you for reading!

If you enjoyed this book, please consider leaving a review on Amazon, Goodreads, or wherever you spend time online. Even a few words can make a major difference to an author.

Look for other novels in the Art of Murder series: *Boat Camp Killer*, Book 2, and *The Double Magpie Murders*, Book 3, are available on Amazon.

Find news of later releases at www.PamFoxAuthor.com.

Comments? Email the author at PamFoxAuthor@gmail.com or follow her on Twitter at @PamFoxAuthor.

www.ingramcontent.com/pod-product-compliance
Lightning Source LLC
Chambersburg PA
CBHW021224130626
46554CB00004B/1362